# Acclaim for the Wo
## of REX ST

"Rex Stout is one of the half-dozen major figures in the development of the American detective novel."
— *Ross Macdonald*

"Splendid."
— *Agatha Christie*

"[Stout] raised detective fiction to the level of art. He gave us genius of at least two kinds, and a strong realist voice that was shot through with hope."
— *Walter Mosley*

"Those of us who reread Rex Stout do it for…pure joy."
— *Lawrence Block*

"The story has everything that a good detective story should have—mystery, suspense, action—and…the author's racy narrative style makes it a pleasure to read."
— *New York Times*

"One of the most prolific and successful American writers of the 20th century…The writing crackles."
— *Washington Post*

"Practically everything the seasoned addict demands in the way of characters and action."
— *The New Yorker*

"One of the master creations."
— *James M. Cain*

He became suddenly aware that his hand was again in his overcoat pocket, closed tightly over the butt of the revolver. His hand came out and the revolver with it, and he stood there with his forearm extended, the weapon in plain sight, peering around, downstairs and up, like a villain in a melodrama. If the door of the landing had at that instant opened and one of the art students had appeared, he would probably have pulled the trigger without knowing it.

His hand returned to his pocket and then came out again, empty, and sought the railing as he mounted another step, and another, and then stopped once more.

Oh you would, would you, he said to himself, and he felt his lips twist into a grimace that tried to be a smile. No you don't, you don't go back now, this time you go ahead, if it's only to point it at her and let her know what you think she's fit for....

# HOW Like a GOD

## a GOD

by **Rex Stout**

A HARD CASE CRIME NOVEL

**A HARD CASE CRIME BOOK**
(HCC-164)
*First Hard Case Crime edition: June 2024*

Published by

Titan Books
A division of Titan Publishing Group Ltd
144 Southwark Street
London SE1 0UP

in collaboration with Winterfall LLC

Print edition ISBN 978-1-80336-486-5
E-book ISBN 978-1-80336-487-2

Design direction by Max Phillips
*www.signalfoundry.com*

Typeset by Swordsmith Productions

The name "Hard Case Crime" and the Hard Case Crime logo
are trademarks of Winterfall LLC. Hard Case Crime books
are selected and edited by Charles Ardai.

Printed and bound by CPI Group (UK) Ltd,
Croydon, CR0 4YY.

*Visit us on the web at www.HardCaseCrime.com*

*HOW LIKE A GOD*

# A

*He had closed the door carefully, silently, behind him, and was in the dim hall with his foot on the first step of the familiar stairs. His left hand was in his trousers pocket, clutching the key to the apartment two flights up; his right hand, in the pocket of his overcoat, was closed around the butt of the revolver. Yes, here I am, he thought, and how absurd! He felt that if he had ever known anything in his life he knew that he would not go up the stairs, unlock the door, and pull the trigger of the revolver.*

*She would probably be sitting in the blue chair with many cushions, reading; so he had often found her. He shivered so violently that he almost lost his balance as his foot found the next step.*

*His mind seemed suddenly clear and intolerably full, like a gigantic switchboard, with pegs in all the holes at once and every wire humming with an unwonted and monstrous burden. A vast intricacy of reasons, arguments, proofs—you are timid and vengeless, you are cautious and would be safe, you would be lost even if safe, you are futile, silly, evil, petty, absurd—he could not have spoken in all his years the limitless network of appeals, facts, memories, that darted at him and through him as his foot sought the third step.*

*He heard them all....*

# 1

You are timid and vengeless.

When you first saw that word you were in short pants and numberless words in the books you read were strange and thrilling. Many of them have long since been forgotten, many more have lost their savor. To become common and flat is sadder than to disappear; but this word has escaped both fates through the verses you wrote, using it in the first line of each stanza. Afraid of your father's and mother's good-natured criticism, you showed them only to Mrs. Davis, the Sunday School teacher.

"Vengeless," she said, "is not used for men and women, only for impersonal things like time and tides."

That was before she invited you to her house in the afternoon, but already she was smiling at you. You were mortified at having misused the word and tore the verses up.

That was timid, and you hated yourself for it without really knowing it. You were always hating yourself without knowing it; the tiniest spark was enough to set off that firecracker. Jane, who had the trick of being aware of things before they quite happened, was always on to you, not unkindly, but that kindness could crush you. Did Jane know that? Years later she did, of course, with Victor and her children, and her friends and committee meetings, but at raw and gawky twelve, just outgrown her dolls, did she already mysteriously know what she was doing to people? She would be peeling potatoes and would turn to your mother:

"Better give Billy a cookie; he's done something in school."

"Let me alone," you would almost whimper. Then your mother, with that pretense of equality which you resented without understanding why:

"Don't you want to help your sister do the potatoes?"

You always intended to refuse the cookie, but you never did. Come to think of it, there was no reason why you should; but it always seemed a surrender. In youth the sources of ignominy were everywhere, or you more tenderly felt them.

The most blatant and poignant timidity of those young Ohio days was when, with the boys down on the lot below Elm Street of a summer afternoon, you would try to steal second base. Why in the name of god did you ever try it? That was peculiarly not your dish, you always knew that and yet forever you tried it. There were three moments of agony: do I go on this pitch? Just that one instant too long on the decision, the bad delayed start—but the running was splendid. You could run. The slide, torture, whether headfirst or hook. A kicked face or a turned ankle? The essential wild precise plunge. You knew what was required, but you didn't have it. There you were, a yard away from the base, with the ball on you, and from all sides the friendly triumphant jeers. If Jane had been there doubtless she would have offered you a cookie, and you would have killed her.

*Oh, that!*

But during this period that vague and oppressive timidity had its usual seat at home, at the little house on Cooper Street. Probably its unknown focus was Jane, for your father and mother were from first to last nebulous and ill-defined; they seemed to float around you; and your other sisters and brothers existed only as pestiferous facts, hardly yet as persons. Larry was only five, and Margaret and Rose were being born or at least scarcely out of the cradle.

How easy to see now that that house meant Jane. There was the time, somewhat later, that you stumbled into the bathroom with a bleeding nose, bruised souvenir of a visit of the lime-kiln gang to peaceful Cooper Street, and found there your mother and Jane, both naked, one fresh from the tub, the other just getting in. It was a dilemma. Outside was the carpet, not to be bled on; here was your imminent pain. They helped, somehow, hurriedly; Jane handed you a towel, or was it your mother? It was an exciting and confusing experience, and the memory is blurred. There was throughout a portentous embarrassment, even after your mother got a robe around her. Jane didn't bother. That night the pink living skin you saw behind closed eyelids was Jane's; also the other nights; never your mother's. Timidity? You shrank from the warmth that crept tingling into your own skin at the forbidden memory. You at once invited it and denied it. Not so would Jane have done! Was she embarrassed that day? You wondered about that ceaselessly, until the dignity of new juices and new purposes drove it underneath.

With your father there was timidity too, but as you see now perfumed with contempt. Not even you could have been really timid with that little herring of a man who meant invariably well and went around with the air of one who is always expecting to hear a bell ring. There is not more good will in all heaven than he carried in his heart; The first dream you dreamt that was in touch with reality came when his business and his health lost step together and you were shocked and pleased to find yourself taken seriously as a member of the family.

"Bill, it's up to you," said your father, after your mother's tears were dried and the younger children had been sent from the room. "Doc's crazy. I'll be at it again in a month. You're nineteen, and big enough to handle two real drug stores, let alone that little hole in the wall. Nadel can do the prescriptions, and, with all the afternoons and Saturdays you've had there..."

"He can't do it," said Jane, home for the summer from Northwestern. No, she was through then, and was teaching Latin in the high school like a goddess waiting at a railroad station for a train. Anyway, "He can't do it" was what she said, and when you grunted protest she added:

"You know you can't, Bill. It's not your line, and anyway you're too young and it's not fair. I'm the one for it, and Dad will have to let me."

Your father, curiously persistent, had Mr. Bishop come in and empowered you to sign checks, but no one was fooled by that empty symbol except your mother. The summer dragged endlessly, with the intimate and inane activity of the leading drug store of a growing town. You resented Jane bitterly as she competently kept patent medicine salesmen where they belonged while you mixed ice cream sodas and washed the glasses; and by July you found it almost impossible to talk to her. It was just then that Mrs. Davis went to Cleveland—ah, you still wonder, how much of that did Jane know? At all events, the whole world was dark. But your father, to the pleased but professionally discomfited surprise of Doc Whateley, pulled on his trousers again, "slightly disfigured but still in the ring" as the editor of the weekly *Mail and Courier* put it, and you went off for your second year at college.

That was the year that saw your legend created and made you a man of mark. You have never understood that episode, especially not when you were acting it; it was an astonishing contradiction of all timidities and inadequacies; what would have happened and where would you be now if Mrs. Moran had not done your washing and sent little Millicent to fetch it, and deliver it, twice a week? It was on her second or third visit that you noticed her and became intensely aware that that pale child was handling the things you had worn. It was indefinable and incredible; she was exactly ten, half your own age, pallid and scarcely alive, barely literate; but as she calmly and silently rolled up your soiled shirts she did something wise and terrible. There was no action in it, no gesture, not even a look, certainly not a caress; there was really nothing, and yet it was a profound and suggestive impertinence. At the time you were aware of nothing but an inexplicable discomfort. You twisted in your chair; your body needed moving and you got up and opened the door for her.

"I'll come back Friday," she promised.

It must have been three months later that there happened to be a crowd in your room when she came; by then you were always making sure to have candy for her and to be always there when she arrived. That day you didn't want to give her the candy with the other fellows present, and without even a glance she somehow let you know that she understood perfectly and sympathized.

When she had gone somebody remarked that it was a pity that so young and delicate a child had to carry bundles around.

"Oh, that little bitch," said Dick Carr, known as the Mule. "Nothing's going to hurt her. She's got a nasty line."

Two or three protested in the name of innocent childhood. No one seemed to see you trembling.

"You're nuts." The Mule spat a rich tobacco brown. "She used to come for my stuff, but I changed over to the Chink. Honest, I was afraid. Hell, Bill, she might seduce you."

Without willing it you were on your feet and advancing on him. "Carr, you're a dirty low-down skunk."

The words weren't so bad, among friends, but your tone and attitude made them gasp. The Mule, a seasoned halfback with nothing left to prove, was contemptuously surprised but undisturbed.

"My god, you aren't tilting your little lance for her, are you, Bill?"

Blindly you slapped him in the face and as he leapt out of his chair a dozen restraining hands clutched him. Here of course tradition stepped in, not only of dear old Westover, but also of all the manly centuries. Time and place were discussed and courteously agreed upon. There wasn't a lot of excitement because it was taken for granted that the Mule would hit you once and then watch you bleed.

It was agreed afterward that no one could adequately describe that encounter. The Mule certainly did hit you and you certainly bled; but long after you were logically extinct, with your face a mass of pulp and your ribs trying to escape by way of your backbone, you still poked your bruised fists somehow at that gigantic shape which must be annihilated before you went down to stay. You were not aware of either weariness or pain, though you did think that surely all the time in the world had been used up. Probably now the Mule could easily have given you the coup de grace, but he seemed to be sick of it. Perhaps aware at last that his real opponent here was something that had no blood to lose, and that to knock you down again was pointless.

You were held, finally, not only from combat but also from falling, while the Mule stood panting, wiping his face with a handkerchief, his undershirt splotched with dirt and blood not all yours; and when you had been half led and half carried back to your room you collapsed utterly. Late that night, too gone to move, you lay and watched your admiring visitors eat the candy you had bought for little Millicent.

Skinny Porter, who is now an actuary for a life insurance company here in New York, said that the battle lasted eighteen minutes, but within a few months the legend had grown to over an hour. At any rate no one had ever before stood up to the Mule for any appreciable time whatever, and you were suddenly famous. Kept in bed for a week, you were visited on the third day by the Mule himself.

"Well, Bill, you old bastard," he said affectionately.

Not long after that you began to call him Dick instead of Mule, specifically at his own request, and thus became a man of note not only for having stood up to the Mule, but for being chosen as his chief intimate. Whether there was then, or ever, an authentic bond between you is unknowable. As well as you can judge through the jungle of the years, on your part it was probably a smirk at opportunity. He was the most popular athlete of the year, universally liked, even by Old Prune, and he was by far the richest man in the college. Fabulously rich; motor cars for undergraduates were at that time unheard of, but Dick had one. On parties he would flash hundred dollar bills, not offensively; and spend them.

All the spring semester you were inseparable, and when you went home in June you had promised to visit him during the summer. Home was flat. Jane had gone to Europe with one of the early schoolteachers' crusades for culture; Larry and Margaret and Rose were still floundering in the jelly of childhood; your father and mother were more obviously than ever conveniences of nature. Not that you felt this then. At that time it was still understood that you would go to the College of Pharmacy, and you still contemplated a safe and complacent career in the leading drug store of the growing and bustling Ohio town without real aversion, chiefly perhaps because you saw no alternative. Besides, those few weeks were filled with expectation of the visit to Dick Carr's home in Cleveland; and Mrs. Davis's Cleveland address had been in your little red memorandum book for more than a year.

You had not been in Cleveland twenty-four hours before Mrs. Davis was entirely forgotten.

You fairly and visibly trembled with timidity that first afternoon in the garden when Dick introduced you to his sister Erma. Yes, you were always timid with Erma Carr, damn her! Partly perhaps it was the house, the servants, the motor cars, the glistening fountains, the clothes-closets lined with fragrant cedar? Perhaps, but god knows Erma was enough. You see now that you resented her and felt her cold presumption that first day. Then you were charmed and submerged and inexpressibly timid.

By the end of the third week she asked you to marry her. Yes, damn it, she did, though she may have left the question marks to you. How many times you have wondered why Erma picked you, suddenly, like a flamingo darting at a minnow, out of all that were offered to her. It is amusing, your irritated concentration for more than twenty years on that trifling *why*. Yes, you were handsome after a fashion, with your large and mild but not stupid brown eyes, your diffident and awkward torso and shoulders, your thick tumbled hair that left the line of your head to be guessed at, and your angular, slightly delicate face. Your legs always had, and still have, a free fine swing. That first day, the first hour, Erma told you how well you walked. But none of that answers your question. What caught her was the timidity, not the timidity of a fool or a coward, but of a stag not quite willing to leave the set of his horns to nature and still not heroic enough to adjust them himself.

You were driving with Erma along the lake shore the afternoon the telegram came, and when you returned it was waiting for you: *Father very ill come home at once Whateley*.

As you hurriedly packed with Erma and Dick standing by sympathetically you suddenly remembered with a shock that

Jane was still in Europe. When you got home, after midnight, your father was already dead; had, in fact, been dead at the time the telegram was sent. A greater trial than the bereavement was your mother, in whom a thousand unsuspected springs of suspicion and resentment were suddenly released. She held against you unreasonably and implacably the fact of your absence when your father had breathed his last, and she seemed always to be saying, from breakfast till bedtime, though of course never uttered, "You are not the man to take his place and steer this ship." Larry, far more masterful than you even then, offered an alliance, but you were too timid for it. Male rule was done in that house.

When Jane came come it was like Napoleon back from Elba. Your mother contentedly retired again into her mist, and from that day faded perceptibly. Margaret and Rose stopped their incessant squealing, and Larry, with a shrug of his shoulders, sought other worlds. With the perfection of tact Jane considered and felt the difficulties of your position, and your mature admiration of her dates from that time.

"You don't have to decide now whether the drug business is the best thing for you. You've got to finish college. I can run the store for a couple of years; it'll pay better than ever; you'll see. Please, Bill, you've simply got to finish. With some kinds of men it wouldn't matter, but for you it's important."

In a letter you had sent Jane to Paris, from Cleveland, written on the Carrs' engraved paper, you had said a good deal of Erma; but though Jane asked about her now at length you did not mention the engagement. You felt strongly that the counter of that drug store was the place for you, and the real truth—one of your favorite bits of irony—is that you shrank from so formidable a task! Jane undertook it blithely, as one goes for a walk, and you packed up and went off for your third year.

The knowledge would put out no fires in hell, it would change nothing either in the lost years or the present torture, but what would you not give to know how much of the power pulling you back was the desire to hear little Millicent knock at your door! The thought is entirely too grotesque for any credit, but now you suspect even that.

Only one thing was then in your mind. You had accepted Jane's generous offer, and you had bowed to the necessity of postponing the fulfillment of your own responsibilities, only because you were going to have a career as an author. You knew that words had always excited you, verses of yours had been published in the local weekly, and in your second year you had been placed on the staff of the college paper. You rejoiced that finally you had had the acumen to perceive to what all this clearly pointed. Famous writers can marry even the wealthiest and most beautiful women without a thank you. Or even refuse to marry them because they have more important business in hand. Of course, under this plan, even if you and Erma did eventually marry (you were thinking that with her it might already have become a hot weather episode), it could not happen for many years. You were twenty-one; she was twenty-three. You could easily write a book a year. By the time you had written eight books (only half of them perhaps outstanding successes), she would be thirty-one and you twenty-nine. That would be all right, provided you hadn't decided by then that marriage was a mistake anyway.

That winter you did write two or three stories, and one day read one of them to Millicent, with whom you were by now enmeshed in a strange and peccant intimacy. Still you wanted pathetically to call her Millicent, but she wouldn't have it; Millie she detested; you called her Mil and at the sound of it she flew to you. As you read the story, she sat like a diminutive mother-of-the-world watching her man-child play silly games; when you had finished she said:

"I like it, but I'd rather…"

She was never verbal.

A leap of nearly two years to the next marked and fateful hesitation. You and Dick Carr were seated in a café on Sheriff Street in Cleveland, having just come in from a ball game. Dick was proceeding with an argument he had been carrying on for a month.

"I can't understand why you don't see it, Bill. It's so obviously the thing to do."

"It would mean giving up my writing," you protested for the hundredth time. You had had two stories published in a Chicago magazine. At the title of the first one, when it appeared in print, you had stared for a total of days; you had kept the magazine open so you could see it while you were dressing, and you can see it yet, in large black type:

## THE DANCE AT THE LAZY Y
### by
### William Barton Sidney

"Hell, that game isn't worth a damn, I think you can really do it, but it isn't worth a damn. If you do it for money there's not really much in it, and if you don't do it for money what the hell do you do it for? Anyway, I'm asking this more for my sake than for yours. I'm over twenty-one now, and I'm going to be the works down on Pearl Street all right, but I want you along. If Dad hadn't died when I was a kid I suppose I'd be going to Yale or taking up polo, but that's out. I see where the real fight is, and I'm going to be in it."

"You don't have to fight so hard, do you, if you're worth five million dollars?"

"You bet you do. Old Layton at the bank told me yesterday that the business has been going back for two years. He said young blood was needed. Right. I've got it. So have you. Of course I'm dumb as hell but I'll catch on and then watch the sparks fly. There's going to be the devil to pay when I start firing those old birds down there about a year from Thursday. I want you in on it, Bill. It may be a real battle, but that's all right. I know you don't mind a fight."

Oh. That. Dick was prouder than you of the Battling Bill legend at Westover, perhaps with better reason. Your silence encouraged him to go into other details.

"The set-up down there is that I own half the stock and Erma owns the other half. She's more than willing to let me run the thing provided her dividend checks come along. I'm going to be elected to the Board, and President of the company at the meeting next week. What I want to do is get the whole thing right in my fist. I'm going to spend most of the winter in the plant at Carrton, and meanwhile you'll be picking up all you can here at the office. You can start in at any figure you want within reason—say five thousand a year. Later you can have any damn title there is except mine. You can trust me to come through when the time comes."

In his brusque and eager sentences, Dick was already the Richard M. Carr who is new on forty directorates. And already he was saying *within reason*—but that's unfair for his offer was generous and uncalculating: A hundred dollars a week was to you affluence. You should have accepted it quickly and eagerly and confidently. Or you should have said "Start me in at two thousand, though I can't earn even that at first. When I'm worth more I'll take it fast enough." Or you should have refused: "No, Dick, I know I can write and I'm going to do it, but for god's sake invite me to visit you now and then for I'll probably need a good meal." Or you should—oh hell. The five thousand coaxed you onto another bridge you weren't sure of.

And yet none of the bridges has ever really collapsed—not till now, not till this moment.

It was like Erma never again to have mentioned the garden episode. Either you could see that she had changed her mind or you were too stupid to bother with. At the time of her first trip to Europe she probably still intended to take you eventually—possibly not. One of your longest sustained curiosities was to see that unlikely husband of hers, whom she claimed to have picked up in a fit of absentmindedness on a beach somewhere east of Marseilles. The winter they spent in New York you were not yet there.

Did you or did you not marry Erma because you saw conscription coming and wanted to escape it? As Treasurer of the Carr Corporation, one of the big metal industries of the country, you could certainly have been exempted anyhow; there is too the fact that you were genuinely tempted to enter the army notwithstanding. There is of course one other explanation of that reluctant venture, that it might be desirable for the salaried treasurer of the Carr Corporation to be married to half of its stock.

You are determined to grant nothing to the loveliness and fascination of Erma herself, and yet she was lovely enough as she unexpectedly opened the door of your private office in New York that December morning. Off came her hat, as it did invariably under all possible circumstances, allowing the clipped ends of her fine yellow hair to fall on either side of her face. Her dear pink skin glowed with its perpetual nervous excitement. You had not seen her for nearly three years.

"Here I am—isn't it silly? To come back from Provençe at this time of year! I must be getting old, I honestly think it was

the thought of Christmas that brought me. Last year it was terrible, at Tunis—Pierre had hives or something and couldn't eat
anything but cheese. I'm so sorry Dick's out of town—they just
told me. How do you like having the office in New York? My,
but you look up to almost anything! Really elegant!"

Now, of course, you would never see the unlikely Pierre,
since he had died the preceding spring, somewhere around the
Mediterranean, possibly in the middle of it. Erma's infrequent
letters, which Dick would usually give you to read, were never
very precise. He had handed you this one at lunch one day and
when you had finished reading had said with a grin:

"Now why don't you and Sis go through with that little affair
you started in Cleveland once?"

You had never known before whether Dick knew.

It became apparent that Erma did intend to go through with
that little affair. She had not been in New York a week before
she told you that she was "fed up with that 'sieu-dame stuff,"
and it may have been as simple as that, but that did not explain
why she again selected you. By that time you had become much
more articulate than in the day of the famous garden scene in
Cleveland, and on the morning that she made the announcement, across the breakfast table, you put it up to her squarely.

"I haven't the faintest idea," she replied brightly. "Do you
mean that you feel yourself unworthy of me?"

"I'm not making conversation," you said.

"Oh. Well. Ask the flower why it opens to the bee, or if you
prefer, the lady-salmon why she swims a thousand miles to that
particular creek. If she's properly brought up she'll tell you, but
it won't be true."

"I don't believe it's that kind of a reason. I honestly can't
imagine what it is."

It took only a little of that to irritate her, and no wonder; you were never a greater fool. To end the argument she took things into her own hands, and the following autumn there was an effective climax to what the newspapers called a youthful romance. This whole thing had been consummated without your having reached a decision of any kind. That seems preposterous, but it is literally true. You never agreed to marry her; you never decided to marry her. That was worse than timidity; it was the act, or rather the passivity, of an imbecile.

If in that passivity you unconsciously had your eye squinted at a more solid footing in the unreal world you inhabited, you had your trouble for your pains. Erma's stock has remained in her vault to this day; and tonight, and tomorrow (oh yes, there will be a tomorrow) you will still be the salaried treasurer. Forty thousand a year. Erma pays sixty thousand rent for the place you and she call home. Twenty thousand a year you save. The six cars in the garage were all bought by Erma, though there is another she doesn't know about. Over two hundred and fifty thousand you now have in your own vault, by god! Erma pays the servants, fifteen of them, not counting the country. Last year her dividends—oh hell! Once started this sort of thing can go on forever, as you've discovered before. Essentially you don't care a hang about money anyhow. You would certainly be hard put to prove it, but it's seriously quite true.

There was one other time when you might have got the thing in your fist, as Dick says. One other time…that evening about a year ago…it would not then have been too late…but there is so much bitterness concealed here that when you think of it you must take care to do so with the utmost calmness and restraint, otherwise you would lose your last and only friend and be within reach of insanity.

This is scarcely the picture of a man who would execute a

desperate and hopeless enterprise. What are you doing making another gesture in a last effort to impress yourself? She doesn't believe in it, and she knows you far better than you know yourself. Last night she said:

"I'm afraid well enough. But not that you'll hurt me that way. Call it contempt, it doesn't matter what you call it. There's nothing in you that makes you get even with people. Don't ask me again what we're going to do, as if we were two wheels on a cart. We've been fitted for what we've done together, but I've been me and you've been you. There's nothing changed now if you don't bring words into it. You know I have always lied to you and always will. It isn't the truth you look for in me."

That is the longest speech you have ever heard her make. When at its end her eloquent hand lifted a little and her eyes softened and faintly offered to close, you stumbled back as if in terror of your own threats. She let her hand fall and smiled a patient assurance.

"Come back tomorrow night."

# B

*Not halfway up the first flight, he stopped and listened. That was the basement street door closing. Mrs. Jordan putting out the milk bottles. He almost called to her. She would have called back, what d'ye want, in a tone that advised him to want as little as possible.*

*His right hand left his overcoat pocket and took hold of the rail; when it left the handle of the revolver it felt as if it were letting go of something sticky and very warm. The wires hummed and buzzed in his head.*

## II

Just what is it you expect to accomplish? One of your favorite
and best-articulated beliefs is the futility of anything we may
do to other people. The things that are done to us are the only
ones that matter, especially the things we do to ourselves. Of
course our own acts mostly have a rebound, but not this fatal
act you are now considering, knowing all the while that it cannot
be consummated.

All the futility of Jane's thrusts at you, for instance, did not
arise from your antagonism and parade of independence. The
futility was inherent in the material she was trying to work
with. The question of motive need not enter. What considera-
tions moved her are entirely beside the point as far as you are
concerned.

The fact is that she is the woman for you. This is true in spite
of society's traditional attitude, first brought to you the day that
red-haired boy (whose name you have forgotten) taunted you
with being tied to your sister's apron strings. And later shouted
at you incessantly from across the street until the shocked
neighbors made an issue of it:

"He drinks his sister's milk, he drinks his sister's milk, he
drinks his sister's milk!"

Very well, tied to your sister's apron strings. That is worse
then than being tied to the ribbons of Erma's rue de la Paix
robe de nuit, or chained with steel to the black and impenetrable armor of the woman upstairs? Bah. The world of course
is thinking of incest and hasn't even the courage to say so.
The concern is authentic, physiologically, but who is talking of

physiology? Not you. You are not responsible for what you may or may not have dreamed as an infant and a boy, but you know what you think as a man, and when you say that Jane is the woman for you, you mean that all the security and peace you have ever known, all the gentle hours of content, all the exciting assurances that the world was made for you too, have come from the touch of her hand and the sound of her voice. Anyone who tries to translate that into that which may be bought at any street corner for two dollars has very little to do.

But you've never thanked her for it, and it has always been futile. The time you went home from Cleveland for your things, having definitely agreed with Dick, Jane listened quietly to your grandiose plans and exaggerated enthusiasm, along with the rest of the family. She gave you your father's old place at table that evening, and you noticed that your mother accepted the arrangement calmly and even with a mild pleasure, because it was Jane's.

The following morning Jane came into your room while you were packing

"Bill, I'm afraid you're being driven into this by your feeling that you've got to do something for the family. You shouldn't, really you shouldn't. The store's doing better than ever and I'm honestly having a lot of fun with it. You must come down this afternoon and see all the new stuff I've got. The fountain is a peach. I'm only twenty-five, and you don't need to think I'm going to get covered with moss. The way this town's growing we can sell the store for a lot of money in a few years."

You wouldn't admit anything. Superficially you were offended.

"Gosh, you might think I was taking a job cleaning streets. This is the real thing, Jane. Five thousand a year for a man of my age isn't to be sneezed at."

"It's not your line. I'm glad and proud you've got the offer; I suppose it would rush nearly any boy off his feet. But I'm even prouder of that second story you wrote. I think it's pretty darned good."

This made you glow, but you protested:

"It was about the twentieth, and most of them were terrible."

"I mean the second one published. Oh, Bill, don't let yourself be gobbled up. I expect you think that it's just that I want to manage things, but it isn't. If you were older than me it would probably be the other way around. The store can keep all of us nicely. What if you don't make much for two or three years, or even five?"

Futile. In your pocket was the five hundred dollars Dick had advanced, more than you had ever seen before. Most of it went to pay off ancient personal debts around town of which even Jane knew nothing.

She tried again four years later, when the store was sold and you went down to help take the sucker off the hook as Jane put it in her letter. In reality there was nothing for you to do but sign papers; Jane had made an impeccable deal. She was now mature, in full flower, radiant and assured. Her own future was perfectly indefinite, but not with the mist of doubt or hesitation.

"I'm going to New York and take Rose and Margaret along. Mother wants to stay here with Aunt Cora. Thanks to your generosity Larry can go to college next month without anything to worry about."

As neat as that. The talk you had with Jane that night was the closest you and she had ever got to each other. You admitted your regrets and she appealed to you with tears in her lovely eyes. You longed inexpressibly to say:

"Take me to New York with you. Let's be together. There's no one but you anywhere that's worth a damn. I'll write or I'll get a job or I'll do anything. Maybe some day you will be proud of me."

Well why not? Tied to your sister's apron strings. No not entirely that. Drawn as you were to her, you were at the same time repulsed. Surrounding that seductive haven were difficult and dangerous shoals. Perhaps underneath all her tact and competence and beautiful strength you felt an avidity of power which would at length leave you a naked and pendent slave of her compassion and her will. Or perhaps it was something much less elaborate; some feeling deeper than anything you have words or thoughts for.

At any rate it was again futile. When you departed for Cleveland the next day everyone but Larry was in tears; this was different from other departures; it was the beginning of the end of the roof and that family.

Even more to the point by way of futility have been your own efforts at Larry. They have affected him of course in super-ficialities such as his place of being, his momentary companions and his intellectual opinions; once he even willingly followed your advice regarding the choice of a suit and you can't get closer to a man than his clothes. But in no essential have you left a mark on him.

How differently from you did he pass from the morning twi-light of college into the bright day. He bounded out of the west into New York like a calf confidently and arrogantly bumping its mother for a meal. This was only a week or so after Erma had returned from Europe widowed of the unlikely Pierre, and you had just had lunch with her. Larry was pleasantly impressed but not at all overawed by your elaborate office. Almost at once he was telling you that he had never properly thanked you for putting him through college, that he was really tremendously grateful, that he would pay you back as soon as he could, and that he was glad it was over.

"It's mostly horseplay. They don't really know any of the stuff they tell you, except football. That's the only thing they've found out for themselves. I'm glad it's over. Have you decided where I'm to start blowing up the buildings?"

He was leaving it all to you, and you were thrilled by this, unaware that it was only because to his youthful eagerness and ardor details were unimportant Also it had already been decided. Dick had been extremely decent about it, regretting that he hadn't a younger brother of his own to start along the line, and welcoming Larry as a substitute.

He spent six months in the plant in Ohio, six more in the Michigan ore mines, some few weeks in New York, and then was suddenly interrupted by the war.

Larry's letters to you and Jane were your only intimate contact with the insane ultimate consumers of the steel and iron toys which were causing the stock in Erma's vault to increase in value at the rate of six thousand dollars a day. Being treasurer of the corporation, you were in a position to contemplate that insolent accretion with fitting ironic admiration. But for the censor Larry's narratives from the trenches would have served excellently as frontispieces for the imposing rows of journals and ledgers which were locked each evening behind those massive steel doors on lower Broadway.

Back as a decorated captain, Larry returned to his desk as if nothing had happened. It was easy to see in his eyes the questions that had not been there before, but he left you to guess at them. Was that true of Jane also? You wonder about Larry and Jane.

He proved himself, young as he was he rose in importance by his own ability and force, but during all those months that became years you felt a vague uneasiness about him. All the time you wondered what it was and why it disturbed you so, not aware of the deep significance which his presence and progress in that environment had come to hold for you, as vindication of your own acceptance of it.

The explosion came at a difficult moment, and unexpectedly.

Only the previous week Larry had won new laurels by bringing
to a successful close the Cumberland bridge negotiations, down
in Maryland. You had heard Dick offer him praise of a different
character from any you had ever earned. The difficulty though
had come through Erma, whose pretty teeth had shown themselves for the first time the night before in a most inelegant snarl.
You didn't feel like lunching with anyone and were annoyed at
Larry's persistence. When, immediately after you and he had
been seated at the usual corner table in the Manufacturers'
Club, he announced that he was going to leave the Carr
Corporation, you were at first merely irritated, as if he had said
he was going to put a fly in your soup.

"Of course you don't mean it. What's the joke?"

"There's no joke. I'm going to chuck it."

"But good heavens, you're crazy. What's the matter? What's
the idea?"

Larry took a drink of water and unfolded his napkin. He
looked uncomfortable.

"This is the only hard part of it, Bill, trying to tell you why.
You've been so damn good to me and from your standpoint this
must seem insane. I'm afraid I can't even be very definite about
it. Only it's not the life for me. It's not what I want to do. I suppose I'll get into a rut no matter what I do—everyone seems to
nowadays—but this is the wrong kind of a rut."

"You might have found that out seven years ago, before Dick
and I took all the trouble we've taken, and made room for you—"

"I know it. I know all you've done. But my mind wasn't made
up till quite recently. At that I don't think I owe the company
anything. If I could only tell you exactly how I feel about it,
Bill, I think you'd understand. You certainly have a knack of
understanding people."

He went on explaining with words that explained nothing

while you scarcely heard. You were filled with anger and even
with a sort of terror which you now comprehend much better
than you did then. There was indeed nothing trivial about this;
it was a major and almost a vital casualty for you; it meant that
Larry was spewing out in disgust that which you found no great
difficulty in swallowing and digesting. Essentially that was what
it meant, and it threw you almost into a panic. You had often
suspected yourself of a finer nature, too fine to be really comfortable in this den of hyenas, but not Larry. It was intolerable.

There he sat, for all his expressions of gratitude and regret
and his embarrassed concern for your feelings really quite
imperturbable. Unshakable. You asked him with a sneer:

"What are you going to do?"

"I don't know. I've got a good deal saved, thanks to your and
Dick's generosity, and I may buy the Martin place out in Idaho
where I went last summer. He'll sell cheap."

"Going to raise cattle?"

"Perhaps. Or get a job in the forest service. I don't know."

Evidently he had been considering it for some time.

That evening you went to see Jane, at the house on Tenth
Street where you always felt incongruous, like a pig on a silk
cushion, despite Jane's presence. You were recurrently indignant at that feeling and tried to bully yourself out of it. What
the deuce, you yourself were not precisely illiterate; you read
Norman Douglas and Lytton Strachey and went to the concerts
of the International Composers Guild. But in this Tenth Street
intellectual sea you swam with difficulty, or more commonly
stayed behind on the shore, for they were always beyond your
depth almost before they started; you listened to their jargon
with uneasy contempt, and loathed Jane when she undertook
to explain to you who Pavlov was. Your visits had become more
and more infrequent.

This evening you expected to find there the usual crowd, Jane's husband (if he were not away lecturing on god knows what), a writer or two, at least one experimental actress and an assortment of parlor radicals. You intended to take Jane off somewhere and persuade her to bring Larry to his senses. But when you arrived the rooms on the ground floor were dark, and proceeding brusquely upstairs, past the faintly protesting maid who had let you in, you found Jane and Larry alone in Jane's room.

Larry was as startled at your sudden appearance as though you had caught him rifling your desk. Jane seemed merely glad to see you.

"Bill! It's almost a family reunion."

In the six hours since lunch you had somewhat recovered your balance, and for that matter you did not yet suspect the depth of this wound; so you went to look at the baby with proper appreciation and waited till you had all gone downstairs before you remarked:

"I suppose Larry's told you of his contemplated renascence."

"Yes. Oh yes."

"We've just been talking about it," Larry said. "Jane thinks it's all right."

"So it's a conspiracy."

"Not actionable." Jane came and sat on the arm of your chair and put her hand on yours. "Don't cut up about it, Bill, there's a dear."

"It would make a lot of difference if I did. I think it's crazy and I think it's a pretty rotten way to act. After all I've done…"

"What have you done?" But instantly Larry's voice changed. "I don't mean that. I mean you might think I was letting you down. Good lord, I'm of no importance down there. You've got dozens as good as I am."

"We've not got dozens who have your opportunities and your future. And who prepared it and made it easy? Oh, I know you've worked and you've made good. Quite probably you'll prove to be a better man than me, but that isn't what gave you the inside track."

Larry opened his mouth and closed it again. Jane, whose hand had remained on yours, rose suddenly and went to him.

"You run away, Larry, and let Bill and me talk. Please. Go on."

He went, observing that he would see you in the morning at the office. Jane came back to your chair.

"Meaning that you'll smooth out my childish irritation," you observed.

"Yes," she agreed unexpectedly, putting her hand again on yours. "Only I don't know how childish it is. It's a darned shame."

"That I'm so unreasonable, I suppose."

"Oh don't do that, Bill. It's not a question of anyone's being unreasonable. This was bound to hurt you. I told Larry so the first time he spoke to me about it, and at the same time I told him I approved."

"So it's been cooking for a long while. I like the picture of you and Larry calculating the chances of my eventual recovery."

There was no reply. You looked up, and for the second time in your life you saw tears in Jane's eyes, as lovely as ever. You moved your hand restlessly.

"You're the only person I've ever cried about," she said finally. "I don't know whether it means anything in particular. I seem to feel more touched by what things mean for you than by what they mean even for myself, let alone anybody else. With Victor for instance I can discuss at length what Larry should or shouldn't do, and get quite heated about it. With you it's impossible

because nothing matters except that Larry is going to go and it
makes you unhappy. I think I know every single thing you feel."

There was nothing left to say to that. You suddenly forgot all
about Larry and had to choke an impulse to tell Jane about the
night before with Erma, the humiliation of your position at the
office, even your inner humiliations which you never discussed
with yourself. You were silent; the crust had become too thick.
A moment later Victor's voice was heard in the hall, with Rose
and Margaret and other people.

A month later Larry was on his way west. If Jane had been
futile with you, how much more futile had you been with him!

You could dance around in that cage forever. There was the
first man you ever fired, out in Cleveland many years ago, the
fellow with the big bony white hands who always smelled
faintly of mingled perfume and himself. When you learned a
week later that he had committed suicide you were so stricken
with remorse that you couldn't sleep for two nights. That was
the conceit of your youth. A man who will kill himself merely
because he gets fired is bound to lose his job, for that reason if
for no other. There was the manicure girl downtown who was
so intelligent and sympathetic that you paid her way through
business college, gave her a job in the office, and promoted her
out of order. She married your assistant office manager, and
within a year he was arrested and convicted of embezzlement
of the company's funds. Thirty thousand dollars of the money
had disappeared and could not be accounted for, but the intelligent manicure girl played the role of deceived and disillu-
sioned wife with complete success. The futility begins when?
Hardly in the cradle. There is probably a gradual progress toward
immunity from the time of the first breath until that day when
the ego makes its curt announcement, I have room for no more
scars. There will be a universal variation. With some it will come

almost with the first syllables, with others it will be delayed to full bodily maturity. These would be the extremes. With you it had almost certainly arrived, for instance, by the time you went to the home of Mrs. Davis that first afternoon. You were fifteen, seventeen, no matter.

You went to Sunday School willingly for the sake of the intellectual excitement. Mr. Snyder, the teacher, detested you because you insisted on questioning the feasibility of water having been turned into wine, a thing which you said could not be done even in the best equipped modern laboratory. You voiced many other skepticisms, but this was the best fortified, on account of your father, who as a practicing druggist and chemist resented that miracle with an unwonted violence. Into the Sunday School discussion you would bring technical terms direct from your father's lips, reducing Mr. Snyder to a cold and speechless fury. You always flattered yourself that you drove him from the class; it is undeniable that he left and that Mrs. Davis took his place.

Her advent ended the free play of the intellect. You tried once or twice to start an argument, but she merely turned her soft blue eyes on you and said that after all the Bible is true, isn't it? But you didn't stay away, though your father would have been more than willing and your mother indifferent. You continued to go, and for the most part sat silently watching Mrs. Davis's face and hands. As time went on, she would ask the boys to run errands for her, and when the choice fell on one of the others you were conscious of a painful and disagreeable sensation unlike any you had ever known before. More and more often it was you who were chosen.

One winter Monday afternoon, as soon as you could make it after the close of school, found you on her porch with an umbrella which she had left on some previous day at old Mrs. Poole's on the other side of town. She herself opened the door.

"How do you do, William. Thank you so much." Then, as you flushed and twirled your cap, "Won't you come in a little while? Please do, and cheer me up. Mother is spending the week in Chicago and my husband won't be home for hours and I'm feeling lonely and not at all in a good Christian humor."

You had several times previously crossed the moat of the lawn and advanced as far as the pure white portal, but never before inside the castle itself. You felt admirably adventurous and keen, though you did stumble a little on the rug in the dimly lighted sitting-room, where the curtains were drawn and a fire was glowing. You were grateful to Mrs. Davis for not noticing; your mother would have scolded your clumsiness and Jane would have asked if you had hurt yourself. But you were a little taken aback when she observed:

"We can sit here on the couch and go over next Sunday's lesson." She was probably watching your face, for she added almost at once, "Or would you rather just talk?"

You blurted out, "Just talk," and sat down on the edge of the couch beside her.

She began to ask you questions, and though your tongue gradually loosened enough to form sentences you could not look at her face. You wanted to and dared not. You could see her small soft white hands lying in her lap and you thought of her face, also soft and white with its lips that were never still, even when silent, and its blue eyes with long dark lashes. Sam Boley had said once that she had a double chin, and nearly got killed for it, though not by you.

She had asked you what you thought about when you were not in school or playing games with the boys, and you were struggling for courage to tell her of the poem you had written about her, when suddenly she put her hand under your chin and turned your face squarely toward hers.

"Goodness, can't we look at each other? I like your face so much. It's so sensitive and strong, for a boy. There, we have looked at each other." She took her hand away. "Now go on and tell me."

But you had been made dumb again. At the touch of her hand you had almost fainted with pleasure. You hoped she hadn't noticed it, for you wanted her to think that you were far from being a puppy to play with. To mention the poem now was impossible. She gave it up and got an album of snapshots which she and her husband had taken on their honeymoon trip to England, nearly ten years ago, she said. You turned the leaves together, your hands touching and your warmth mingling. You were feeling rather gone and miserably inadequate by the time she arose and said it was time to get her husband's dinner.

On your way home you thought, so that's what experience is, is it? You felt ineffectual and at the same time expectant and unashamed. You wondered how old she was and finally settled on twenty-seven.

The second time you went, invited without the excuse of an errand, she told you all about her husband. It seemed that although he was a fine man, he had more or less deceived her into marriage by concealing from her girlish ignorance some of its more difficult and profound aspects. He was now doing his best to atone for that early betrayal, but try as she would she could not abandon herself to a complete and true union with such a man—not that there was really anything to be said against him. There was a great deal of this, of which you understood perhaps a third. It seemed however to be leading to something when the doorbell rang and Mrs. Davis went to open it with a Bible in her hand. Especially apropos, for it proved to be the pastor making a call.

The next time, only a few days later, you took the poem. She

discussed it only as literature, and at her suggestion you changed
a word here and there. Then she asked you to read it again and
you did so, seated on the chair by the little desk while she was
on the couch. When you had finished and folded the paper and
put it in your pocket she said quietly:

"Come here."

You went across to her.

"Do you like me?"

You nodded, trembling; no word would come.

"Sit down by me. Here, put your head in my lap, like that.
Don't you like to be near me and put your head in my lap? You
are a very dear boy, only you are nearly a man. Nearly a man,
aren't you? Why not pretend you are a man, and kiss me? Do
you mind if I kiss you? Will you kiss me?"

You discovered then that the girls at school knew very little
about kissing, and you yourself, as a matter of fact, knew less.
Nor had particularly cared about it. Mrs. Davis's arms were
around you, and you held her tight, your lips on hers; she
kissed your neck and your eyes; you kissed her eyes, her nose,
her chin, her throat, through inexpertness and excitement not
always hitting the precise spot, but aim is unimportant when
it's shrapnel. Easy enough now to smile at that sprawling
urchin, uncouth, drinking with noisy gulps at the unknown
pool, but then your blood was a true torrent of fire.

Granting all your neat formula of futility, it is strange that
you have never been curious as to the nature and depth of Mrs.
Davis's attachment to you. Was it for her an episode among a
hundred, or was it all that her avowals in transport declared?
You have never bothered to guess. Under her you served a sexual
apprenticeship conventionally complete; it lasted over two years;
there were many moments when the bodily fusion was utterly
sweet and terrifying; and yet, except for those moments your

attitude was essentially as if she were merely one more school-teacher and it was all a part of the course in physical culture.

How clever she was at arranging meetings, with what admirable sangfroid could she dispose of an inopportune caller, and above all with what fine gallantry did she carry herself when the explosion came and the whole pack yapped and howled at her heels!

For months you had felt sure that Jane suspected something, nevertheless you were startled when she suddenly said to you one afternoon:

"Bill, you'd better be careful about Mrs. Davis. There isn't a woman in town that doesn't know all about it, and now the men are beginning to talk. Dad heard someone say something at the store yesterday that he didn't understand, and he asked Mother, and he's going for you as soon as he can get his courage up. I heard him talking with Mother last night."

You thought the thing to do was to appear innocent and ignorant. Jane snorted:

"Don't be a fool. It might as well be in the paper."

It might indeed. Or among the public notices on the doors of the courthouse. It finally reached even Mr. Davis, in his law office across the square from the drug store. You were requested to call upon Mr. Davis, and your father instructed you not to go. Your father, of course, questioned you with what was for him unexampled severity, but in the meantime you had seen Mrs. Davis and you did exactly what she told you to, even perhaps a little more. In effect you denied all facts of your physical existence, save that you had been born and that you were of the male sex. The dramatic climax was a conference arranged to take place at the Davis home among Mrs. Davis, Mr. Davis, your father and yourself. You went with your father, who you suspected was at heart enjoying the whole affair as a colorful adventure in an otherwise dull life. There was a great deal of talk between your father and Mr. Davis. Though rather hard-pressed by the lawyer's cross-examination, you maintained your general denials and refused to go into details. Mrs. Davis was no longer present, for she had said:

"William, I am sorry that people are so determined to make life ugly. Mr. Sidney, I regret that you are having all this trouble, and I know you regret that I am. Jim, when you finish with this silly business I want to talk with you."

And had left the room.

Whether it was she or her husband who finally found the pressure too great you never knew. Off they went to Cleveland with nothing but a trunk; their furniture followed later by freight, with suggestive and insulting notices pasted on the bedstead. The whole town learned of this kindly godspeed to its departed citizens, and the authorship was hotly disputed, especially of the placard on the foot of the bed which read: Handle With Care Willie May Be Under It.

Its echoes were heard as long afterward as the elections the following autumn, when old Doctor Culp, who had stoutly defended Mrs. Davis throughout, was a candidate for the Board of Education and in spite of his popularity squeezed through by the narrowest of margins.

Superficially the affair seemed to place you in a difficult and ridiculous position, but in the circles which bore most closely on your daily concerns the effect was far from deplorable. Among the fellows you were regarded as a man with a past, and the attitude of the mothers whose daughters you escorted to parties merely accentuated your evil eminence and fed your vanity. There were certain jibes which you resented acutely, but altogether the experience did you no harm and was not unpleasant.

As regards that kernel, that ego, that stubborn infinitesimal entity which resists all definition and all seizure and which alone is you if you exist at all, what did Mrs. Davis do? Nothing. What would her husband have done if, differently constituted, he had shot you dead, as the most vociferous townsfolk said he should have done? Nothing. What do you do to her upstairs if you achieve all that your despair contemplates and she lies before you bloody and annihilated? Nothing.

Nothing…nothing….

# C

What if Mrs. Jordan had heard him come in? Or even seen him? She might very well have been standing by the grill, her hands full of milk bottles, when he turned and went up the stoop. He had first reconnoitred from across the street, but it was so dark in that confounded basement entrance that one couldn't see anything.

His hand still on the rail, he half turned about there on the stairs. He opened his mouth to call to her. But that would make everything impossible. True, it would establish whether she had heard him, but it would make everything impossible. He stood undecided.

Timid, futile, vengeless, actionless...

# III

There has not been one major experience in your life in which you were the aggressor. You have never even invited one. At the bottom of the sea there are said to be organisms against which food must float by the chance of nature if it would be devoured and assimilated—strange and stubborn masochism down in the slime beneath the oceans. Without its counterpart, infinitely more intricate and subtle, here on the crust, infused even into nature's supreme two-legged achievement, you would have perished long ago.

The Davis affair was her doing. Each crisis in your economic and business life, which means the Carr Corporation, has been so little guided by you that you might as well have been at home asleep. The fact of your not marrying Lucy Crofts was determined by a Cleveland street car which, a little behind its schedule, refused to stop when you waved at it. In all the weary kaleidoscope of your life with Erma there is not a single picture that was composed by your will. With Jane, nothing; Larry, nothing; Dick, also nothing—except that one amazing episode which not only contradicted timidity but indicated also an aggressiveness and a violence of will unique and inexplicable. It fooled Dick and it fooled everyone but you; you were merely bewildered and still are. It is impossible that it could have been you who slapped the Mule in the face, stood up to him and blackened his eye, and got the name of Battling Bill.

It is curious that Dick never mentioned Millicent again, not then or at any subsequent time, not even when it was generally known that Old Prune had spoken to you about her, and some of the other fellows were not so reticent. Can it be that he shared—but that neither he nor she would tell you, and there's no sense in beating your brain about it. At the time you appreciated his silence and sensitiveness.

It is curious too to reflect that but for your knightly ardor in defending her innocence little Millicent might have gone on indefinitely rolling up your soiled shirts, however wisely and terribly and never have touched you. But it is unlikely and it would be intolerable to believe it. If that was pure chance, sheer accident, then there is no slightest significance in anything and life is nothing but an obscene hocus-pocus.

It was your bruised face though that she first touched, as you reclined in the big armchair, still none too comfortable on account of your ribs, after you had been confined to your room for a week.

"I'm sorry you got hurt," she said in her thin even monotone.

"Thanks. So am I. And I'm sorry there isn't any candy for you. The fellows ate it all up the other night."

She was gently rubbing your still swollen jaw, her fingers firm and sure and alive.

"I don't care. What was you fighting about?"

"Oh, he called me a liar and then he said he could lick me."

"Could he?"

You started to grin, but your bruised muscles and bones brought you up.

"Don't I look like it?"

"Yes. You look pretty bad."

"Your hand feels very good. You ought to be a nurse when you grow up."

"No. I hate sick men. That ain't why my hand feels good."

You were suddenly aware that you didn't want her to tell you why. You moved your head a little, and she took her hand away and gave a sharp little sigh.

"I guess I've got to go."

Thenceforth the course of that business proceeded, slow, insidious, inexorable. The details of its progression are now mostly blurred and vague, more so than other contemporaneous affairs, for instance your friendship with Dick. Where in fact was the evil? To judge not from your own scanty experience, but from what is freely discussed in technical jargon and whispered here and there in the vernacular, life can include a most strange and varied repertory without creating anything more damaging than a mild disquietude. Certainly not dishonor nor damnation. But god knows in this case the evil was there, and if it was not in the suggestive stillness of her little white face, or the constant concentrated expectancy of her dark eyes, or, above all, the somehow irresistibly thrilling movements of her hands and fingers, where was it? Was it after all in you? But where in the name of heaven did it come from? What put it there, and why?

Not to be explained.

Some of the later details are not blurred at all; you have in subsequent years so frequently repeated them in fantasy that you could more precisely describe that sequence of gestures than you could those of dressing yourself. Then, less than two years ago, like being awakened by thunder out of a dream which was caused by it, fantasy again became reality....

The original awakening, which abruptly terminated the affair, was due merely to the existence of other realities than your own. You were completely unprepared for it, and that sunny morning as you walked across the campus toward the imposing new brick building behind the pine grove, in response to the summons from the dean's office, you wondered mildly what was up.

Seated at his shiny glass-topped desk was Old Prune himself, appearing uncommonly disturbed, and in a chair facing him was a poorly dressed, tired-looking, but compact and energetic little woman whose face seemed vaguely familiar to you.

"Good morning, Sidney. I suppose you know Mrs. Moran." Old Prune was brusque with irritation at the unpleasant task. "She has made a complaint about you which she says is based on information she has received from her daughter."

You were stunned. The woman saved you by breaking in:

"It ain't exactly a complaint. As I said, if it's all a story it ain't Millie's first. I just want to ask Mr. Sidney about it."

"I'll do the asking, Mrs. Moran." And to you, "Have you been guilty of misconduct with this young girl?"

How fortunate that surprised indignation too is incoherent! You stammered, "No, sir. I—I've given her candy, of course. No, sir."

"It's you that gave her the candy then," said Mrs. Moran gloomily. "That mixes it all up again, for she says that the gentleman that gives her the candy is nice and handsome, but wouldn't do anything his mamma told him not to. She told your name, sir, when I had her by the ear, and she stuck to it, though it was afterwards I noticed it was there on the package on the chair ready to go back to you and it might have come into her mouth that way. But it was in one of the books you gave her."

"I never gave her any books." Nor had you, as was evident from your tone.

"You didn't!" Mrs. Moran sank back discouraged. "Sure, the little devil has mixed it all up." She sat up again. "Do they call you the Donkey?"

"No. I don't think there's anybody called the Donkey. There's a fellow they call the Mule."

Afterward you wondered why you had been fool enough to say that.

A few more of Mrs. Moran's questions and observations
made it evident that little Millicent had so confused the issue
and more especially the identity that almost anyone might be
involved, including two or three members of the faculty. Old
Prune was disgusted and became skeptical. He would probably
gladly have told Mrs. Moran to go home and mind her own
business and lock her brat in the cellar, but there was too much
explosive in this material for that, particularly since it appeared
that Mrs. Moran had been sent to him from the president's
office, where she had first carried her tale. In the end he
arranged with her that he should question Millicent himself, and
you were dismissed with what almost amounted to an apology,
and with a strict command to speak of the affair to no one.

You were pretty sick, and the vague uneasiness which had
been constantly with you for many months was now acute and
intolerable; but you did something that was for you rather
clever. You calculated that if you had been innocent you would
almost certainly not keep still about it, and that therefore if you
observed the dean's imposition of silence it would bear an
implication of guilt even with him. So you imparted some of
the details, here and there, selecting the recipients with due
regard to the requirements, and overnight the morsel was being
rolled around on a hundred palates. Unquestionably it would
get back underground to Old Prune, whose chief concern then
would be to suppress the unseemly tale.

Summoned again to his office a few days later, it was at once
obvious that you had nothing to fear. Chiefly he was angry with
you for letting the thing out, but he couldn't prove it and had to
accept your comments regarding other possible channels of
publicity. The main charge was dismissed with a curt and not
enthusiastic apology.

"I have questioned the girl," he went on, "and discovered a

prodigious native talent for mystification and obscurity. It would be beyond any human power to unravel the tangle she has manufactured. I make this explanation because it is due you. The incident is closed, and I hope the gossip also."

Little Millicent, of course, was no more. You did not again hear on your door that firm low knock which you had grown to await with so sharp an expectancy. You were even compelled to make your own guess among the various rumors regarding her; the one that seemed most likely was that Mrs. Moran had been seen holding tightly to her daughter's hand as they boarded a westbound train. By inquiry you might have learned more about it, but that was dangerous and not to be thought of; besides, it would have been pointless. She was gone.

That was only a month before your diploma and farewell, the return home, and the subsequent third visit to Dick in Cleveland.

You are not concerned to place blame either on that pale slim child or elsewhere; you would gladly assume it yourself if you could only feel that you are worthy of it. You would be proud to convict yourself of a pursuit and a seizure even of that shameful diminutive prey. But the will was hers, the first gestures were hers, it was her show. Superb spectacle, you! That's funny; you were the prey.

It was so again with Lucy Crofts in Cleveland.

The very first days at the Cleveland office, before Dick went out to stay at the plant, are too dim for recovery. You were of course introduced to all the heads of departments, but you don't remember any desk those first few weeks; you were a great deal with Dick. You have never had any trouble understanding what things were about, nor for that matter people either, and it was easy to see that Dick was pleased with your curiosity, your eagerness, and your quick comprehension. It encouraged him to offer you a certain defined authority, with the title of Assistant to the President, before he went away. You didn't want it.

"I'm too young, Dick."

"You're my age."

"You're the owner. You're god by the incontestable right of signed stock certificates."

Dick didn't like that quotation from one of your stories; he thought it was socialistic. He retorted:

"Nevertheless I've got to live up to it."

"And nearly everybody here is old enough to be my grandfather. It would make them all my enemies right at the beginning."

"They're that already. They've been looking forward to me for ten years with dislike and suspicion, and now they find there's two of me. That's what it amounts to. A title more or less doesn't matter. Anyway, I'm not going to the North Pole; I'll be in at least once a week. But have it your own way. It's unimportant."

He was faintly disappointed.

The next day your name, in gold block letters, William B. Sidney, was placed on the door of a room across the hall from Dick's, but you continued to spend most of your time in the various departments. The distribution of emphasis differed considerably from the present. Then, for instance, the only person concerned with publicity was the man with a moustache, at a desk back in a corner, who spent his mornings at the office of the Simmons agency editing copy which had been prepared for the trade journals. Now there is that elaborate room downtown occupied by the Public Relations Counsel with a salary not less elaborate than the room.

You made yourself a nuisance in the accounting rooms day after day, with eventually a fair grasp of the principles but never quite getting inside the details of cost distribution, depreciation and the like. Nothing was withheld; you learned the intricacies and dubiosities of rebates, territorial agreements, preferred contracts. Those were the days of early exploration in the possibilities of by-products; this you found more exciting and stimulating than anything else, and you missed another chance of action here, for, in spite of your lack of proper training, your intelligent and genuine interest might really have accomplished something. You had the thought, but you funked it.

The export department interested you too, but differently; it aroused your romantic imagination to handle those slips of paper which told of the shipment of thousands of tons of steel for the construction of a railroad bridge in the heart of the Malay jungle; you even wrote a story about it, those lonely evenings in your room, a biography of a bit of iron ore from the time it left the Michigan mine until, become part of a girder, it supported the foot of a hungry and inventive panther who decided to try out the possibilities of ambush in this strange new tree. You thought rather well of it and wanted to show it to Dick, but decided that it would be just as well not to.

Throughout the first months, and even years, you served as an information channel between Dick and the intricate parts of the vast organism he was getting into his fist. For that function you were well fitted and you fulfilled it excellently. Unquestionably, that bewildering mass of facts and movements and personalities was more rapidly and easily assimilated by him, strained through your quick and fresh observation and reaction, than if he had gone himself to the sources. Most important of all, for his purpose, was your intuitive feeling for men and their interrelations, though Dick learned to place reliance on it only after it had been variously and without exception verified by the event.

He would get in from the Carrton plant usually on Friday evening late, and you and he would go to the café on Sheriff

Street, because he said he could relax there more easily than at home; an arrangement which suited you, for Erma would often be at home and you found it embarrassing. This was the period when the scene in the garden had apparently slipped her mind and she seemed entirely indifferent to you.

Dick, having ordered a three-inch steak, would gulp a stein of beer without stopping, lick the foam from his lips, settle back in the big leather chair and sigh contentedly.

"Well, how are the old Megatherii of Pearl Street? I've had a swell week—twelve hours a day—pretty soon I'm going to make it twenty. Like hell. I'm half dead. I'm going to take three of those ancient furnaces and throw 'em so damn far out in Lake Erie they'll be nothing but pins in a bathtub. It's not so much fun now there's nobody left to fire. Old Skinner is gone, gave him a pension. He and Dad made the first coupling-pin west of the Alleghenies, or something like that."

He looked far from dead; fresh and vigorous as a young bull. You felt overwhelmed.

By the time the steak arrived you would be reading from sheets of memoranda neatly arranged on the table before you.

"There are nine Class A companies in Utah and Colorado. In 1900 there were six, and three of them were on our books. Now none of them are, but one of them uses a little of our stuff through a Kansas City jobber. We haven't any of the three new ones, one of which is tied up with Bethlehem. Net loss of two, practically three."

"Who covers it?"

"It's handled mostly by Byers from San Francisco, but Harper was in Denver and Salt Lake in 1907."

"What does Jackson say about it?"

"His usual line; expansion, natural shifting of territory, drop one here and pick up another one somewhere else."

"What was done this season?"

"Not a thing unless Byers wrote some letters. Jackson never
checks up on Byers, I think he's afraid of him. He talks vaguely
about an offer from Farrell he heard of once. We don't have a
thing on it here, not even a list of operations."

"When did we lose them?"

"The last order from one of them was 1903, the other one
1905."

It had taken you most of two days to dig all this out; it took
only fifteen minutes for Dick to get it. But usually this sort of
data was not communicated orally; he would take your memoranda to Carrton and devote his evenings to them. Together
you would talk mostly about the men, their attitudes, their
capabilities, their energies. You are astonished now to remember
how impudently those two youths passed judgment on a generation, and how nearly right they usually were. Your own lack of
discretion in those reports to Dick, which seemed bold and
spirited but in reality proceeded from your immature disregard
of implications and effects, made you many enemies. And a few
friends, like Schwartz, who on your recommendation was placed
in charge of an export section over the heads of older men.

For months, a year, two years, you found a live and exciting
interest in all this. There were not many lonely evenings, for
you commonly used four or five of each week digesting and
arranging the day's work, and were with Dick for the remainder.
The happiest days of your life? That's meaningless, but at least
the days when you most nearly approached the joy of feeling
that between you and life you were more a source than a recep-
tacle. While he was away at Carrton, Dick arranged that one of
his cars should be always at your disposal, and the arrangement
was continued even after his return permanently to Cleveland,
but you seldom took advantage of it. The social side of life he

entirely ignored, refusing even to appear at Erma's Sunday teas, and you were pulled along with him.

"You'll both die of ingrown dispositions," Erma would observe indifferently. "Damon and Pythias, victims of the Iron Age— I'll erect statues of you in the Square."

"Go on and deposit your dividend checks," Dick would reply with equal indifference.

Gradually, after Dick's return to Cleveland, you began to find time on your hands. Erma went to Europe and Dick closed the house and took rooms at the Jayhawker Club. He spent most of his evenings at the office, where you were usually with him, but he soon began to find friends among the young bankers and businessmen, and in this circle you somehow didn't seem quite to fit, though you were always welcome.

There was the affair out at Courtney's on the road to Conneaut. You wanted to go, and yet were reluctant.

"Come on, Bill, you've got to," Dick insisted. "It's my first blow-off in two years. My god, think of it, I haven't raped a single duchess for two whole years. I don't suppose you have either. Come along."

You left town around midnight in two of Dick's cars and four others. In your car were two young brokers whose names you can't remember and four or five girls from the show at Wright's Theatre which you had all attended. You drove, and one of the girls, short and plump, sat with you and kept saying:

"It's too bad it isn't moonlight."

At Courtney's, when the six cars had all arrived the gate was closed and the place was yours. Couples, already affiliated during the brief ride, began to drift away, only to be immediately reassembled in the main room where a long narrow table was prepared, completely covered with silver, glasses and flowers. The guests were seated, for the most part decorously, but with some confusion, for it appeared that the girls considerably out-numbered the men.

"I certainly wouldn't go anywhere I wasn't invited," said the girl on your left in a loud challenging voice.

"Then you'd better go on home," said the girl on your right, across the back of your neck.

You had never been drunk except once or twice at parties with Dick at college, and then more sick than drunk. Now you did not want to drink. You made no decision in the matter, you certainly were conscious of no feeling of revulsion or superiority, but you didn't drink. The girls beside you tried to pour it down your throat, then finally gave it up and emptied your glass themselves. Dick by this time had a red-haired girl on his lap and was feeding her soup with a fork.

The feast dragged along, punctuated by toasts that were not heard, songs, a little dancing which grew more and more uncertain, shouts and screams, a game of leapfrog. Couples again began to drift away, but were called back peremptorily by Dick for what he said was to be the climax of the evening. Meanwhile he was furiously pulling off the stockings of the red-haired girl, who was giggling and squealing and trying to wriggle out of his grasp. She broke away and ran.

"Hey, Bill, catch her!" Dick yelled. "Catch her! Hold her!"

He proceeded to explain indignantly to all who would listen. It appeared that the red-haired girl had agreed to dance naked on the table for the sum of one hundred dollars and was now trying to repudiate her contract.

She called from the corner of the room, not at all drunkenly:

"I'll do it for two hundred."

"Hundred an' fifty."

"Two hundred."

Dick started for her like an avalanche. "You little red devil, I'll tear every stitch off your back!"

She sprang to the other side of the table and yelled at him: "All right. One-fifty."

Off came her dress, her petticoats, her corset. Somebody started the piano. Champagne bottles fell off the table as Dick lifted her up. Everybody cheered; someone threw a stick of celery at her. A man who tried to catch her foot as she danced got kicked in the face and went sprawling. Applause.

You stood a little off, alone, furious with yourself for your soberness and detachment. This was fun; this was real fun; what was wrong with you?

Hours later, driving back to Cleveland in the early morning sun, you thought that nothing could be quite as unlovely as the amorphous mass of your cargo, a loose and twisted face showing here and there, and you envied them.

About this time Dick put you in at the Jayhawker Club and suggested that you take a room there. You could easily have afforded it, for your salary had been doubled the first of the year, but it didn't come off, though you never decided definitely against it. Dick didn't insist. More and more you began to find time on your hands. You read a great deal, went to a show now and then with someone from the office, usually Schwartz, and would often drive out along the lake shore after dinner, or into the country, mostly alone. There was nothing much in any of this; you felt aimless and dissatisfied.

One evening you looked through the little red memorandum book and found Mrs. Davis's Cleveland address, placed there six years before from the only letter you had ever received from her.

You supposed that she would probably have moved. In any event you couldn't very well call, in the evening, when her husband would probably be at home. You thought of the telephone, and from the directory learned that she had moved and got the new address and the phone number. But the phone's audacious immediacy repelled you—number, please...click, and there

you are, after six years and all their content. You would have to
write. You did so, on the letterhead of the Carr Corporation
with your name engraved in the corner, asking if she would
dine or go to the theatre with you.

There was no reply. Two days, three days, four days. The
next afternoon you telephoned, and there she was. Her voice,
perfectly. You were made aware that you were more deeply
interested than you had suspected by the fact that your own
voice trembled with excitement. Had she got your letter?

"Yes, oh yes, I got it, it was very sweet of you to send it. It
was so nice of you to think of me."

Would she—that is—how about going out to dinner?

"Well, you see, I'm afraid I can't. Of course I could manage
it I suppose, but there are so many things always to do, and I
always eat dinner at home with my husband…"

You idiotically asked after Mr. Davis's health.

You reflected that chorus girls, though terrifying and meaty in
the mass, were not necessarily impossible as individuals; in fact
you had seen some that were quite attractive. When Schwartz
said it was his turn to treat and suggested a musical comedy,
billed for the following week, you declined on some pretext or
other and later got a single ticket as near the front as possible.
Once there, the seat seemed much too close, the paint and
wrinkles were terribly obvious, but there were three or four
more than passable who looked young and capable of tender
sympathy; you were sure that one of them smiled at you. When
the curtain fell for their first intermission you decided that it
was time to act. You didn't leave your seat; the plan was to send
a note by an usher, and you had made sure to come equipped
with a dozen of your cards, a fountain pen and some small
envelopes. But confronted with the moment the difficulties
appeared insurmountable. You certainly could not call an usher

to you and explain matters in full view of the entire audience. When the curtain went up for the second act you had not even written the note.

At the second intermission you sought an usher in the rear and in the lobby. The first one you found was surrounded by people who would certainly overhear you and smile at you; the second, alone in a corner, looked unapproachably solemn and forbidding. Clutching the note in your hand you went for a drink of water, and downstairs to the men's room, then resumed the search. But the gusto was gone; you were like a hunter with all his cartridges soaked still watching wistfully and listening for the whirr of the rising bird. After the last curtain you went around and stood by the stage door, desperately summoning your courage, watching dark forms hurriedly emerge, until two men whom you knew suddenly came out with laughing girls on their arms, when you melted away. You thought that you had recognized the girl in front as the one who was to have received your note, but that was probably fancy, it was really too dark to tell.

You perhaps remember that evening so vividly because it was so complete, so neat and so characteristic. Your life in miniature, all in three hours. There have been others, only more extended, like the winter devoted so completely to Lucy Crofts, or like the summer, only four years ago, which you and Erma spent at Larry's ranch.

It was Erma's idea, suggested by a rodeo she saw in New York, and impelled of course by her constant restlessness. At the time you were on good terms with her, partly because of your gratitude for the splendid support she had given you in the difficulties at the office. You were a little doubtful of Larry, since the only news he had had from you since going west had been through Jane, but when his reply arrived it was most cordial and urged you to come.

The preparations interested you more than anything had done for years. Erma took seven trunks, one of them containing three saddles and a red bridle with silver studdings and bit set with turquoises.

When you finally arrived, late in June, riding a hundred miles from the nearest railroad station in an old rickety Ford, you were somewhat disconcerted by the bareness of the house and the absence of all accustomed conveniences. Erma thought it was charming. By comparing with the rest of the house the room that had been prepared for you it was easy to see that Larry had been at great pains to arrange for your comfort, and he was obviously pleased at Erma's delighted appreciation. This same room, with its large double bed, was one of the causes of your discomposure. You and Erma had never slept in the same bed. She accepted it without concern, as one of the necessary hardships of primitive life.

Except for the cook, Maggie, the wife of the rheumatic half-breed who went around fixing corral fences and repairing saddles and harness, there was no woman within thirty miles. Erma thought that was charming too. By the third day she was perfectly at home, out at the branding chute, declaring that the smell of the burning hair was delicious, and coaxing Larry to let her handle the iron.

For you that summer was unique, a blessed piece of life lifted for you out of the general mess and made intimately and peacefully your own. In effect you were alone, with yourself, among the hills, the endless forests and the clear distances, for between you and Larry it was soon evident that there was nothing but the shadow of a bond, not even faintly exigent; and Erma, having got you there, cheerfully forgot your existence. You were content not to remind her. She and Larry seemed to have hit it off; she was given the best house on the place, and usually she was out riding the range with him or off for a day's fishing if she could persuade him to go. At times you suspected that he was being a bit harried, but you had been chronically suspicious of Erma for so long a period that this was merely the continuation of a basic state of mind and not unduly disturbing.

You were in effect alone, and yet not alone, for Jane, who had been there the preceding summer, had described much of the surroundings so well that you were always recognizing spots that she had made hers. Riding along the narrow trails or exploring on foot a canyon inaccessible to your horse or splashing up the middle of Elk Creek with a fly rod, you were always feeling her presence and imagining her voice. You felt that all this perfectly belonged to her, which was odd, for it was as alien to the facts of her life as it was to yours. It was on Elk Creek one day, after you had eaten your sandwiches and cold coffee and were lying on the grass smoking a cigarette, that you had a peculiar and unnatural experience. You floated off into a fantasy about Millicent, something you had not done for a long time, and suddenly, nearing the climax, became aware that Millicent had gone and it was Jane! You were startled, horrified. You got up and washed your hands and face in the icy water of Elk Creek to get the grease of the sandwiches off your fingers and lips, and when you had got your rod ready and a new fly put on, you angrily observed that you were still trembling a little.

One evening somewhat later at the dinner table you noticed that Larry and Erma scarcely spoke to each other. All you got out of it was a faint amusement and an even fainter irritation, for you had long since grown accustomed to Erma's talent for creating tensions with almost anyone when she was in certain moods. She was unusually voluble with you, telling of a calf that had fallen down a slide and got caught in a pine tree,

where it perched bawling and kicking until it was yanked loose
with a rope. Larry, who had done the yanking, remained silent,
turning on a grin now and then as a concession to appearances.
He went to bed shortly after dinner, and you and Erma soon
followed his example.

Sometime in the dead of night you awoke out of a dream, a
thing not at all out of the ordinary for you. You pulled the
covers a little closer, turned over and recomposed yourself, and
in a few moments were again half asleep. Suddenly you became
aware that something was wrong, at least there was something
you didn't understand. You opened your eyes to the black
night. What was it? You kicked out a foot: Erma wasn't there.

At once you were wide awake, not at all startled, but awake.
You thought she had gone to the bathroom and at the same
moment remembered there wasn't any. You heard a noise
somewhere, a faint mumbling trickling through the thin bare
walls. You started to call her name but instead lay silently a
moment; then, without any clear thought in your mind, you
got out of bed and groped your way to the door and softly
opened it.

The mumbling instantly became voices, loud enough to be
recognized. You tiptoed in your bare feet down the narrow hall,
which with no windows was blacker even than the room had
been, to the door of Larry's room. The door was closed, but
through its flimsy boards and the cracks between them the
voices became words. You stood right against the door, beginning to shiver in the icy air of the mountain night.

"You're a little fool," Larry was saying. "My god, can't you
take a hint?"

Then Erma, somewhat louder and much more calmly:

"Come, Larry, you're the fool. Why do you pretend I'm not
attractive to you? Such conceit. Don't you know that I made

you kiss me the first time I decided it was worth the trouble?"

"The first and the last. Erma for god's sake go. You've no sense of decency."

"It would be nicer to kiss me now—like this."

"You're crazy! You must go! Bill might wake up any minute."

"I've told you he won't. Even if he does he'll turn over and go to sleep again. Even if he knows—he isn't like you, Larry—come—come—"

You heard a quick movement, and another. Larry's voice came, "I tell you to go, I mean it," and immediately you heard something that you would have given a great deal to see—a loud sharp slap, the smack of a heavy open palm, a quick angry ejaculation from Erma, someone bumping against a chair....

You tiptoed swiftly back down the hall to your room, now almost freezing. You got into bed shivering and pulled the covers close around you. It seemed but a fraction of a moment before you heard the door open and someone enter. You lay as quietly as possible, trying to breathe evenly, while you felt the covers being pulled down at your side and Erma crawling in.

Here, you told yourself the next day, is the chance to do something with that woman. This is really too much. This is beyond forbearance; uncouth; utterly disgusting and degrading, and even she must feel it, here in the sunlight among the hills. Well, you could tell her that, and she, tortuous, might easily agree, and then what? As a matter of fact there was no point in all the abuse you heaped upon Erma and yourself. If she had no roots in you deep enough to hurt when she tried some transplanting you were under no compulsion to bleed. You have enough authentic grievances against yourself without hauling in pretended ones.

It has never been in her power to inflict on you the kind of suffering that withers the heart, nor the kind that compresses itself dangerously into an explosive. What if it were Erma up there now in that room; imagine yourself here on these stairs, equipped, desperate, with death in your heart! Bah, you wouldn't even bother to slap her as Larry did that night. Ha, can it be done anyhow? Bitter dilemma. Schwartz's hot iron. The irresistible necessity, not conceivably to be argued with, and at the same time the hopeless conviction that in all your flesh and bones and blood there is no such glorious violence....

# D

He stood there, trying to force his brain to consider and decide the instant problem, whether to call to Mrs. Jordan. He was completely confused. If he called to her, that settled it, that was easy; but if he did not call to her, how was he to know whether she had heard him come in, or seen him? She was still moving around in the basement hall below, three steps in one direction, then a pause, then four in another direction; he felt intensely irritated with her and wished to god she'd quit fooling around and go back into her room.

He stood there without moving a muscle, still less than half-way up the first flight, and all at once he heard a voice from a great distance calling to him, well, aren't you coming up?

You fool, he told himself....

# IV

You fool, to stand here on the edge of hell and listen to dead voices, to her dead voice.

You did so stop on those stairs, though, that night in Cleveland many years ago, and Lucy Crofts did call down to you as you stood hesitating whether to bother to go back and turn on the lights of the car:

"Well, aren't you coming up?"

At that time you would rather hear Lucy's voice than any other sound in the world.

You decided, after the fiasco that evening at the theatre, that chorus girls were impossible anyway, that the thing to do was to find a nice Cleveland girl and take her for a mistress. While smiling since at that decision of a youth of twenty-five, you have also been puzzled by it. You were conscious of no aversion to marriage, either in theory or as a specific and practical solution. In fact you do not seem consciously to have thought of marriage at all. Can it be that within you was a hope which you did not dare to articulate, that Erma might again change her mind? At that moment she was away on her first visit to Europe; that is certain, because you reflected that you might have met a likely candidate at her house if she had been there. You had received a letter from her.

You went over your scanty list of friends and acquaintances; there was no one.

Of a late afternoon, as you walked from the office in Pearl Street to the Jayhawker Club, where you dined sometimes with Dick but usually alone, the sidewalks were filled with girls.

Working girls, high-school girls, fur-coated girls, fat girls, slender girls. In a swift comprehensive glance your eye would note each of them, label them, devour them. Sometimes you would see one that looked a little like Jane, and your heart would be warmed and hungrier than ever. Walking or driving about in the evening after dinner, again they were there, in front of theatres, coming out of restaurants, on the sidewalks.

You knew that three out of five of these girls could be picked up, for Dick had said so.

The easiest way would be with the car. You began to leave the office a little early, get the car and drive around the Square, up and down Euclid Avenue, through the narrow crowded crosstown streets. You had often seen it done; one drove slowly, against the curb, and at just the right moment, with a quick direct glance, one said in a low tone, rapidly but clearly, "Hello, want to ride?"

You never did actually pronounce those words. They never came out, though a thousand times they were on the end of your tongue. Once a grinning toothy woman in a red hat called to you, "Hello, dearie, want a passenger?" You felt yourself blushing clear to your collar as you pretended not to have heard. There were other solicitations, but that sort wasn't what you were after. You decided that the car was too public and too obvious, and you tried it on foot, with no better results. You did make some attempts, but either you didn't speak loudly enough or they thought you were talking to yourself; no one seemed to hear you, except the girl in Hahn's bookstore, who did not reply but looked directly at you with amused disgust, as though you were a monkey scratching itself. You were indignant, and crushed.

Late one rainy afternoon in April, you were driving the car slowly along Cedar Avenue, aimlessly aware of the wet glistening pavements in the gathering dusk, the clanging street cars, the forest of bobbing umbrellas on the sidewalk at your right. Under the dark umbrellas white faces were in sharp contrast, some so close you could almost touch them, eyes glancing momentarily at you with a cold and impenetrable indifference....

Suddenly there was a sharp cry ahead, and other shouts of alarm as you automatically jammed your foot on the brake and the rear wheels skidded gently to the curb. You jumped out. Almost under your front wheels a girl was being helped to her feet. In an instant you were there beside her, helping another man hold her up. She was half laughing and half crying. A crowd was collecting around you.

"It's my fault," the girl was saying. "I'm not hurt. I stepped right in front of the car. Where's my music?"

A search disclosed a black leather roll lying in a puddle of water against the curb. You picked it up and handed it to her. The other, a big man with a red moustache, was still holding her arm. She pulled herself away.

"Really I'm not a bit hurt. I'm glad you found my music. Heavens, it's soaked!"

"I'm terribly sorry," you said. "That's the first time I ever hit anybody."

"I don't think you really hit me, I think I just slipped. Goodness, I'm soaked too. I can't go like this. I'd better get a cab."

"There's a stand just down the street, I'll get one," said the man with the moustache, and pushed off through the crowd.

"I'd be glad to take you if you'll let me," you offered hurriedly. "I promise to be careful not to kill anyone."

She looked at your face, and down at her dress. "I suppose I'll have to go back home. It's quite a distance."

You grinned, assured. "Anything this side of Painesville."

"I'll get your car all dirty. Look at me."

You helped her brush the water and mud from her skirt as well as you could, helped her in the car and wrapped a robe around her. The crowd had begun to drift away into the forest of umbrellas. Just as you drove off the man with a moustache arrived in a car, and the girl shouted her thanks at him. Even raised thus above the din of the traffic her voice was clear and young and pleasant.

She gave you the number, far out on Rosedale Avenue, and said that she was afraid it was an imposition.

"I haven't a thing to do," you assured her. "I have all the time there is. I was just fooling around watching the rain."

She gave you a quick glance and sank back into a silence which was scarcely broken during the long ride, except when she directed you to the best route. You wanted to talk but were afraid of making a false step. She was quite young, you guessed not over eighteen, and very pretty. You couldn't see her now, under her big drooping hat; you were determined to drive carefully. Once she mentioned her music roll and glanced at the rear seat to make sure it was there, and said something about having been on her way to a lesson. You asked her, violin, and she said no, piano. That was about all. A sense of embarrassment; which had not been there at all when you started, seemed unaccountably to develop as you rode through the gathering twilight.

Finally you drew up at the curb in front of a large house set behind a wide lawn. It was still raining.

"My name is Will Sidney," you said abruptly. "I work downtown. I'm the assistant treasurer of the Carr Corporation. I wonder if you would care to go to the theatre with me sometime?"

She looked directly at you and said promptly and simply: "I'd like to very much." Suddenly she smiled, "You know I've been arguing with myself the last ten minutes whether you'd say something like that to me."

"How did it come out?"

"I didn't decide, only I thought you might, and then I didn't even decide what I would say. I really would like to, only it wouldn't be easy, because I live here with my uncle and aunt and they are very strict with me. Much more than my father and mother, but then of course a big city is different from the country."

"You could tell them we met somewhere."

She frowned. "I don't know. I could tell them something."

"We could meet downtown and you could tell them you were going—oh, anywhere. We could have dinner downtown."

"I couldn't do that." She frowned again. "If they ever found out it would be awful. I'll tell them I met you at Mr. Murray's. Then you phone someday and then we'll decide."

"Couldn't we decide now?"

No, she thought the other way was better. It was arranged. You wrote down her name, Lucy Crofts, and the telephone number, and the name of her uncle, Thomas M. Barnes. Then you unwrapped the robe and handed her the music roll and helped her out, and she ran through the rain across the sidewalk and up the gravel path.

On your slow way back downtown and through your leisurely dinner your mind played all around her. You pictured her in your arms, you composed in fancy a dozen scenes of capitulation and devotion; or, turning to cool realism, you decided that she was a little country prig and that it would be best to forget her. Underneath all this surface play-acting and intellectualizing there was herself and her genuine impression on you, already faintly manifest, especially the loveliness and the integrity of her voice. You were irritated that this genuineness kept intruding itself into the free play of your fancy.

Next day, at the lunch hour, you went to the Hollenden and got tickets for a play the following week; but you waited four days before telephoning her, as agreed. By that time you were in an agony of expectancy, and inexpressibly relieved when you heard her voice telling you it was all arranged.

"But I changed it a little. I couldn't say I had met you at Mr. Murray's, and anyway they might have seen the car out front, and I had to explain why I was such a mess and why I hadn't had my lesson, so I just told them all about it. I suppose Uncle will want to talk to you, but it's all right."

She couldn't come to dinner; you were to call for her at the house at a quarter to eight. You supposed you were in for an extended interview with an aggressively protective uncle, and were tempted to call it off; but when the evening arrived it proved not to be so at all. You did meet the uncle and aunt, but only for a brief introduction in a dim parlor, and they seemed friendly and unconcerned.

When she took off her hat at the theatre, and patted her hair and looked around at the audience, you realized that she was even better looking than you had thought, and a little nearer maturity. She had a great mass of light brown hair, coiled in braids at the back of her head; she seemed more hair than anything else when you glanced at her with her face turned towards the stage. When she moved her head to direct her frank grey eyes at you the braids became only a subordinate frame for the smooth wide brow, the straight, small positive nose, the not too large mouth with its full red lips. She was excited and interested in the play; she had been to the theatre only three or four times in her life, she said.

On the whole the evening was a disappointment. She didn't care to go to supper afterwards, and driving home through the spring night she talked mostly of her father's farm near Dayton, until she learned that you too came from downstate, when she wanted to know all about your father and mother and sisters and brother. She had three brothers, two older than herself, but no sisters. She said that Jane must be very attractive and that she would like to know her; she had often wished she had a sister.

At dinner that evening you had decided that at a minimum you would kiss her goodnight at parting; but as she stepped out of the car at the curb without waiting for you to help her, and held out her hand, nothing seemed more violently improbable. You drove off feeling dignified and aggrieved. You reflected that she certainly was nice, and attractive, you had seen lots of people looking at her in the theatre, but that was nothing in your pocket. She hadn't even thanked you for taking her; probably she didn't know she should. "Good lord she spent twenty minutes telling about a calf that some damn cow she called Sapho had down on the damn farm."

A day or two later, receiving through Dick an invitation to a dance at the Hollenden, you phoned Lucy and asked her to go. That was more like it. She danced well, and so did you; and it was especially satisfying to keep her mostly to yourself against the protests of those smart and assured young men among whom you had felt so inept and insignificant. You looked around at the girls, no less smart and assured, and were amused to see here and there one who had been on the list of candidates you had made up, and rejected. At the time the reasons for some of the rejections had been dubious; now you looked at Lucy and said they could all go to the devil. She was indeed charming, fresh and lovely; if you had not been there she would not have wanted for partners. Dick danced with her once and afterwards observed to you:

"If she needs her shoes shined or anything and you're too busy let me know."

On the way home Lucy said:

"They're pretty silly. I had a wonderful time. This is the latest I've ever been out. Of course I'm only nineteen. Mr. Carr dances very well, but not as well as you. You dance much better than I do."

This time you helped her out of the car and went up the gravel path and unlocked the door for her, and though the kiss seemed as improbable as ever you felt neither dignified nor aggrieved.

You took her to the theatre again, several times, and to another dance or two. On one of those occasions you were invited by Mrs. Barnes to dine with them, and on the appointed day you called for Lucy late in the afternoon at the house on Orchard Avenue where she took her piano lesson, and drove her home. You were no longer inventing fancies about her or imagining easy triumphs; with her the pose of a triumph had become absurd.

Lucy's Uncle Tom was a shrewd little man with a bald head and pleasant brown eyes. He was in the wholesale grocery business, and was also a director in a small neighborhood bank out on the edge of the city. That evening in the parlor before dinner he said that he didn't want you to think he was careless about his niece; he had looked you up all right, and had been informed that you were one of the steadiest and most promising of the city's young businessmen. "Very satisfactory," he said, "and very typical of the new century. When I was your age I was behind a little grocery counter down in Greenville at four dollars a week."

There was none of his blood in Lucy. Aunt Martha, who was the sister of Lucy's father, with all her serene acceptance of this childless household as her authentic anchorage, had a little the air of having sometime or other missed a boat somewhere. You felt pretty sure she didn't like you, though you were always cordially welcomed by her. Lucy, obviously, she idolized. As you got up from the dinner table that evening she said:

"Seems to me your parties begin about the time they ought

to be over. Don't you dance till you're all tired out again. You'll bring her home early, won't you, Mr. Sidney?"

Uncle Tom and Aunt Martha bored you completely.

Towards the end of May Lucy began to talk of going home for the summer. In three weeks, she said, her music teacher would leave for Europe, and she was going home to the farm to remain until he returned in the fall. Or perhaps she would then go to New York; she supposed that was really the best thing to do, if her father could be persuaded. Just now she wasn't much concerned about it, what she wanted was to get away from the city, which she never really liked.

"I've heard of a place down south of here," you said. "Down near Cuyahoga Falls. A deep canyon, with walls two hundred feet high, quite wild. Let's go down there next Sunday. We can drive it in two hours, easy."

Her aunt and uncle didn't like the idea, but they knew that a whole generation was against them, and early Sunday morning saw you off with a huge lunch basket and a thermos bottle of coffee. A leisurely two-hour drive through the sunny fields and villages brought you to the crossroads which Schwartz had described, but you had a good deal of trouble finding the canyon, or rather the approach to it. You had to park the car at the edge of a little wood and explore on foot. Finally a narrow path led you to the brink of a precipice, almost sheer, down which a descent apparently had to be made by clinging to roots and saplings. There was evidence of its having been done. At the bottom was a clear rapid stream, with grassy banks and trees, so far down that the tops of even the largest trees were quite a distance below. You stood at the edge and looked doubtfully at the almost perpendicular trail.

"It would be simple if it weren't for this darned basket," you observed. "Do you think you could make it?"

"Sure, easy," she declared. "I've slid down haystacks all my life, that's nothing. Let me take the basket."

"I expect I'd better go first," you replied, ignoring the offer, and not at all offended by it, for there was no irony in her. "So if you fall I can catch you. I'll manage the basket."

You always shrank from heights, and you were more than a little frightened, but with her grey eyes on you over you went, clinging to a sapling, having first made the basket secure with a belt around your shoulder. Lucy came immediately after, and you scrambled down as fast as possible, with her keeping so close above you that you were every instant afraid she would slide into you and bump you loose. A dead branch came off in your hand and you caught wildly at a projecting rock, and Lucy called to you to be careful not to break the thermos bottle. Suddenly and surprisingly you were at the bottom, upright and unhurt on the soft green grass, with the little stream rushing merrily by, and Lucy was beside you. You looked at her face; it was flushed a little with exertion, and beautiful and friendly.

"I didn't break the thermos bottle," you grinned.

"No, wasn't it fun! This is lovely, I wish we'd come here before. Doesn't it smell good!"

She bent down to the stream and washed her hands, and took your handkerchief to dry them.

You left the basket under a tree, and together explored the gorge downstream a mile or more, to where it narrowed and the stream became a torrent between two straight cliffs of rock, impassable. You threw twigs into the shallows above and watched them disappear, whirling, into the foam. The sun, now almost directly above you, filled the gorge with a soft golden warmth almost like midsummer.

"I'm hungry," you observed.

"And lunch a mile away," said Lucy. "Good heavens, what if someone has taken it!"

You raced back along the bank of the stream, jumping over rocks and fallen branches, arriving laughing and breathless to find the basket still there untouched.

You liked to watch Lucy eat. You had remarked this to yourself before, and now, sitting on a rock in the warm sun, with her in front of you on the grass, you munched sandwiches and looked at her. You remembered how Mrs. Davis used to nibble uncertainly at the thin little sandwiches she would sometimes bring from the pantry, after you and she had got yourselves arranged again and returned to the sitting-room. You remembered Erma's nervous gestures with her knife and fork, and her habit of always starting to say something just when a bite had been scooped into her spoon or impaled on her fork, leaving the morsel of food cruelly suspended just short of the fulfillment of its destiny. More especially and vividly you remembered Millicent with the candy you gave her, how back and forth from the box to her mouth her slender little fingers would go, deftly, silently, methodically, remorselessly. Now that movement appears to you monstrous and horrible; then you were amused by it. You were at the time enthusiastic about Omar, and you made a parody and recited it to her:

"The Moving Fingers light. And having lit…"

She had no idea what you were talking about.

You liked to watch Lucy. She sat there on the grass with your sweater under her, and the sandwiches and pickles and cake disappeared, and as far as her consciousness was concerned she obviously might as well have been picking wild flowers or sewing on a button. Beyond that was her grace, the leisurely precise movements of her small strong hands, the flash of her white teeth biting out a neat and considerable semi-circle with unaffected conviction.

"It's funny there aren't any violets around here," she said. "Do you suppose we're too late? It seems just right for them.

There's a hillside down home, not far from the house, that's always covered, every year."

"Do you know yet when you're going?"

"June nineteenth, that's two weeks from Tuesday. I'll be glad to go, but I'll miss you. I've been in Cleveland two winters now and everybody's been very nice, but I've never really liked anyone I've met there except you."

You moved from the rock and knelt to pour some coffee from the thermos bottle. She leaned over to hold the cup and there was her face close to you, and you turned a little and kissed her on the mouth. She took the kiss, briefly but completely; then not at all startled she drew away and said quietly:

"You're spilling the coffee."

So you were; a thin trickle was running directly into your shoe-top. To set the bottle down and put your arms around her, as you wanted to do, seemed suddenly too complicated. You filled a cup and handed it to her.

"That's the first time anyone has ever kissed me," she said, quietly as before

"Not really!"

"Of course." Her grave grey eyes shone a little humorously. "I guess it's the first time anyone ever wanted to."

"Not your father or brothers?"

"Oh, that. On the cheek maybe."

"But—you don't mean—there must have been boys—"

She laughed. "Once a high school boy tried to and I turned away so quickly my hatpin scratched all the way across his cheek. He thought I did it on purpose."

"Did you like me to kiss you?"

She sipped her coffee without replying.

"Did you like me to kiss you, Lucy?"

"Yes, I liked it." Then a little hurriedly as you moved to her

side and bent over her, "But don't do it again now. I think probably I would like to be kissed very much. I've often wondered if
you would kiss me. I know I like you, I know I care for you."

She took your hand in hers and held it tightly, and before
you realized what she was about raised it and pressed it to her
lips. Then she sprang up and away, laughing, and dared you to
catch her, knowing well you couldn't. You tried, though, and
when you tripped over a fallen limb and fell headlong you gave
it up and went back to your cup of coffee, now almost cold.

A week later you drove into the country again, but it rained
most of the day, and early in the afternoon you surrendered
and returned to a roadhouse just outside the city, wet and
chilled and hungry. Lucy didn't seem to mind it, but you were
unduly miserable, and when she asked you what was the matter
you observed gloomily that it was only a little more than a week
before she would be gone and you would be alone.

"Alone!" she exclaimed. "You have more friends than I ever
heard of."

"I haven't a real friend, anywhere, except you."

She was silent. Her eyes were on you with their curious trick
of saying nothing and yet offering all their secrets.

"Where are you going this summer?" she asked suddenly.

You replied importantly that you had to work.

"Don't you get a vacation?"

"Oh, I suppose I'll go down home for a week. I could get a
month, but there doesn't seem to be anything to do. I might go
to New York. I've never been there."

Another silence. Finally she said:

"Would you care to come down to our place? It's very nice
there in the summer. I'll teach you how to milk and I'll let you
ride Babe."

This was surprising; it hadn't occurred to you even in your

numerous fancies; but now that she said it, it was so natural and obvious that it almost seemed as if you had deliberately planned it.

"But I couldn't," you protested. "Your folks never heard of me. It would seem funny, wouldn't it?"

"Oh, I've told them all about you. Anyway it wouldn't matter if I hadn't. There won't be anyone there except Father and Mother and Jim. They'd love to have you."

"I don't know," you said doubtfully. "Maybe you could write to your father and make sure it would be all right."

You knew that of course you were going. It meant nothing to you but that you would be with Lucy, which was enough. You can see clearly now how true that was from the beginning to the end. She was the only person you have ever known who needed no justification beyond herself. What she did and what she said never seemed of the slightest importance as compared with the vital fact of her being. You could not now tell what she wore on any occasion, not even the color; you probably could not have told immediately after leaving her presence, though you do commonly notice women's dresses and can recall numberless ones, of Erma, of Jane, of Millicent, even some that Mrs. Davis wore twenty-five years ago—especially the changeable silk that you tore one day, and she cried, and then laughed when you pretended to sew it up. What did Lucy wear? She always had on large hats, but so did everyone else. You don't remember what she wore at dances, You don't even remember what sort of dress it was she took off, that remarkable afternoon....

Of course, all this wouldn't prove anything about Lucy but for the fact that it is you. Take Dick, probably Dick has never observed a woman's dress in his life, except to notice whether it was easy to unfasten, and not even that unless it was an immediate and practical problem. He has never been interested in meanings or even appearances, nor in the moral or imponderable implications of an act, only in the activity. That summer, when you told him you would like to take a month away from the office, he was completely indifferent to your intentions until their specific probabilities amused him, and not even in that until his own active intentions had been disposed of.

"Sure, I took it for granted," he said. "But I hope you haven't anything arranged. Three or four of us are going to the North Woods and let the flies eat us up, and we're counting on you to go along. Harper and Pete Moreland and maybe Slim Endicott. Leave about the middle of July. I should have told you before. You'll come, won't you?"

You were tempted; particularly you were pleased to find that Dick had figured you in as a matter of course; you had suspected that on the whirling disc of his widening regard and interest, with its ever-increasing momentum, you had begun to slip a little away from the secure center towards that edge whose jagged saw-teeth you had more than once already seen in action. You were relieved to feel yourself as safe as ever, but this put you in a dilemma.

"I did have something planned," you said hesitantly. "I wish I'd known about this, I'd certainly like to go. Now I don't see how…I was figuring on being away all of July.…"

"Oh, forget it. We're going to catch all the fish there are north of the Great Lakes. Four canoes and a whole tribe of guides—Harper's arranging it, he's been up there before. Come on, we'll have a regular damn flotilla."

You seemed undecided; you were tempted, but you knew very well what the answer would be. Dick went on:

"What were you going to do, go down home? You were there Christmas."

"No. Oh, maybe for a week," you replied. "I thought I might go to New York, but Lucy Crofts invited me to spend a month down at her home near Dayton."

Dick's eyes opened wide. "The hell she did! Why you old Romeo. You'd better watch out, Bill. She's the kind that gets chronic."

"Maybe she already is. I've told her I'll come."

"You'll go all right. I'm not so sure I wouldn't pass up the North Woods for that myself, but I'd get sick of it in a week."

He grinned, and went on:

"You know, she turned me down flat. Out at the Hampton Club, about a month ago, you remember, you brought her of course, I asked her to go to dinner and a show, and she said she couldn't. I told her to make it any old day she wanted, and she said no, and I asked her what she had against me, and she said nothing at all, she just didn't want to go. She handed the same package to Charlie Harper."

So Dick had tried to take her away. And that big bum Harper, that big fathead…well, that was all right. Nor was there any code which warranted the indignation and resentment you felt against Dick, but you felt it.

"It will be all right then for the first of July?" you said.

"God bless you. If you ask me I think you're hooked. Not that she'd insist on your marrying her, any more than a bottle of wine insists that you get drunk. That's just the way it works."

That evening, the eve of her departure, you told Lucy you would come for the entire month of July.

You resented Dick, you resented all of them, you resented anyone knowing anything about Lucy. You were sorry you had ever taken her among them. But Dick particularly. You have never understood where Dick really is within you, he is too deep somewhere. Where would he finally be found if somebody cut you open and sorted out all those entities and personalities that have become imbedded in you? In the gall, perhaps. In the heart, god is there anyone in the heart? Jane, Lucy, Larry—a ghostly hall in which always someone was but no one ever is. "You live in my heart." What a dirty cheat, that's where you die! Not that Dick was ever there. You see now that that feeling of resentment has never been absent, not from the first day. Or is it that your present fury, diffused backward over all the years, deceives you?

That's an amusing fancy, that idea of cutting you up and finding people where they belong. It should be an accepted routine, the result to be read at the funeral. "Ladies and gentlemen, the official autopsy. Heart, empty, except for unrecognizable vestiges. Liver, John Doe and Richard Roe. Gall bladder, the following thirty persons…Stomach, Mrs. Hetty Hill, widow and chief mourner. Reproductive glands, the following seventy-one…."

Well. Yours wouldn't be so far off, if you were really as mad as you seem, here now. You go on, you open the door, you kill her, dead, forever dead. Then they kill you. That seems neither real nor possible, and of course it isn't. You add this exquisite masterpiece to all the other enigmas of conduct you have presented to yourself, what are you doing here?

# E

He was still conscious of an irritation at Mrs. Jordan's persistent noises below, but he found that he had mounted another step, and another. His eyes were now level with the first landing, one flight up, the floor where the two art students lived, two girls, one of whom looked so much like his sister Margaret. Another step, and he could see the grey plaster figure in the niche in the curved wall, beside the flimsy little electric lamp that always got knocked off when he passed it with his overcoat flapping. He had picked it up a hundred times. There it stood on its perilous edge, its silly imitation parchment shade, with a silhouette of a dancing girl playing a flute, a little askew as always.

He looked at it, really looked at it, as if he had never seen it before, and yet he did not now see it. His ears acutely registered the movements of Mrs. Jordan, and yet he did not hear them. He did hear himself, in his brain somewhere, do you realize that you are going on, going ahead? Do you realize that you don't at all know what you are doing?

# V

You have felt this before, less acutely, that day for instance you ate dinner at the club with your son. What if he had known, what difference would it have made? What if the men around you, friends and acquaintances some of them, had known? They would not have been more than mildly interested; possibly some of them had done precisely the same thing at that same table.

Paul, his name is. You called him Paul. That didn't seem real either. More than two years ago.

No surroundings anywhere were more familiar to you, since for a long time you had dined and spent many of your evenings at the club, but his presence made everything grotesque and strange. Not that you were affected in any way that mattered; it was as if he were a character in a play, and you had been unexpectedly called from the audience to go on the stage and sit down and talk with him, without knowing any of the lines.

You can still see that note, on a square piece of blue paper, which you found on your office desk one morning in the pile of personal mail.

"Dear Mr. Sidney," it said, "if you can spare me an hour, some day this week, I would like very much to ask you about something. It was a long time ago, but I believe you will remember my name. Sincerely, Emily Davis."

At the top was an address and telephone number.

You speculated about it idly, with little real curiosity. It was too far away, too dead, and it was even a little unpleasant with its reminder of old fires and hopes now extinguished, unrealized, and in retrospect ridiculous. You did not telephone, you had your secretary do it, and an appointment was made for the following afternoon.

Something unexpected came up at the office the next day, and you had to keep her waiting. When she was finally shown in and stood there uncertainly, just inside the door, you were genuinely shocked. She was an old woman. Everything about her admitted it; the plain unobtrusive dark brown dress, the formless little hat, the way she stood blinking in the bright light, her faintly dragging step as she came forward to meet you. But there was a firm strength in the shake of her hand. As she looked at you frankly and pleasantly, you could see anxious years in her eyes, and a present anxiety, too.

"Little Will Sidney," she smiled. "Now that I see you, I know I was foolish to take so long to make up my mind." She looked at you and around you. "What a fine office, and how fine you look!"

You tried to say that she too looked fine.

"Oh, I'm done for," she replied, not sadly. "It's like you to want to say it, you were a nice boy. I'm nearly sixty years old. That may be pretty hard for you to believe, but it's not hard for me."

You escorted her to the big leather seat in the corner, and took a chair in front of her. Only vaguely, and by an effort of the imagination, could you make the pretty, soft Mrs. Davis of those far-off juicy days out of this little dried-up woman. The eyes, perhaps; the rest was impossible.

She seemed to know a good deal about you, the year you had come to New York, the date of your marriage with Erma, the fact of your having no children. She told you, briefly but completely, of her own journey through the many days. Mr. Davis had practiced law in Cleveland, never very successfully, for seven years, then they had moved to Chicago. There it was even worse, he never squeezed more than a scanty living out of it; and there was nothing but a modest insurance payment left for his wife and little son when one winter he took pneumonia and died. Mrs. Davis managed to get a position as a teacher in the Chicago public schools, which she still held; she was in New York only for a visit, having come, it appeared, expressly to see you. She had somehow kept her son Paul fed and clothed to the end of High School, and he had worked his way through the University of Chicago.

"Anyway, I didn't treat you the way you treated me in Cleveland," you said with a smile. "Remember when I telephoned you, and you wouldn't see me?"

She looked a little embarrassed. "I didn't answer your note either. I wanted to. I cried that night for the first time in years. But it was as plain as the nose on your face. You were twenty-four and I was over forty, and Paul had come and I was no longer—well, I was pretty once. I was so glad, you have no idea, awfully glad you thought of me."

She glanced at you, and then away.

"It's Paul really I came to see you about. He graduated from the university two years ago; he's twenty-four now. He's a good boy and he's not lazy, but I'm afraid for him. I thought you might help."

"Where is he?"

"In New York, he's been here over a year. He has a job now and then, but he thinks he wants to be a sculptor. He studied in Chicago a while, and now he works at it so hard, he can't keep a job very long."

This began to sound ominous, and you wondered what was going to be proposed. Did she want you to give him a job? You asked questions, with a careful lack of enthusiasm.

By no means a job, he probably wouldn't be any good in any job, she explained. What he wanted, and what she prayed for him to have, was a chance to learn and practice his art, his sculpture. She was of course no judge, but he had had high praise from his teachers. He had won a prize in Chicago, and on the strength of it had come to New York. It was a terrific struggle. What he wanted, more than anything else, was to go abroad for two or three years. That was really what she wanted to talk about, she thought you might help.

You considered.

"If he has real talent he certainly should be encouraged," you agreed judiciously. "Of course, my opinion on that point is no better than your own. If he has, the next problem would be to find a rich man—or woman—to stake him. That might not be very difficult, it's often done. I might speak to Dick—Mr. Carr—about it."

It seemed to you that this should sound rather encouraging but she appeared almost to be thinking of something else. She looked at you, directly.

"I thought you might do it yourself," she said. "You see, you're his father."

You stared at her.

"I wasn't going to tell you," she went on, "but after all why shouldn't I? Jim's dead, and it's nothing to be ashamed of. He was born a few months after we got to Cleveland That was really why we went away, I knew it was coming, and that would have made things worse than ever."

You stammered. "Can you—that is—I don't see how you can know—" How odd to be talking like this to this strange little grey-haired woman.

"I know well enough. Oh, it's sure."

"What does he look like?"

"Not much like anyone." She smiled, she was really amused, and that persuaded you more than anything else. "You'll just have to take my word for it; it's funny it never occurred to me that you might doubt it. His eyes are a little like yours, but he's not as handsome as you are. He's intelligent though, really intelligent."

She had said he was in New York. He might be in the outer office at this moment. You felt a bit harassed.

"But honestly I don't see—of course I don't doubt, I don't really doubt what you say—but, good lord, I was only a kid, I couldn't have been more than seventeen—"

Her eyes met yours directly, a little sharply, a little surprised.

"I really am sure, Mr. Sidney," she said.

"Well." You got up from your chair. "Well." You walked to the window and looked down into the street, thirty stories below, and to your desk, and back again. You stood and looked at her, and suddenly laughed. "My god, he's nearly as old as I am," you observed. "Do you remember how I always called you Mrs. Davis, and you wanted me to call you Emily and I couldn't?"

Her answering smile, humorous and friendly, had a tranquility which showed that for her those days were even farther off than they were for you; she had crossed a peak which you had not yet reached.

A thought struck you; a curiosity, no longer a doubt.

"Why didn't you tell me about it then?"

"I just couldn't," she replied. "Once or twice I meant to, but I couldn't, I don't know why. It wouldn't have done any good." Then, with a flash of that homely playfulness she showed so rarely even in the old days, "Maybe I was afraid you might brag," she chuckled.

"Of course he doesn't know?"

"Good heavens no!" She looked at you, her eyes reflecting

the quick anxious suspicion in her mind: what if this rich child-less man should want not only to help his son, but also to claim him! "No, he doesn't know. He mustn't ever know. There's no reason why he should."

"None at all," you reassured her. "It was a foolish question. Of course he mustn't know. As for helping him—yes, of course. I'd like—"

You hesitated. Certainly there was no more harmless and honest person in the world than this grey-haired schoolteacher, but still, should you perhaps first consult a lawyer? Common prudence...Oh well...

"I'd like to see him," you said. She agreed at once.

The details were arranged. You and Paul would have dinner together, alone; she thought that would be better. She would tell him that you were an old friend, a former pupil in the Ohio days before he was born, which had the advantage of being true. The evening and hour were agreed upon. You were given Paul's address.

She arose and held out her hand.

"After I've seen him, we'll meet again and talk things over," you said.

She nodded, still holding your hand. "You're a good boy, Will Sidney. You've got a good heart. If I don't want to tell my son who his father is, it isn't because I'm ashamed of it." She smiled, but her eyes had tears behind them. "If it weren't for you I wouldn't have Paul, and he's all I've got in the world."

After she had gone you let callers, who were already waiting to see you, wait even longer while you walked back and forth across the room, or stood looking out of the window. This was indeed a voice out of a past which had for long seemed so dreary and monotonous that if the future were to be merely a projection of it, you might as well be dead. So you were a father, you had a son. You found no particular thrill in that; indeed, without having seen him you felt vaguely that you disliked and resented him. But undeniably, here at last was something real, something that you could put your teeth into, something intimate to you with none of that ghastly phantom quality of hollowness and nothingness that had somehow crept into all your relations with people and things, and clung there.

A son twenty-four years old! He wanted to be a sculptor. It was a damn good thing he wasn't looking for a start in a business career, you'd had enough of that with Larry. This really opened up all sorts of possibilities, which you contemplated with keen pleasure. You could leave Erma and you and Paul could live in a flat somewhere in Greenwich Village. Erma wouldn't care, or what if she did? Or you could leave the whole damn outfit, the business too, and you and Paul could go abroad and stay there. Apparently that was what Paul wanted to do. You had plenty of money to live on, not of course as you were then living, but still really plenty. Or, as far as that was concerned, you needn't leave at all; you could tell Erma that you had found a protégé, a promising young sculptor, and that you wanted to bring him to live with you. There was plenty of room. Surely there were teachers for him in New York as good as any in Europe. Erma wouldn't object, she was always indifferent to that sort of thing.

Suddenly the flow of your thoughts stopped and you laughed aloud, heartily, there in your office alone. No, Erma wouldn't object. It pleased you, ironically, to put it to yourself in the barest possible words; you couldn't invite your son to come to live with your wife and you, because she would most certainly seduce him!

You phoned Miss Malloy that you were now ready to see those who were waiting.

Two days later you met him. He stood there in the lobby of the club, hesitant, hat in hand, as an attendant approached him. You knew him at once, and hastened over and extended your hand.

"Mr. Davis? I'm Mr. Sidney."

Later, seated in the dining room with soup in front of you, you examined him critically. He was rather poorly dressed; his hands were big and strong and not too clean, and his coat-sleeves were too short. His hair and eyes were dark, and his large face gave the impression of having so many features that it hadn't quite decided what to do with them. Certainly, he didn't look at all like Mrs. Davis; you thought that he did perhaps resemble you a little, particularly in structure.

"This is fine soup," he observed. His voice was a little husky, pleasant, and not at all timid.

Now that he was in front of you, no longer to be imagined, you felt much relieved that you hadn't spoken to Erma, that you had kept all those idiotic schemes to yourself. You were more than ever willing to accept his sonship as a statistical fact, somehow his mere bodily presence seemed to establish it; but at the same time, it demolished the feeling of intimacy your fancy had built up. Hearing him speak and seeing him eat, he was as much withdrawn, as completely circumscribed within his own alien circle, as any of those others.

He seemed perfectly at ease as you talked at random of indifferent things, until with the salad you decided it was time to broach the main subject.

"Your mother tells me you would like to study abroad," you observed.

"Yes, sir. I would like to. It's almost essential." Until then he had not said "yes, sir" since the first few moments.

"Are there better teachers over there than in New York?"

He explained that it wasn't so much a matter of teachers, it was the stimulation, the atmosphere, the tradition, the opportunity to see the great works of the masters. He talked of all this at length, in a sensible and straightforward manner, you thought, but with an underlying nervousness that betrayed the depth and intensity of his desire. You reflected that at his age you could not have spoken half so clearly and intelligently of your desire to write—nor could you now, for that matter. Also, there was in this boy a purposefulness, a sort of concealed arrogance, which—you smiled—which he certainly had not inherited from his father.

"I suppose," you observed, "you could make out over there on three thousand a year."

"Less than that," he replied quickly, "surely much less. I should say two thousand would be ample. That's forty dollars a week.

"If there really is a chance of your helping me out," he went on a little awkwardly, "of course, you would want to find out if I'm likely to deserve it. I haven't much stuff, a few figures and a group or two, but if you could come down some day and look at them...I told Mother naturally you would want to do that."

You replied that you would like to see his work, but that it wouldn't mean anything, you weren't competent to judge.

Apparently your mind was already made up, for as he went on talking of the difficulties and prospects, and of technicalities of which you knew nothing, you heard little of what he said. You were thinking that three thousand a year—certainly it should be three, it might as well be done right—wouldn't make any great difference to you. Even if it all had to come out of the half of your salary you were saving, seventeen thousand added every twelve months wouldn't be so bad. And maybe you wouldn't have to do that at all. Perhaps you could cut down a little here and there—better still, Erma would certainly contribute half of it, if you cared to ask her, or the whole thing for that matter. But that thought you almost immediately rejected, in disgust. You would do it all yourself, he was your son, wasn't he?

By the time you parted that evening, you had practically given him your promise, and had arranged to visit his studio the following afternoon but one.

It wasn't much of a studio—a small room with an alcove on the top floor of an old house in one of those obscure and unsus- pected streets west of Seventh Avenue, below Fourteenth. Apparently he both worked and slept there, and perhaps ate too; there was a rusty gas plate and a small sink in a corner, behind a screen made of painted burlap. Clay and plaster fig- ures were scattered about; there was a bronze bust of a young girl, without hair, and two marble groups, one, quite large, of workmen lifting a beam. It seemed to you very big and smooth and impressive.

"I worked nearly two years on that," Paul said, "and it's all wrong. See, look here."

You listened attentively and nodded your head from time to time. He moved a chair for you out from under some sketches and pieces of black cloth, and brought you a cigarette and lit it. After he had finished talking about it you still thought the group big and smooth and impressive. He brought out some portfolios.

"By the way," he said suddenly, "I almost forgot. Here's a letter from Mother." He took an envelope from his pocket and handed it to you.

You opened and read it. It was almost as brief as the one that had come to the office a few days before. She thanked you, and said she knew she need never again worry about her son, and bade you goodbye.

You looked at him in surprise. "Where is she? She hasn't gone?" He nodded. "Back to Chicago. Yesterday. You see she only had a week off, she has to be back in school Monday morning." He grinned. "Lord, I'll bet she's glad to have me off her hands."

He opened one of the portfolios and began turning over the sketches, pointing and explaining. You nodded approvingly, thinking of the little grey-haired schoolteacher hurrying back to her bread and butter, leaving her son and her son's father to wrestle with these deeper problems. You wonder why she hadn't come to you years before, and whether it would have made any difference. What if she had brought Paul to you before you had married Erma?

He finished with the portfolios and stood in front of you.

"Mother suggested something before she left," he said doubtfully, "but I don't know whether you'd care about it. She made me promise to ask you. You see, of course, it doesn't matter when I leave, and she thought I ought to stay on a month or two and do a bust of you. That is, if you wanted it. I don't know how good it would be, but I'd like to do it. You have a fine head and a strong face, not at all ordinary. Quite interesting."

If you had been at all undecided before, which as a matter of fact you weren't, this would have won you completely. How clever she was, in a simple, direct sort of way.

"She wanted me to propose it as my own idea," Paul continued, "but I was afraid it would sound impertinent. I'm by no means a mature artist."

You thought it would seem ridiculous to have a bust made of yourself. A statue. One of Erma, perhaps, and let her pay for it. Or Dick. Or old Mrs. Stanton, she was vain enough, and had more money even than the Carrs. But perhaps Paul wasn't ready yet for jobs like that. After all, if he wanted to practice on you, why not? If he could do that girl who apparently had had no hair, why not you? Would it be marble or bronze? You had always liked marble better, white marble, you loved its feel, the suggestion of possible movement beneath its firm hardness.

The sittings began the following Monday afternoon.

You told no one about it, not even Erma, particularly not Erma. Not even Jane, though you were at that time seeing more of her than you had for years, on account of the recent illness and death of your mother, the journey to the funeral in Ohio, and Margaret's difficulties.

None of you had been back to that town since leaving it, though your mother had made several visits to New York. Each time you and Jane had tried to persuade her to stay, and each time, a little older and feebler, she had refused and returned to Ohio, to her sister Cora's big white house under the maple trees.

You and Jane and Margaret and Rose went out on the same train, and Larry came from Idaho, his first trip east since his departure, five years before. Everything was done before you arrived, nothing was left but the dismal role of polite mourner, for there could be no sharper grief for one who in all essential respects had so long been dead. With Jane, perhaps, for between her and her mother there had doubtless been a closeness of understanding of which the younger children knew nothing. Margaret's thoughts were obviously back in New York, concerned with her own immediate and pressing dilemma, Rose was as usual preoccupied with her own appearance, and Larry merely sat about helplessly for want of something to do, moving restlessly from the porch to the parlor and back again. The day after your arrival you drove out to the cemetery with a long line of cars behind you, and saw the coffin lowered into a hole beside the mound of your father's grave.

The following morning, at Jane's suggestion, you walked

down to the square, to the drug store, with her, and stood around for an hour while she conversed with the proprietor— the sucker she had asked you to help take off the hook twenty years before—inspected the counters and shelves, and commented on the additions and improvements. You were invited to go behind the fountain and mix yourself a soda for old times' sake. You watched Jane with wonder and envy. She actually got a kick out of this! She was genuinely interested to find that the decrepit old cabinet, which had held horse medicine and Villater's 300 Pills, had been replaced by a shiny new rack filled with little leather books, and to be told that over three thousand of these books had been sold in the preceding twelve months, at a profit of more than six cents each.

You walked back up Main Street together, arm in arm, returning the respectful and compassionate salutations of old friends and acquaintances.

"We sold that store too darned cheap," observed Jane. "It's the best location in town, a regular gold mine."

And yet she was less interested in making money, or having it, than anyone you knew.

That evening all of you left for New York, walking from the big white house where your mother had died to the new brick railroad station, only three blocks away. You had engaged a drawing-room for the three girls and a compartment for yourself and Larry, who, having got as far east as Ohio, had been persuaded by Jane to come on to New York for a visit.

"What's up between Rose and Margaret?" asked Larry, as you were stowing the bags in the corner of your compartment and taking off your coats, after the train had started. "They act as if they'd like to bite chunks out of each other."

"They would," you replied. "Maybe they will. There's a hell of a row on."

"What about?"

"Margaret's going to be a co-respondent and Rose doesn't want her to."

Larry, stooping to get a magazine from his bag, straightened up to stare at you.

"Don't ask me," you went on hastily. "I really don't know an awful lot about it, but we're both due to find out. You might as well chuck your magazine, this trip is reserved for a family council. Jane asked me to come back, and bring you, as soon as we got settled."

Larry evidently relished the prospect even less than you, and, as a matter of fact, neither of you had any legitimate concern or authority in the business; your embarrassment proceeded naturally from your total lack of function. Jane had been dragged in, inevitably, they had both appealed to her, and it was really Jane you were trying to help. Trying to help Jane!

Your ring at the door of the drawing-room, and your entrance in response to Jane's summons, evidently interrupted Rose in the middle of a speech. She was curled up on the long seat, smoking a cigarette, her eyes flashing and her mass of short, dark hair artistically rumpled. Margaret, on one of the cross-seats, made room for Larry beside her, and then turned her eyes again on Rose.

"Say it again, so the head of the family can hear you," she drawled with a glance at you. She turned to Larry. "I don't really know you, though you're my brother, but you look like a nice man. Do you believe in sisterly love?"

"Count me out," said Larry so hastily that everybody laughed, including Rose.

"As far as that's concerned, me too," you put in. "There's no occasion to dig at me, Margaret, I'm the head of nobody's family. We came back because Jane asked us to."

"We'll each talk ten minutes and then we'll vote," drawled Margaret sarcastically.

"A lot of attention you'd pay to anybody's vote but your own," snapped Rose.

"Bill may not be the head of the family," said Jane, "but he's got a better head than any of us. I wish you two Indians had gone to him in the first place. I suggest you leave it to Bill and do as he says."

"Not for me," declared Margaret.

"Nor me," said Rose.

"Thanks," you said, "I didn't ask for it." You made to get up, but Jane put her hand on your arm. "I don't know what it's all about anyway," you went on, "except that somebody's wife is going to get a divorce by proving that Margaret stole her husband, and Rose is sore, because if her sister's name is dragged in the mire, she may have trouble marrying a noble scion of the wholesale leather trade."

This produced a double explosion. Rose shouted above the train's roar that her fiancé wasn't a business man at all, that he was of an old and fastidious family, and that, since she had originally met him at your wife's home, it ill became you to sneer at him; while Margaret declared that she had stolen nobody's husband, and that he wasn't just somebody, he was an internationally known scientist and a great man.

"Sure," agreed Rose, "that's why it's such a mess. What the tabloids won't do!"

"They make the mire, we don't," returned Margaret.

"They put you in it, and me too." Rose appealed to all of you. "I'm not asking her to give up her great man. Though if you could see him…"

"I've seen him," said Jane. "That sort of thing isn't going to do you any good. That's what offended Margaret in the first place, and I don't blame her."

"Oh, he's all right," Rose conceded. "Anyway, all I ask her to do is to keep it quiet somehow, till after I'm married. She could go away for a few months, or at least let him alone and go to live with you or something. She could spend the spring and summer at Larry's ranch, couldn't she, Larry?"

Larry stirred and cleared his throat. "Of course, if you want to, Margaret." He looked extremely uncomfortable.

Margaret had turned in her seat to gaze directly at her younger sister. "Rose, you have a remarkable talent for using offensive and provocative phrases. I don't know, if it weren't for that I might have been willing to make a lot of sacrifices for your convenience—but, the lord knows, I'm as petty and human as anybody. 'At least let him alone!' Jane knows all about it, but Bill and Larry don't, and you deliberately try to prejudice them against me, maybe you think they'll bully me. I'm not going to be bullied, and Doctor Oehmsen and I are going to do exactly what we've decided to do, though it will cost him a lot more than it will you or me." Her voice faltered a little, she bit her lip and stopped. Suddenly she exploded, "You're a selfish outrageous little beast!" and began to cry.

Larry patted her shoulder with his fingers' ends, gingerly. Rose, scornful and unmoved, lit another cigarette.

"You are, of course," said Jane to Rose, "but you always have been, and you know it, so that doesn't help any. If only Mrs. Oehmsen had made up her mind a year ago it would all be over now." Jane sighed. "I'll just have to go and see her."

"You shan't!" exclaimed Margaret. "We're asking no favors from her!"

This started Rose off again. Jane got up to go and sit by her, and you moved next to the window in the cross-seat, looking out at the swift panorama of fields and houses and trees, dim in the twilight, listening to Margaret's and Rose's verbal scratches and bites, with Jane trying vainly to soothe them into understanding and decency. You marvelled at the turmoil and fury, at

Margaret's tears and Rose's flashing eyes; whence, you wondered, all this hot concern with things which in the end freeze
us with their indifference?

   In a way you envied them. Do you envy them now? Ah, that
would be more than tolerable now, that would be blessed, to be
again frozen with indifference! What will Rose and her fastidious family say when they hear of this? What will Margaret and
Larry—Oh,—Oh, there will be nothing to hear of. Nothing
happens, nothing is going to happen that they or anyone will
hear of. What if they were all here now, what if they suddenly
appeared on the stairs around you? Larry would pat you on the
shoulder with the ends of his fingers, and Rose would say, "A
nice mess you've got the family into! We'd better all stay here
while Jane goes upstairs and talks to that woman." Only, being
given to abusive words when aroused, she'd probably say, that
whore. So would you, so would you. Jane would go, god bless
her. Of course that can't happen, but you can go to her. You can
turn now and go out and go to her, and put your head in her
lap—if you could only leave it there forever....

# F

He stopped, and again stood still, and his lips moved as though he were talking to the little parchment lamp, for he was looking directly at it, but no sound came from them. He was pronouncing Jane's name.

He turned and looked behind him, downstairs, and started at sight of a dark form against the wall in the hall below, but saw at once that it was the side of the high black frame of the mirror and coat-rack. He had avoided looking into the mirror as he passed, and he wished now that he hadn't; he wanted to know what his face looked like; in the street he had felt that people were staring at him.

There were still sounds of Mrs. Jordan in the basement, but now he thought he heard another noise, above, and he turned quickly to look at the door facing the first landing. It was closed; it had not moved; there was no light under it. Those girls would not be at home anyway, he reflected, they were always out at night. That was one of the things he had counted on.

You counted on, a bitter voice said to him; yes, you might count on that, you might count on anything except yourself...

# VI

You have always betrayed yourself, most miserably at those moments when you most needed the kind of fortitude that can neither be borrowed nor simulated. Yet even that is a gloss, that is too kind, for often it has not been a question of fortitude at all, but simply a matter of permitting your authentic impulses to live and grow. You have played with them as a cat plays with a mouse, and to the same end. Neither the heroism of the ascetic nor the courage of the hedonist. Bah, phrases, what have heroism or courage to do with it? If that were all you lacked! All the petty fears and hesitations, all the ignoble withdrawals! Afraid by god to swallow your own saliva.

Not a fear, exactly, either; more an avoidance and a denial. Certainly you weren't afraid of Lucy, nor were you afraid of the delights she gave and promised, and you doubt if the hopes that were dazzled in front of you by Erma's return and her unexpected renewed friendliness had really much to do with it. They appeared to have, and you don't resent the idea; quite the contrary; you would accept with relief a conviction of cool practical calculation, that at least would be no weakness, nothing that a man need be ashamed of. No, it wasn't a positive choice, even of a slender hope. It was a denial and a rejection.

You felt pretty sure you were going to marry Lucy, that day as you leaned back in the pullman chair with an unopened magazine on your lap, while the train roared its way through the flat fields towards Dayton, where she was to meet you. She had left Cleveland twelve days before, and they had been empty days for you. You tried to decide what it would be like to be married to her, and were irritated to find how elusive it was; it didn't seem to be like much of anything. But it was clearly impossible to contemplate being without her. You were glad you had had sense enough not to go with Dick; to be up north there with them for a whole month, knowing all the time that you could have been with Lucy, would have been unbearable.

She, alone, met you at the Dayton station, and in a little dark blue roadster drove you west, into the setting sun, some fifteen miles from the city. You had not known before that she drove, and decided that she was better at it than you were. You were surprised at the extent of the farmhouse and buildings; you knew that Lucy's father, publisher and editor of a newspaper somewhere, had at middle-age suddenly given it up and purchased a farm and begun raising thoroughbred stock, but you hadn't expected to see anything so elaborate. On one side of the road was the house, in a grove of fine old trees; on the other, somewhat removed, a dozen or more sheds and barns and enclosures, all shining with white and yellow paint.

Of all the people you have known, you have understood Lucy's father and mother least. They were obviously healthy and happy, on excellent terms with life, yet they gave the impression of having no contact with it, not even with those aspects that most closely touched them. Unquestionably Mr. Crofts took a strong and active interest in the rare and fine animals which filled his barns and sheds, and was uncommonly successful with them, but when you led him to talk about them he did so as if they inhabited another world and were no concern of his. He had a large library and read a great deal, but when questioned about any book he would always reply that he had read it a long time ago and had forgotten what it was about. Mrs. Crofts was the same, she said the same things in the same tone of voice. They were always together, working with the men out in the barns, riding around the fields and country roads, sometimes playing tennis on the well-kept court back of the apple orchard.

Their attitude toward Lucy was therefore nothing special, it was a part of their whole. It was plain that she wanted for nothing, she was not in any sense neglected, but there was none of that rubbing intimacy which is always associated with parenthood. She might have been a privileged summer boarder. With some nervousness you had anticipated an embarrassing reception: an over-hearty handshake and a lengthy appraisal from the father, a suggestive and emphatic friendliness from the mother, the general atmosphere of a try-out for two-year-olds. It was not so at all. You were courteously made welcome; beyond that you were strictly Lucy's business, it was no affair of theirs. You had the feeling that if Lucy had suddenly announced to them that she was pregnant they would have said:

"Well. Indeed. What are you going to do? Can we be of any help?"

Not that anything was happening which was likely to place Lucy in that classic predicament. You rode a great deal, you on her little mare Babe, Lucy on one of the more unmanageable beasts from the general stables; you played tennis, read, picked berries, went fishing once or twice. Sometimes you were accompanied by her young brother, a silent slender lad of eleven or twelve, but usually he was somewhere out of sight and you and she were alone. Challenged, you tried to milk one of the big brown Guernseys, with Lucy holding her tail so she couldn't flick you in the eye. The enormous bag looked as if it must hold at least ten gallons, but you couldn't make it come.

"She won't give it down that way, you're pinching her," said Lucy. "Here, let me show you again."

The creamy streams sizzled into the pail, forming a thick billowy foam.

The fishing was no good. The first time you drove to a lake, rather a pond, some twenty miles away, where there were said to be bass, and returned at nightfall empty-handed, wet and muddy and tired. The second time, less ambitious, you walked through the fields and over a wooded hill to where a small stream wound through the meadow and disappeared into a rocky ravine among some shrubbery. You worked your way down its bands for several hundred yards, trying the holes, and got two or three small bullheads.

"I don't understand it," said Lucy. "Just last summer it was full of sunfish as big as your hand. This is all on our land, and no one ever comes here."

You sat beside her on the bank, idly throwing pebbles into the pool, the largest pool you had yet found. On that side the bank was grassy clear to the water's rim; the opposite side was a high ledge of rock, crested with small trees. It was quiet and hot and drowsy there in the ravine, with nothing to be heard but the low murmur of the riffles upstream and some crows arguing far off, out of sight.

"Does your father own clear down to here? He has a lot of land," you observed.

She nodded. After a silence she said:

"I read a book last summer that said that nobody ought to own any land."

You lay back on the grass and looked at her. "Do you believe that?"

"I don't know," she frowned. "I guess I don't believe anything about what people ought to do. I don't see what right anybody has to tell us what we ought to do,"

"I've got a right to tell you you oughtn't to pull my hair, haven't I?"

"You have not. You only have a right to pull mine back—if you can."

Quickly she reached down and grabbed a handful of your thick brown hair and gave it a sharp tug. You yelled and seized her wrist, and straightened up, and struggled and clinched; and locked together you rolled over and over on the grass, almost tumbling into the stream. She was nearly as strong as you. You ended sitting on top of her, holding her down, dipping your hand into the water and trickling it onto her face from the ends of your fingers, and demanding surrender.

"I like that, it's nice and cool," she said, lying quietly; but for some reason you got up and moved a little off and sat down again on the grass. She too sat up and patted at her hair and pulled her dress down, and then got on her knees and dabbled at the water with her hands.

"This is where I go swimming," she said presently. "When we were younger we always used to come together, my two older brothers and I, but when Mart got old enough to go to High School he said we couldn't do that any more unless we wore bathing suits, and I wouldn't wear one and he wouldn't let me go in. He would stand in the edge of the water, there, and wave a stick at me. John took his side, and I had to give in. But I wouldn't wear a bathing suit, so I came alone after that."

You remembered something, and suddenly said:

"This is where you were the other afternoon when I couldn't find you!"

She nodded, as if it were of no importance, and took her hands out of the water and dried them on the hem of her dress. Flushed a little in the warm sun, and with a faint suggestion of freckles showing on her soft creamy skin, she was lovelier than you ever had seen her. You fancied her in the water, standing in the water; was her skin like that all over?

Without any consciousness you said to her, looking into her face, "You are very beautiful, like that."

She replied immediately, returning your look:

"I like to have you think so. But what do you mean, like that?"

"I don't know…I mean, sitting there, in the sunshine…I've never seen anyone so beautiful."

She was silent. After a pause you said:

"Look here, Lucy, let's go swimming, will you?"

"You mean take our clothes off?"

"Sure, why not? What's the difference?"

For an instant she regarded you with a surprised glance, then her eyes twinkled; suddenly she laughed.

"Wouldn't it be fun! I'd love to. But I guess I won't."

"Why not? Come on, what's the difference? Please."

She had stopped laughing, but her eyes were still amused.

"I don't know. Of course there isn't any reason, I just don't think I will. I'm sure I'd feel silly."

You argued and pleaded with her, but she was firm, she wouldn't do it. You gave up, and sulked, ostentatiously, but she appeared not to notice, and again ultimately you gave in; it was impossible to maintain a bad humor with her. When she suggested taking the rods downstream, towards the willows, to try once more for some fish, you went side by side, your heads bent together over the bait-can, trying to see how many worms you had left.

That night in bed you reflected that this was the first faint disagreement, the first slight friction, between you and her. You reflected this because you felt uncomfortable and wondered why. It was so easy, so almost unavoidable, to be on good terms with her. What if you had really tried to quarrel with her about it? You couldn't imagine her quarreling, but you couldn't understand that either; certainly she wasn't too cold or too insipid or too pliable. You went to sleep on the pleasant enigma.

There followed a couple of rainy days; you drove into Dayton and back, and in the evening you tried a game of chess with Mr. Crofts but found him much too good for you. Lucy was better, but he could give her a rook and beat her. This he did with an air of detachment which implied that the little wooden pieces were being moved about by accident of nature and that he found a mild amusement in wondering where they would go next.

That night it cleared, and the next day was sunny; by the middle of the afternoon it was hot, pleasantly hot, with a soft breeze stirring the air just enough to make the goldenrod buds faintly nod on their long stems. You were glad, for it was nearly the end of July and soon you would have to return to Cleveland and you wanted to be with Lucy in the woods and fields, in the sunshine. That afternoon she suggested a walk, and you strolled together to the top of the wooded hill, and from there ran a race pell-mell down to the bank of the stream in the meadow. You followed its course into the ravine, past the thicket of shrubs, and found yourselves at the edge of the pool where you had sat two days before. You were a little surprised, for you hadn't realized you had come so far. Lucy had led you there deliberately. She said immediately and without preamble:

"I was silly the other day. Let's go in."

Almost before you knew what was happening she had removed her shoes and stockings and slipped off her dress and underthings and splashed into the water. Under she went, then rose to the surface and swam to the other end of the little pool, where she stood dripping, tugging at her braids of hair, the water only up to her knees.

"Aren't you coming?" she called.

With trembling fingers you somehow got your shoelaces undone and your buttons unfastened. You placed your clothes in a neat little pile, then stood at the water's edge, feeling extraordinarily naked. She had her hair loose now and was shaking it down over her shoulders, clear to her waist and below.

"Can I dive here?" you asked.

"Yes, it's deep, over your head."

In you went, but too flat, landing on your belly. You swam to the other end and came up beside her, pressing the water from your eyes.

"I forgot about my hair," she said ruefully. "It will take hours to dry."

"There's plenty of sun," you observed. "Isn't the water warm! I thought it would be colder."

You wanted to turn and look squarely at her, but could not; nor did you at all, really, though together you splashed in and out, and sat on the grass in the sun, and dove in again, for a long time. You had glimpses of flashing white arms and legs, firm small breasts, the lovely curve of her back. As you sat beside her you gazed at her feet, you noticed the regular shapely toes with pink translucent nails, and the way the calf slid smoothly and gracefully into the ankle. She was not in fact undressed, for as she sat there the long strands of brown hair, shaken out but still glistening with water-drops, fell around her in all directions, the clear warm wet skin shining through here and there like sunlight through a vine.

"I wish I'd brought a towel," she said. "My clothes are wet too. We splattered them."

You didn't reply. You were thinking how exciting it would be, how original and natural, if you were to turn and look at her as she sat there beside you all unclothed, and say to her, "Lucy, I love you. Will you marry me?" You wondered what she would reply. You thought you knew. You said nothing.

A little later, dressed again, you strolled leisurely back toward the house through the still hot sun, by way of the apple orchard. Mr. and Mrs. Crofts were playing tennis, and you and Lucy sat in the shade of one of the crooked old trees and watched them. Abraham, the Negro cook's little boy, appeared with a pitcher of lemonade and some glasses, and the game was suspended.

"What's the matter with your hair?" asked Mrs. Crofts.

"It's still wet," said Lucy. "We went swimming."

Mr. Crofts smacked his lips with enjoyment of the cold sour lemonade, and remarked that tennis was better exercise than swimming because it made you sweat.

A few days later, on the last day of July, Lucy drove you to Dayton to catch the afternoon train for Cleveland. Her father came along, having some errands in town. You were expected back at the office the following morning.

Nothing had happened, and you couldn't understand it. What did you want, what were you waiting for? You said to yourself that Lucy was interested in her music, that what she wanted was a career, but you knew that was twaddle. She had said it was her vacation too and hadn't practiced once while you were there, and had scarcely mentioned it. You wondered if she really had any talent and guessed probably not, though you knew nothing about it. At all events, it was plainly inevitable that you would marry her. There was no special hurry, she was only nineteen. Six years younger than you, that was just right. In the meantime, you would be lonely in Cleveland, during the six weeks that would elapse before she returned.—But why, after all, had nothing happened? You had kissed her just once, that day last spring when you spilled the coffee. How many wasted opportunities! Perhaps she didn't expect to be married, didn't want to be. She had unsuspected wisdoms and maturities.—But no, it was plainly marriage. A curious father-in-law and mother-in-law they would be—well-off apparently, and no one to be ashamed of. Different from that awful uncle and aunt in Cleveland.

Was Lucy in love with you? Yes. No. What would she say if you asked her, do you love me? Probably that she didn't know, and then if you asked her to marry you she would say at once, yes, of course I will. Were you in love with her? Yes—oh yes— hell, you didn't know. All you knew was that nothing seemed to happen; there in the train, toward the end of the journey, you felt all at once tired out and used up. You decided you would write her a letter, and ask her, and have it done.

At the office next day you found yourself surrounded by difficulties. Dick was not due to return for another two weeks, and various questions which ordinarily he would have decided, were put up to you. You suspected malice in this, for in fact the extent of your authority was questionable and had never been clearly defined. It appeared later that in the Pittsburgh deal, Jackson had deliberately set a trap for you.

In the course of the afternoon Dick's secretary entered and handed you a letter.

"I've attended to most of Mr. Carr's private mail," she said, "but there didn't seem to be anything I could do about this. I've sent a wire to Mr. Carr, but he may not get it for a week."

The letter was from Erma, mailed in Vienna. She said she was leaving for America, and after spending a week in New York would continue to Cleveland and probably spend the fall and winter there. Would Dick, like a good brother, give the necessary orders to have the house got in readiness? She was sick of hotels.

The next morning there was a telegram, saying that she would arrive on Thursday. You immediately drove out to Wooton Avenue to see that your instructions of the day before were being executed.

One of your most vivid memories of Erma from the early days is that August morning in the dingy old Cleveland railroad station. She came down the board platform like a fairy princess in lace and flowers borne on a breeze, surrounded by porters loaded with bags and parcels. You had expected to see a crowd, but apparently she had notified no one but Dick.

She waved from a distance and called, as you hastened forward:

"Bill—how nice of you!"

You explained that Dick was out of town. She kissed you on the cheek, and you felt yourself blushing.

"I've got to kiss someone," she declared, "do you mind? Anyway, you look so nice you should be kissed. I think Americans are better-shaved than Europeans, they always look a bit stubby. Dick ought to be ashamed of himself, off in the woods when I come home. Heavens, I've been away over a year!"

She was gorgeous, distracting, overwhelming, with her dark red close-fitting traveling dress, her dark red shoes with incredibly high and pointed heels, her dark red velvet hat, and above all the air and perfume of strangeness that clung to her. You told yourself that she was the real thing, she was different from those smart and assured girls who always made you feel at once inadequate and contemptuous.

You rode out to the house with her and spent some time explaining the arrangements you had made, regretting that the time had been too short to see them all carried out, and finally you stayed and lunched with her before returning to the office. That afternoon you sat at your desk and thought that if you had married her you probably would have gone to Europe too.

When Dick got back you heaved a sigh of relief; things at the office were getting too thick for you. He plunged into the midst of it with a boldness that fairly took your breath when you remembered how much he had had to get from you, only two years before. You were worried about the Pittsburgh deal, as was everyone else who knew about it. There was a meeting the evening after his return, lasting far into the night.

The next morning you were summoned to Dick's office. When you entered he was alone, walking back and forth with his hands in his pockets, looking sour.

"Bill," he said abruptly, "what the hell did you mean by that letter to Farrell? It showed our hand, and they've double-crossed us. It's the biggest thing we've had a crack at for two years, and we've lost it. I didn't want to say anything in front of the others last night, but by god, I don't understand what you were thinking about."

You had known this was coming, and you had resolved to keep entirely calm and show no indignation.

"It's not as simple as it looks," you replied, "though I suppose it does fall on me. Look here."

You took from your pocket the telegrams that had come, the day you returned, and copies of Jackson's previous letters. Dick read them through, while you explained that they had not been shown to you until after your own had been sent.

"Where were they?"

"I don't know. I didn't go to the files myself."

"Are you accusing Jackson of deliberately—"

"No. I have no proof of anything. It may have been only carelessness. Those are the facts."

Dick started to reply, but you went on hastily:

"I know there's no excuse for it, I should have known better, but the truth is they had it already so balled up that I was desperate.

The first bid had been recalled, and that looked bad to begin with. Why did Jackson send a new man down there? Why didn't he go himself? He says the new man was a pal of Mellish's, as if that would do any good."

Dick looked thoughtful but unconvinced. You knew that he suspected you of a grudge against Jackson.

"That letter was terrible, Bill," he said, "there's no getting around that. God, it was dumb. But you're right, it was mismanaged all the way through. I said that last night."

Nothing more came of it. For some time you fancied that Dick was a little off with you, but after all he was friendly enough, as friendly as he was with anyone. What did come of it was that you began to keep an eye on Jackson, which was not difficult since you still had free access to all departments. The only person you discussed it with was Schwartz, who agreed that there was something underneath it somewhere; Jackson wouldn't deliberately stir up such a mess just to spite you.

Late one afternoon, about a week after Erma's return, called to the telephone, you heard her voice. It was raining, she was lonely, she needed intelligent conversation, would you come out for a tête-à-tête dinner?

You would.

It is difficult to recapture the impression that Erma made upon you then. Certainly you were flattered by the attention she gave you; just as certainly you were not in love with her. You always tell yourself that, with Mrs. Davis, with Millicent, with Lucy—then you have never been in love? No, has anyone? Some people seem to feel differently about it—oh to hell with that! You were at least willing to accept Erma's cordial gestures, partly perhaps because you knew that any one of the smart assured young men would have given a good deal to be invited to dine with her alone.

She was very nice to you that evening; she can be nicer than anyone else when she wants to. The dinner was perfect, and you both drank enough wine—just enough. Afterwards you sat in the little room beyond the library, with the windows open on the garden, and she played and sang some *chansons populaires,* which you had never heard, and later came and sat on the divan by you and told you about things in Europe—people and cities and rivers and the shore of the Mediterranean. You felt that you had little enough to tell her in return; but you might as well be fair to yourself, as a matter of fact you have always talked very well when there was nothing at stake. She has always enjoyed, and still does, your maliciously embroidered accounts of captains of industry leading their embattled forces of pale bookkeepers and pretty stenographers to the conquest of a foolish and bewildered world. You do, after all, know fairly well what's going on; it's only when you presume to take a hand in it that you become an idiot.

You sat on the divan that evening, and talked, and listened, and admired Erma's firm white arms and graceful neck and her pretty fluttering nervous gestures. She had not yet cut her hair; it was a soft yellow mass on top of her head, a little loose and escaping here and there from the nest.

She had just finished telling you of a young Frenchman who had followed her twice across Europe, dying of love, suddenly reaching his emotional climax in Cannes with a request for a loan of ten thousand francs, when all at once she stopped and looked at you and said:

"There's one thing I've admired you for a lot. Do you remember that we were once engaged to be married?"

It was without warning, but you managed a smile.

"No," you said, "were we?"

"And you've never even told Dick, at least I don't suppose you have—"

"I haven't."

"And when I—well—overlooked it, you just overlooked it too."

By now your smile was quite all right.

"I couldn't very well yell at you, hey, you dropped something—and I was too bashful to pick it up and hand it to you."

She kissed her finger and then touched your lips with it.

"You're a darling. I hate explanations. Of course, it may be that you were glad to be out of it."

"Unspeakably. I was going to be a great writer and was afraid it would take my mind off my work."

She pretended to shiver a little. "Ugh. Don't. That sounds as if it were decades ago. Good heavens you're only twenty-five and I'm twenty-seven. We were both too young."

"Twenty-six next month."

"Yes? We'll have a party and make everybody bring you a present."

You didn't reply to that; Lucy was due to return a few days before your birthday, and you and she had planned a farewell autumn trip to the canyon at Cuyahoga Falls.

After that you received many invitations from Erma—teas, dinners, dances—and you accepted most of them, but you were careful; you had been scorched once by that tricky flame and were shy of it. She was obviously enjoying her position and prestige in Cleveland, and it was reflected on you; it was often you who were chosen to take her in to dinner or sit by her in the theatre. You exerted yourself to be amusing and you achieved in fact a certain modest reputation and standing; people who had scarcely noticed you as one of Dick's business associates began to find you desirable and to be careful to include you. You and Erma were rarely alone together. She was friendly, intimately cordial, that was all; she said you were the only person in Cleveland who could both dance and talk.

One afternoon she telephoned to ask you to come to dinner, early; she emphasized it, early; and when you arrived and had been shown into the library she entered almost at once and explained:

"Dick's coming. He phoned and especially wanted to come, so I suppose he intends to talk about business. I regard you as my business adviser, and I confess I'm a little overpowered by darling Dick's Napoleonic dash, so I want you to be here too."

You were aghast.

"Good god, Erma, I can't do it. You mean he doesn't know I'm here?"

"Of course not. It's a pleasant surprise."

"But I can't. Anyway it's silly. Dick's perfectly all right; anything he suggests will be all right. Don't you see I can't do it? Don't you see how impertinent and impudent it would seem to him?"

Her eyes tightened a little; that was the first time you saw them do it. Her voice was raised.

"Impudent!" she exclaimed. Then she laughed. "I don't need you to withstand Napoleon, Bill dear; it won't be necessary and if it is I'll attend to it. But I'm ignorant, and you know things. Really I insist. We can tell him you dropped in for a handout, or that we're living together to see how we like it, or anything you want."

When Dick arrived a little later he didn't bother to conceal his surprise and annoyance at seeing you. Nor did he trouble to lower his voice when he said to Erma:

"I thought you said you'd be alone."

"I'd forgotten about Bill," she said carelessly. "He often comes out to relieve my loneliness. If it's really so confidential—"

No, Dick said, it didn't matter.

It was the first time the three of you had been alone together since the summer of your second visit. At dinner you talked of that, and of Dick's fishing trip, and of other inconsequential things. You were relieved that Dick had speedily forgotten his annoyance at your presence; seemed, indeed, as dinner progressed, to become more than usually genial.

"I'm surprised that you can get Bill out to this end of town so often," he said to Erma. "Who does he leave to guard his shepherdess? Not that she needs it."

Erma glanced at him, and at you. "Have you got a shepherdess?"

"What, haven't you met her?" asked Dick. "I don't know where he found her, but he brought her to a couple of dances last spring, and she darned near started a riot. Young and sweet and good. Old men sighed for their lost youth. We all offered to buy food for her, but Bill had taken away her appetite. She wouldn't even go for a buggy ride except with Bill. That's why he turned down the fishing trip; she invited him down to the farm to help her with the flocks. You really haven't seen her? She's entirely worth looking at."

He turned to you. "You haven't fried and eaten her?"

You explained that Lucy had remained for the rest of the summer and wouldn't return to Cleveland for another week or so.

"And I thought you told me all your secrets," said Erma reproachfully, "and here you have a beautiful shepherdess that I never even heard of."

"It's no secret," you said shortly, "and I haven't got her."

"The hell you haven't," said Dick with his mouth full of ice cream.

After dinner you wanted to leave and were busy devising a suitable excuse, when you caught a glance from Erma which said plainly that she read your intention and that you might as well discard it. You went with them into the library, and coffee and cigarettes were brought. You felt resentful and uncomfortable, especially when Dick moved to a chair next to Erma and began telling her his errand.

The recent death of old Meynell, the lawyer, he explained, made necessary a new arrangement regarding Erma's stock. During his and Erma's minority all of the stock had been controlled by a committee under a trust agreement, with Meynell as chairman. On Dick's twenty-first birthday half of the stock had been turned over to him; but when Erma had reached her majority two years earlier her half had gone under her control, but a proxy for it had been given by her to Meynell, at the lawyer's own suggestion. When Meynell died the proxy of course died with him.

"The stock should be represented at the next annual stockholders' meeting," Dick went on, "and that's really the point. Of course, you can attend the meeting yourself if you want to, there isn't anything technical about it, electing directors and so on. What I wondered was if you would give me a proxy and let me vote your stock along with mine. That would be simplest. If you happen to be in Japan or Singapore you couldn't very well attend the meeting yourself."

Erma sat comfortably sipping black coffee and blowing cigarette smoke in the short little puffs that were already a habit with her. She hardly seemed to be listening.

"If I give you my proxy you'll vote the whole thing, won't you?" she asked when Dick had finished.

"Of course. I own the other half."

"How long is a proxy good for?"

"As long as you want to make it. Usually there is no stated term. You can recall it whenever you want to, or make a new one."

Erma took a sip of coffee and a puff on her cigarette. What was she teasing him for, you wondered idly.

"It would be fun to attend the meeting myself, if it weren't in that dirty hole," she said. "Why don't we get some decent offices somewhere?"

"It wouldn't be so very amusing," Dick replied, "no one there but me and a lawyer and a stenographer. Of course, do that if you want to, provided you're here."

"No, I guess I'll make a proxy, it sounds more important. Only I think it would be piggish for you to vote the whole thing, so I'll give my proxy to Bill, if he'll promise not to elect the shepherdess a director."

You glanced at her; naturally thought she was joking. Dick also glanced at her.

"You'd better make me promise too," he grinned. "I might even want to make her President."

"I mean it," said Erma. "Bill, consider yourself my faithful proxy. Don't betray your trust, or I'll scratch your eyes out."

"Don't be silly," said Dick. "There's no point to that."

You were flustered; you felt yourself blushing.

"Really, Erma," you protested, "you're putting me in a false position—"

"I don't see anything false about it," she declared. "It seems to me very sensible. You two can run things just as you want to, and two heads are better than one, and you are much more apt to keep me informed of things than Dick would be. Anyway, no matter how it's done Dick will run the show, won't you, Dick darling? This just happens to appeal to me. I like the idea of your going up to him and saying, see here, old man, this won't do, we'll have to get new pencils for the export department, my proxy violently dislikes green pencils."

"You're a damn fool," said Dick.

But she really did mean it; she stuck to it, airily but inexorably.

Dick, once convinced that she was in earnest, seemed to be not at all disturbed—rather amused with maybe a touch of irritation at her levity. The point once decided he made the arrangements for getting the proxy signed; you and young Ritter, from the law office, were to come out to the house the following afternoon. You sat for the most part silent, hardly knowing what to think or say; what was Dick thinking, you wondered. Did he in fact feel restrained and humiliated? If so, you were in a delicate and dangerous position; you would be every moment suspended on the fragile thread of Erma's good will. But with Erma insisting and Dick accepting with outward good grace you were helpless.

When Dick finally rose to go and asked if he could drive you downtown, Erma said no, she wanted to have a conference with her proxy. And then all she did was sit and smoke cigarettes and tell you of the battles she and Dick had had as youngsters; but when you at length crossed to her chair to say goodnight she held out her hand and said:

"I don't know if Dick really thinks I'm a damn fool, but I'm not. He's a brilliant and remarkable person, but it won't hurt him any to feel that there's somebody around with the right to ask questions. What a rotten job for you! I know it, but I'll stick by you."

You walked all the way home, in the mild September night, feeling alternately humiliated and elated. You knew that Erma had sized you up for an intelligent and faithful dog, and particularly you resented her light assumption that you would accept the function without having consulted you. You felt, fearfully, that you had been manoeuvred onto the edge of a precipice; how did Dick really feel about it? After all, as Erma had said, Dick would run the show.

But one thing was a fact: at twenty-six, not quite twenty-six, you held the voting power for one-half the stock of a ten million dollar corporation. You would be elected a director. You would write Jane tomorrow and tell her about it, sort of casually. You would be on equal terms with Dick—but even your fancy balked at that. You laughed aloud at yourself as you swung along on the sidewalk under the maple trees, not with any special bitterness—no, you would scarcely be on even terms with Dick, not if you had a hundred proxies.

But no bitterness for him.

For her…for her….

# G

He became suddenly aware that his hand was again in his over-coat pocket, closed tightly over the butt of the revolver. His hand came out and the revolver with it, and he stood there with his forearm extended, the weapon in plain sight, peering around, downstairs and up, like a villain in a melodrama. If the door of the landing had at that instant opened and one of the art students had appeared, he would probably have pulled the trigger without knowing it.

His hand returned to his pocket and then came out again, empty, and sought the railing as he mounted another step, and another, and then stopped once more.

Oh you would, would you, he said to himself, and he felt his lips twist into a grimace that tried to be a smile. No you don't, you don't go back now, this time you go ahead, if it's only to point it at her and let her know what you think she's fit for.

You go ahead....

# VII

You said that to yourself, over and over again, that night in Cleveland when Lucy was going away. Go ahead, go ahead, you repeated, what in heaven's name are you waiting for?

Or, finally, forget it.

You did neither. You dangled on the peg of your irresolution until a street-car motorman decided it for you.

Why was Erma so curious about Lucy? It has never been like her to show an interest in anyone without a plain and direct profit in sight. All her generosities and graceful gestures have a quality of indifference that renders them lifeless; she is warm only when she is in pursuit, avid and ready to seize. But by exception she was actively curious about Lucy. She insisted on seeing her at once, as soon as Lucy returned to Cleveland, and a dinner party was arranged, informally, only you three and Dick and another couple—that young doctor and his wife who had been Erma's chum at school.

A week later, in the afternoon, she took Lucy to a concert; you were irritated when you heard of it, and remarked that it was amusing to see Erma doing the Grand Duchess.

"She's nice and friendly," said Lucy, surprised. "It didn't occur to me that I was being patronized."

"Do you like her?"

"Oh, all right. I wanted to hear the concert anyway. I don't like anyone very much, except you."

There were no lonely evenings then. You had finally, not long after Dick's return to town, moved to the Jayhawker Club, to one of the large rooms with an entrance hall on the top floor, and every day there would be phone messages, invitations, notes. Obviously, as you see now, you had become an interesting object of speculation in that circle of whispers and surmises and scandals which constituted the high world in that noisy and sprawling municipal monster sitting on the lake shore. Doubtless a picture was composed of you as an aggressive and successful young business executive who could reach out with his right hand and take the lovely Erma with her great fortune, or with his left and gather in the fresh young beauty and innocence of Lucy. Lucky dog. A man who would go far.

You were a great deal with Lucy. There was a trip to the canyon on your birthday—Erma had forgotten about it—and Lucy spent the preceding evening in her aunt's kitchen baking a cake which tumbled out of the basket during your descent down the bluff and was cruelly mangled on the rocks at the bottom. You often took her riding of an evening, or to a dance or theatre.

You had never written that letter....

She had not been back long, it was towards the end of October, when one evening you were dining at Winkler's Restaurant and she suddenly said:

"It looks as if I'm going to New York soon. Mereczynski has opened a studio there and Mr. Murray says he can get him to take me. I don't know if I'm worth it; I've written to Father about it."

You felt at once that she intended to go, that she would go. You were vastly surprised, and you were panic-stricken; not till that moment had you been aware that underneath her simplicity and her quietness was a strength which made her immeasurably your superior. Had you felt it unconsciously and leaned upon it? Had you misjudged also your own importance to her? Were all men always helpless like this with women? But good lord

Lucy wasn't a woman; she was a young girl taking piano lessons whose idea of an exciting experience was teaching you how to milk a cow.

"How soon would you go?"

"I don't know, probably a couple of weeks, as soon as Mr. Murray can make the arrangements. If I am to go at all it might as well be at once."

"In two weeks," you said, and then were silent. Her hand was on the table, and you placed yours on top of it; she laid down her fork and with her other hand patted yours and pressed it, smiling at you. Then she picked up her fork again and went on eating.

"You're certainly casual about it." You spoke almost desperately, feeling that you were being forced into an untenable position without choosing it or desiring it. "I've been wanting to ask you to marry me. Of course you know that. If you go to New York that will be the end of it."

You hesitated, then finished more desperately and rapidly: "Unless you'll promise to marry me before you go." There. Done. At last, settled.

But Lucy laughed! And said:

"Well, you did ask me after all."

"I've wanted to since the first day I saw you," you declared. "I took it for granted you knew. You did know, you couldn't help it. Ever since I met you I haven't cared a hang about anyone else. I didn't even go home for a week this summer, though I'd promised I would. But I've never known what to say to you. I don't know even now how you feel about me—"

She stopped smiling, and her voice was more serious than you had ever heard it:

"I don't either. I never have known how we feel about each other. I like you so much, much more than I've ever liked anyone, but there's something in you I don't like, and I don't know what it is. That's what troubles me about it, that I don't know what it is."

She gave you a warm and friendly smile.

"For a while," she went on, "I thought it was because you couldn't make up your mind whether you cared for me enough to marry me, but then I couldn't make up my mind either, so that couldn't be it."

"Mine's made up now," you declared. "It has been, for a long time."

"Yes. Mine isn't. I don't know about us. Though if you'd asked me last summer I'm pretty sure I'd have said yes."

Yes, she would have, you knew she would have. This did not much resemble any of the scenes of sweet capitulation you had so often constructed in fancy; it did not in fact resemble much of anything unless it were a horse with a bundle of hay suspended on a pole in front of him so that he never quite reached it.

You see now more or less all around yourself, and inside too, as you sat there that evening and confronted the petty barrier of her indecision and made no plunge to demolish it. At the time you felt forlorn and defeated, and probably that was the impression Lucy got; a considerable urnconscious histrionic feat. Much more subtle than any voluntary blackguardism!

On the eve of her departure, two weeks later, you became incautious; your careful cowardice was very nearly broken down by a free and genuine impulse. You had been with her nearly every day of those last two weeks, and had insisted on nothing. Now you comprehend very little of it; then you understood nothing at all. You spoke constantly of the loneliness you would feel when she had gone. You declared, with careful levity, that if she wouldn't stay in Cleveland you would follow her to New York and get a job tuning pianos in Mereczynski's studio. She tranquilly completed her preparations, letting you be with her as much as you would, and as the day approached you found more and more difficulty in meeting her frank and quizzical eye.

She was to take a sleeper Wednesday night. Tuesday evening you dined again at Winkler's. After dinner you drove her home and, arriving there and observing that it was only ten o'clock, it was suggested that you stay a while. Finding the library and parlor occupied by Aunt Martha and a bridge party, Lucy said you could find refuge in her room, and ran upstairs ahead of you. It was then that you hesitated on the stairs, wondering if you should bother to go back and turn on the lights of the car, and she called down to you:

"Well, aren't you coming up?"

You had been in Lucy's room before, without particularly noticing what was in it; either she had the gift of making her surroundings seem colorless, or they were in fact so through her own indifference to them. This night, perhaps scenting danger, you stood just inside the threshold and glanced around at the big, neat, fat-looking bed, the two straight chairs, the pile of music on a table, the enormous trunk in a corner with its lid open, being packed. Lucy had taken off her coat and hat and was seated at the dressing-table, arranging her hair.

"As soon as I get to New York I'm going to get a bob," she announced. "Then I can just give my head a shake and there I'll be."

You remonstrated, declaring that she had the most beautiful hair in the world, to be kept at all costs.

"All right, I'll send it to you," she laughed.

She had some snapshots, taken during your summer visit, which you had not yet seen, and you helped her dig them out of the trunk; and she sat cross-legged on the bed, propped against the pillows, while you sat beside her and took the pictures from her one by one. You hardly saw the pictures, though you looked at them and discussed them and laughed together over them. She had never seemed so close to you, physically; her skirt, twisted up to her knee, seemed not to be there at all; as her fingers brushed against yours, or your shoulders touched, it felt infinitely intimate, like the feel of your own hand on your own body when, relaxed in bed, you give yourself a sleepy careless caress; and she smelled warm and clean and very sweet. You almost held your breath till she touched you again, and you passionately hoped that she would not notice, that she would go on letting her shoulder meet yours as you leaned over to take a picture from her. She must not know that you were lost within her, and she within you, nor feel the divine tenderness that had suddenly overwhelmed you. You struggled to keep it in front of your eyes; if you ceased to be able to look at it you were gone; you could not understand this swift unexpected threat of annihilation; and you could not permit it. Something precious, something without which you could not live, was in peril and must be preserved, though you could neither then nor now give it a name. You only knew that Lucy must touch you again, you must go on like this forever, enfolded in her closeness; and she must not know. This precarious ecstasy was a secret not to be shared; even, shared, would be shattered. Violently must be shattered.

A picture fell from your fingers into her lap. You reached for it together, and your hand closed upon hers, on her soft skirt, on her leg. She looked at you, and her eyes widened and her face became suddenly still as marble. You leaned forward and kissed her. You kept your lips on hers, put your arms tight around her and pressed against her, hard, pressed her back against the pillows. You kept your right arm close around her and, never releasing her mouth, with your other hand caressed with blind and clumsy strokes her back, her hair, her shoulder, her neck and throat.

"My love, oh Lucy my love," you gasped. You twisted around and lay against her and put your lips again on hers, murmuring, "Kiss me, please kiss me."

She was silent, but she kissed you, again and again. She held you close with strong and urgent arms. "My love, my dear love," you whispered. Awkwardly your hand forced itself within the neck of her dress, at the back. She shivered, suddenly and violently, withdrew herself, pushed you away, and sat up, breathing hard and not looking at you.

"I think you tore my dress," she said, feeling at it.

You swung yourself around, got onto your feet, on the floor, and stood there, betrayed and ridiculous, fumbling in your pocket for your cigarette case. She too got off the bed, arranged her skirt, and without saying anything went to the dressing-table mirror, and twisted herself about, first this way, then that, trying to see the tear in her dress.

"I'm sorry if I tore it," you said from across the room. "I didn't know what I was doing. I'm sorry."

She came over and stood in front of you, quite close, and put her hands on your shoulders. She tried to smile and you tried to look at her troubled eyes.

"I'm almost crying," she said. "I can't figure it out. What was wrong? I'm not afraid of anything we might do. I should love to have you tear my dress, but it was no good."

"I'm sorry," was all you could say. "I'm awfully sorry, Lucy." As she stood there with her hands still on your shoulders you thought to take her again in your arms, but she moved away, to the bed, and began picking up the scattered pictures.

"Aunt Martha will wonder what we're doing," she said.

"Yes," you agreed, "I'd better go."

"I can't eat with you tomorrow evening after all, because she asked me to have my last dinner here. She told me to invite you, if you care to come."

You remarked that they would probably prefer to have her to themselves, that they didn't like you anyway. "I'll come later, after dinner, if I may, and go to the train with you."

"All right. Yes, do that. That would be nice."

She went downstairs with you to the hall and outer door. You felt awkward and completely helpless; you had no idea what was happening, what you intended, what she thought or felt. You were pure idiot, without direction or purpose or under-standing. At the door you took her hand and she smiled at you, you said no matter what, you went off down the steps into the dark and heard the door close behind you.

Carrying your concealed and uncomprehended torture. If since maturity you have approached any human being with candor and have been accepted clearly and honestly, surely it was so with Lucy and the result was total bewilderment. There was something in her that frightened you profoundly, or some-thing in you which deeply felt a menace far below the level of reason. When you go digging around in yourself you can uncover almost anything, you have fitted together the pieces of many a complex puzzle; but with Lucy, where the complexity was least, you are most at sea. Good god how simple it was! She offered you everything, everything that you needed and desired....

All next day at the office, that last day, wretchedly nervous, you felt certain that it was at last decided. You would go out to her house immediately after dinner, that would give you three hours with her, the train didn't leave till eleven. There was no other possible course. Say you didn't go until nine, there would still be two hours—and two minutes would in fact be enough.

After what happened last night, if you did not do that, if you did not have the guts to say, there's nothing wrong with it, you are mine, I am yours—you would be too contemptible in your own eyes to exist. You told yourself bitterly that it was not a question of fairness to her; she could do very well without your fairness or anything you might give her; there was merely the necessity that you continue to grant yourself the right to breathe. Desire for Lucy, specifically, or even the suffocating revulsion against a surrender to the fascination in her, had nothing to do with it. Either you had the integrity of your appetite as a living organism, or where was life?

During the afternoon Erma telephoned; she hadn't seen you for a week, she said; how about dinner that evening? You replied that you were sorry, it was impossible. When she insisted you were almost curt in your refusal, which must have been somewhat startling to her. To hell with her, you thought heroically.

You left the office a little later than usual and went to your room at the club. After a rather early dinner, alone, you got the car from the garage; the man there helped you put the top up, for it had begun to rain—a cold determined drizzle. It was then barely eight o'clock, and you decided you didn't want to arrive so early, you would drive around a while; your last drive as a free man. This calculation would indicate that you were still sentient, but that was demonstrably false, for on putting the car away the preceding evening you had noted that the gasoline tank was nearly empty, and walking to the garage only ten minutes ago you had reminded yourself that you must have it filled, but now you drove off without thinking of it.

You stopped first at the club and got the books and candy you had bought for Lucy, reflecting that she might decide to go on to New York and return later, and if she didn't it wouldn't matter. Then you headed south, toward the Heights and the country beyond.

It rained steadily. You decided that you might as well turn at Lewellyn Road, but when you got there you went straight through. You drove slowly and carefully into the black night, the city now behind, watching the straight glistening rain streaks in the rays of your headlights. Were they silver or steel? Steel, you decided.

You did not look at your watch once.

All the time during this sneaking crawl into the night you felt yourself to be thinking, thinking indeed with unusual rapidity and complexity; but no post-analysis has revealed anything that could even with politeness be called cerebration. You considered in careful detail the effect that would be produced on Erma and Dick by the announcement of your engagement to Lucy; how soon you would be married; where you would live; whether Jane would like Lucy. The last, for some reason, stumped you, and you drove your mind away from it—you couldn't imagine any contact between Jane and Lucy. All this as you drove into the rain with the city far behind, your forgotten watch ticking the seconds from one chaos into another, and the last drops of your gasoline tank being sucked into the inexorable cylinders.

A little beyond Myer's Corners, almost directly in front of the white house at the foot of the long hill, there was a sputter from the engine, the car jerked once or twice, and slid gently to a stop as you guided it to the side of the road. You didn't even bother to look at the tank; you knew at once it was empty. You did look at your watch; it was twenty minutes to ten.

You waited five or ten minutes, but no car passed and none was in sight. You got out and stumbled towards the house whose white form showed dimly through the rain and darkness;

there was no light showing, but you finally roused someone, a man in a nightshirt who gruffly said he had neither telephone nor automobile and slammed the door in your face.

You went back to the car and looked at the gas gauge and tried again to start the engine; it spluttered derisively and stopped with a grunt. The first two cars you hailed went by without even slackening speed; the third, going towards town, stopped a hundred feet beyond you and you ran up to it. There was a man in the front seat and dim shapes in the back. He could take you only as far as Myer's Corners, where he turned right towards Fossville. After another wait, in the rain, at Myer's Corners, you were finally picked up by a farmer in an old Ford, and were carried by him almost to the city's edge, to where the Elmwood car line crosses the highway. The cars ran only every half-hour, but one would be due in about five minutes, the farmer said—and headed his Ford around to return to his home, which he had passed three miles back. It was then nearly ten-thirty, and you figured you could just make it to the railroad station if the street-car made good time.

A dazzling headlight came suddenly around the bend, blinding you, there was the rush of the oncoming car, you stood near the track and waved your arms frantically, and it was all over. The car's bell clanged, it whizzed by and disappeared into the night like a scared elephant. You sat down on the end of the wet culvert, at the side of the road, with your feet in two inches of water, and cried like a baby. It was the first time you had cried since boyhood. At those times, in those days, you had always gone to Jane; and now, naturally, you thought of her. You despised your abdication of manhood, and you knew there was no person in the world who would not despise it, except Jane. You sat there in the rain, engulfed in desolation, and bawled for her.

You think it was Jane you bawled for? There doesn't seem to

be much ground under that, does there? When was she ever a
support for your weakness? How about the time you wired her
to come to New York and she didn't take the trouble to answer?
Oh sure, she explained it, she could explain anything. How
about all the times you could have gone to her and never did?
Now, behind your back, impelled by pity—to hell with her.

As for the Lucy business, she didn't seem to know what it was
all about, any more than you did, when finally you told her of it.
It was the following summer, when you took your vacation early
in order to spend two weeks at home while Jane was there. You
hadn't been there more than three days before you were wishing
you hadn't gone. Your mother might as well not have existed;
Margaret and Rose were strangers; Larry was rarely seen except
at meal-time; and Jane was always at the store and expecting
you to be there too. It was on the porch late one evening, when
your visit was nearly over, that you told her of Lucy. You had of
course mentioned her in letters, but at arm's length, making
phrases. Now you spoke of it in detail and with feeling; you
gave Jane to understand that it was a case of a grand passion
unaccountably thwarted by the tragic vagaries of obscure fate.

"I certainly intended to ask her to marry me," you declared.
"It seemed foreordained and inevitable. She clearly expected it
too, felt the same way about it. Surely we were made for each
other if any two people ever were. And yet it was no go, there
was something somewhere that made it impossible. I was with
her out at her uncle's house the night before she left, and we
had a long talk up in her room. I don't want to seem conceited
about it, but she practically put it up to me, and all of a sudden
I saw plainly that it wouldn't do, I'd been kidding myself. I suppose I was a coward not to tell her straight out how I felt about
it, but it seemed so darned brutal I couldn't do it. She was so
lovely, standing there, close to me, looking at me—I wish you
could see her. She was the most beautiful girl I've ever known

—everybody said no one in Cleveland could touch her for looks. You see, I'd introduced her to our set, which is of course the most exclusive bunch in the city, and she made all the other girls look like the run of the mill. Including Erma. I wish you could see her."

"It seems curious," said Jane. "If you did really love her.... How could you help telling her—how could you say goodbye without telling her—have you heard from her? Have you written to her?"

You shook your head. "You see I didn't really say goodbye at all. Oh this is a confession all right, this is no proud tale of conquest, I was a darned coward, I was damn well ashamed of myself. I was supposed to go out the next evening and take her to the train, but something or other came up, I forget what, and I didn't go."

"You just didn't go!"

"Yes. It was pretty bad, I suppose. She's probably forgotten all about me by now but anyway it was a rotten way to act. I honestly think I was in love with her—I must have been. You used to say I had strong intuitions about people, and I think it must have been that somehow unconsciously I felt that it wouldn't work, at least that marriage wouldn't. Remember she's a musician, she's an artist, she has that temperament. Maybe it would have been all right if I'd been realistic about it and taken her for my mistress—"

You said that deliberately, for the sake of the little thrill it gave you; it was piquant, it made your lips feel dry so that you wet them with your tongue, to talk calmly to Jane about taking a girl as your mistress. You had never spoken so frankly to her about that sort of thing, but what the deuce, you thought, we are mature and not prudes....

To your shocked surprise Jane laughed. She stopped swinging the hammock, so she could laugh thoroughly.

"You say that as if it meant cutting her up in slices and cooking her in butter," she declared. "Maybe that's really what she wanted, if she's as remarkable as you say. You certainly ought to be ashamed, Bill, if she really wanted you—you acted like a bounder and a dumb Galahad put together."

You flared up in resentment:

"She was only a young girl, she was under twenty, and I respected her, if that's what you mean by dumb Galahad. To hear you talk you might think you were one of the founders of the National Free Love Society or something."

"I've been to Paris on a Cook's tour," Jane laughed. "Where if you overhear a workman say you have pretty legs, you soon learn there's nothing personal about it, he's just a lover of nature. The first time a man accosted me on the street I acted like a perfect fool, I was mad and flustered, I couldn't remember a single French word, and he walked along beside me, talking right to the point, for blocks, and finally I exploded at him, *depechez-vous!* He was so startled, he went off without even lifting his hat.—Not that spending a month in Paris made me a scarlet woman. At present, alas, no man can truthfully call me his mistress."

"Good god I hope not!" you blurted out.

You reflected that there was more of the puritan in you than you had suspected. You were sorry you had brought up the mistress thing at all, if Jane was going to take it this way and talk as if—well, as if she were just a woman too—that is, a woman with the ordinary vulgar appetites and possibilities....She had not, to your knowledge, ever been in love—though for that matter you had been away almost continuously for seven years. At least, she had never spoken seriously of any man. Presumably she had been kissed—well, on the whole, yes—but at that you were willing to wager that she hadn't except in fun. Probably no man had ever thought her as lovely and adorable as you did, for you, being her brother, were naturally prejudiced. Anyway, the idea of her being anything common, or doing anything, was too grotesque to be thought of at all.

She said suddenly:

"Are you going to marry Erma?"

You were a little startled. "Not that I know of," you replied. "No, not even if I wanted to, which I don't. She's a grand lady, much too grand for me."

"Not too grand to put you in control of her property."

You laughed. "I'm not in control of anything. She can recall that piece of paper whenever she wants to, which might be day after tomorrow. No, she's out of my class."

"You'll marry her, you'll see."

"I'll not marry anybody, at least not for a long time. Maybe never." Something tightened within you as you remembered that night in the cold autumn rain. "I tell you I wanted to marry Lucy. I wanted to. There are things I haven't told you....I cried about it. Cried like a baby."

Jane stopped the hammock again, this time not to laugh.

"You what? You cried!"

"Yes. Sat in the rain and bawled, wishing you'd come along and give me a cookie. If there'd been a good, deep hole handy I think I'd have jumped in."

She came to you, just a step from the hammock to your chair, and put her hand on your shoulder so that her arm slanted downwards across the back of your head.

"Why, Bill," she said. "Why, Bill."

Not a question, they weren't even words. You raised your hand and placed it on hers, there on your shoulder, but you were uneasy and irritated. Why had you told her? Silly, damned silly.

All the same, the feel of her hand was good on your shoulder. "You poor kid," she said.

You patted her hand ostentatiously, and laughed. "I guess I should have married Mrs. Davis," you declared. "As it is, I go now to my chaste and lonely bed. You'd better go too, it's late, and I suppose you have to get to the damn store before sunrise."

No, there was no reason to think she understood anything about it, but what can you expect, neither did you. What does it matter anyhow; things happen and you can stand around forever asking why, you'll never get anywhere. It wouldn't do any good even if you could prove it; the next thing that happened to you would prove you were wrong and you'd have to start all over again. Come to think of it, Jane never tries to prove anything. Neither does Erma. Women don't, mostly. Erma is more apt to give reasons though—just for the sake of the exercise.

How curious she was about Lucy! Did you see her off and how did she look, and have you heard from her, and a list of questions as long as the Miami River. Well, by god, Erma never got her ears full. Strange how far away people are when they seem so close. Only a day or two after Lucy left you went with Erma to a dance, and were so intimate, so familiar, and yet you were as remote from her as the farthest star. Imagine saying to her, night before last I sat on a culvert with my feet in a ditch full of water, and wept. Not only not then, in the first days after Lucy had gone; even less likely now, after being married to her for eleven years. Never could you say that to your wife, though you might, conceivably, to your chauffeur, or the fat little waiter at the Manufacturers' Club.

Or to Mrs. Jordan....

# H

"Is that you, Mr. Lewis?"

It was Mrs. Jordan's voice, from the basement.

Had she then seen him come in? Not necessarily. Perhaps she had heard his footsteps on the stairs; or, since that was unlikely on account of the carpet and the pains he had taken to mount softly, possibly he had knocked the revolver against the rail when he took it out of his pocket or as he put it back.

"Is that you, Mr. Lewis?"

He trembled from head to foot. He turned his head and looked behind him and down, sidewise, looking at nothing, like a treed coon. Well, he thought, for god's sake use your brain if you've got one. Either you answer her or you don't. He opened his mouth and no sound came.

It was only three or four steps to the first landing. He suddenly ran up them, quietly and rapidly, trying to make no noise at all. At the top he whirled around the corner, and as he did so, the tail of his overcoat described a wide semicircle, there was a rattle and a clatter as the little lamp with the parchment shade tumbled to the floor onto the bare wood, beyond the edge of the carpet. It banged against the wall; then silence.

He had jumped as if shot; and now he thought, well you goddam fool what are you going to do? Are you going to answer her or not?

# VIII

You might as well.

Raving imbecile.

Calmly, calmly. You were quite calm three nights ago when you told her that it was intolerable, you could stand it no longer, you were being pushed into insanity, and the only way out was to kill either her or yourself or both. The words were violent enough, but you were quite calm. It didn't faze her; nothing would, except this. What did she say? something about your being excited over nothing!

That's one thing to consider: has she told anyone of that threat? There's no one she would be likely to tell; anyway she doesn't talk. You were an ass to threaten her, but she doesn't talk. If she has mentioned it to anyone that would be fatal. Do you see what thin ice you're skating on—if she has happened to breathe a word of it, to anyone, no matter who, your goose is cooked. Anyone, the woman at the corner delicatessen, for instance. She might, at that. Or there's Grace. No, its not possible. There's no danger there.

They say there are a thousand ways that things like this are traced. That's because the people who do them are either too smart or not smart enough. To do it just right you'd have to know who the man was that was going after you. If you knew it was going to be Schwartz, for instance, or even Dick, you would know just what to do to fool him. It would be easy to be slick enough if you knew who it was going to be. Of course, it isn't any one man, it's the whole damn pack....Why not think of it? You're not going into this with your eyes shut, like a fool,

ready to give up—there'll be no sitting around crying on cul-
verts this trip. They'd have a fine time trying to trace the
revolver in case you were suspected. Over four years now it's
been in that old bag; you had even forgotten about it yourself.

"Take it along," Larry said, when you were starting out for a
day's fishing, one morning on his ranch, the summer you went
to Idaho. "You might have some fun popping at jackrabbits or a
coyote."

You tried it a few times, but never hit anything. No wonder,
the trigger pulled so hard and you'd never had any practice.
Not even that porcupine, the night you heard him fooling
around the saddles and Larry ran over and pointed a flashlight
at him. You didn't get close enough. Larry finally finished him,
and Erma pulled out a lot of quills and stuck them in her hat.
You wouldn't touch him, on account of the smell.

You chucked the revolver away and forgot all about it; discovered it, to your surprise, when you were unpacking after
your return to New York. You meant to write Larry about it, but
never did. For four years it has been in that old bag in the
closet; certainly no one knew of it, not even Erma.

There's no use worrying about the cartridges; there's no
reason why they shouldn't be as good as new. Just three left in
it. You turned it carefully so that a loaded chamber would be in
the right place; not understanding it, you experimented to
make sure and damn near shot the thing off there in your bedroom. Is there any chance of its turning in your pocket? If you
pulled the trigger and it didn't go off....

Dick will presumably know. Of course he'll be suspicious,
and probably he'll know. But he'll keep his mouth shut. You're
surer of that than anything else; He won't care, he doesn't care,
but he'll keep his mouth shut. Is that a weakness or a strength
in him, that you can say, if this happens he'll do that, and be as

sure of it as of tomorrow's light? If he were here now—he wouldn't be here. It would be done, and he would be gone. Where did he get that swift and unalterable conviction that the thing he is doing is the thing to do? Like an oyster, Erma says. Yes, or like the ocean the oyster lives in.

He will say, "You were a damn fool, she wasn't worth it." That's all he'll say, and nothing to anyone else, no matter what happens.

They'll try to get you a thousand different ways if they suspect you. They'll question everybody. They'll ask Erma how you've been acting recently, what you've been doing, whether you've said anything. Erma will be all right; they wouldn't get anything out of her even if she knew all about it, not even after she learns about this place, for of course that will all come out, there'll be no concealing it. They may question people at the office; they'll snoop around everywhere, they always do in a case of murder. The papers tell how witnesses and suspects are taken to the district attorney's office, and they try to trap them.

They'll question you. That's bound to happen whether they suspect you or not, for this place will all come out. You'll have to make up every single answer, you can't tell them the truth about anything, except, of course, when did you first meet her and when did you rent the apartment and what is your name and how old are you. You'll have to make up thousands of answers and make them all sound like the truth. They'll try to trip you up, they'll get you balled up somehow, but if you tried to tell them the real truth about everything it wouldn't be any easier, for you don't know what it is any more than they do. "You were living happily with your wife, were you not, Mr. Sidney?" Oh god yes. "And you took great pains to prevent her learning of this illicit relationship?" Yes, great pains. No, that didn't matter. Whatever you say they'll hitch their chairs a little

closer and lick their lips and think they're digging something
out of you. The damn bloodhounds, the damn fools, as if Erma
had anything to do with it. You could rent all the apartments
from Washington Square to Van Cortland Park and fill them up
with virgins and bawds three in a room and a lot she'd care, as
long as you didn't stay away from Thursday bridge.

They'll want to know everywhere you went and everything
you did. "Tell me, Mr. Sidney, for, of course, you realize that in
an affair as serious as this, it is my duty to exhaust every source
of information, please tell me what you were doing on the
evening of November twenty-first?" He'll talk friendly and
smile at you, the way Dick smiles when he's at a meeting and
putting something over. Or he'll be the other kind, he'll come
up close to you and stare in your face and yell, "Where were
you between ten and twelve Thursday night?"

Dare you ask Jane to do that? "I was at my sister's house on
Tenth Street; I spent the entire evening with her." By god, that
would fix them. "She was alone, and I spent the entire evening
with her." Probably there are people there; maybe not though;
Victor's out of town. It wouldn't be a bad idea to go out and
telephone her now, at the drug store, and then come back. She
would do it if she could. Of course you'd have to give her a
reason. No you wouldn't either; she'd do it if you asked her to.
If you did that it would be grand to hear them question Jane.
Yes, she'd say, or no—and they might as well try to confuse an
oak tree.

As a matter of fact, it might work. You didn't show any signs
of anything at the office; you didn't see Dick after all; you
stayed a little later than usual with those fellows from Chicago.
If only you had taken them to dinner—but that doesn't matter,
you ate at your usual table at the club, everybody saw you, and
Hendricks came over and asked you to play poker. What did

you say to him? If only you had thought of it before and told him you were going to spend the evening with your sister! That would cinch it. What did you tell him? He probably won't remember anyway. You didn't get a taxi at the door; you walked off down the avenue a few blocks, then took a taxi home to get the revolver.

Two or three of the servants saw you, but that's all right, it was still early then, not yet nine o'clock. But you've got to remember that they'll ask about every little thing. All right, after dinner you took a little walk, then you went home, then you went to see your sister. You were only at home a minute or two, just long enough to get the revolver out of the drawer where you had locked it the night before, and the servants saw you enter and leave. "What did you go home for?" What did you go home for. The whole thing may hang on that, that shows how ticklish it is. You went home to change your clothes, but then you didn't change them. You went home to stay and went out again because Jane phoned you—but there wasn't any phone call. You went home to get something for Jane, something you wanted to take to her—any little thing, like a book for instance. "What was the name of the book?" You'll have to talk it all over very carefully with Jane, and get every point decided so you won't contradict each other.

Then you walked away from the house. It will seem odd you didn't have the doorman get a taxi if you were in such a hurry to get downtown. The doorman saw you walk away. It's a good thing you happened to turn south. Well you weren't necessarily in a hurry. You just walked a few blocks and then picked up a taxi on the avenue.

It is vital to remember exactly where you actually did go and whether anyone saw you. You didn't walk on Park Avenue very far; you turned at one of the side streets somewhere in the

Forties, and went over to Broadway where you turned uptown again. You stayed on Broadway quite a distance, maybe Seventieth Street, then went to Central Park West, and turned west again on Eighty-fifth.

Then you were here, in front of the house, across the street. You couldn't come in, you couldn't make up your mind to it. You felt that if you once came in, that would settle it. The next thing you knew you were on Riverside Drive, walking fast to keep warm, and talking aloud to yourself so that passers-by turned to look at you. That frightened you, but you kept on walking fast, though you stopped talking. You got warm and unbuttoned your overcoat, but the weight of the revolver in the pocket made it hang open so you fastened it up again. Somewhere you got over onto Columbus Avenue, and then straight back here and to the door and in.

Almost certainly no one saw you. From the time you left Park Avenue you haven't spoken to a soul. That's a chance you have to take, you don't pretend there isn't any risk. How are you going to get out? You'll just have to stay until you're sure no one heard the shot, and then come downstairs and beat it. Go to Jane's house. You mustn't take a taxi; you'll have to use the subway. That's what Gordon said at the club not long ago, talking about the Farwell case, nobody ever pays any attention to a revolver shot nowadays, they always think it's a backfire from a car. Anyway, you wrap your scarf around it and they won't even hear it. That's what that woman did who shot that dentist in his office with people outside in the hall not thirty feet away. Of course they caught her, but not for a long time. They wouldn't have got her at all if she'd kept her nerve.

What if they do hear it and come in before you can get away? There's no fire escape, there's no other stairs. You can go to the roof. You can't take care of everything; you have to leave something to luck and act when the time comes.

If you do get away, if you really do get clean away, get to Jane's house and later go home, it's even possible that you'll never be connected with this place at all. Nobody around here knows you except as Mr. Lewis. They don't know a thing about you, who you are or where you work or anything else. You've always been careful about that. Why couldn't Mr. Lewis just disappear and let them hunt their heads off? They'll hunt all right, but it's quite possible they'll never connect it up. There's nothing with your name on it anywhere here, no photographs, no letters—

There's that goddam statue!

William the Conqueror. The masterful man, your true character. The artist revealing what everyone else is too blind to see. Erma would enjoy this. Trapped by that piece of junk! Oh no, not on your life. You can take a hammer and knock it to pieces. Knock off the nose and ears and smash the face, smash the whole thing. You should have done it long ago. You should have done it the evening you went home and found Erma decorating it.

They'll hunt, they'll look everywhere.

There's a lot of numbers on the back of that phone book; they'll jump on that: Chelsea four three four three. Maybe your own too; you've never noticed. That one would be enough— straight to Jane! Tear off the cover and burn it; or erase that number. Then they examine the spot with a microscope, and you might as well have left your card. All right, take the book away; take it home and hide it somewhere.

Would it be possible, even remotely possible, to get away with this? It's a temptation, but you want to be careful. There are lots of people around here that know you by sight as Mr. Lewis. Mrs. Jordan and the newsdealer and the two art students—lots of them. And Grace! If one of them ever happened to see you anywhere, at a theatre, for instance, it would be all up.

You could go away somewhere; you could go out to Larry's ranch and stay a long time and maybe grow a moustache, or even a beard. But that would finish you if they ever did find out. Better just to stay here and go on as usual and keep out of it and if someone does happen to see you, it wouldn't be so hard to explain; naturally you would keep quiet, a man of your position wouldn't get mixed up publicly with such a thing if he could help it.

But it would be bad, mighty dangerous. Whereas it would be all in your favor if, as soon as it comes out in the papers you go to the district attorney and tell him all about it and request him to keep your name out of it, if possible. You've only met him once or twice and he won't care a hang about you, but Dick knows him well and you could get Dick to go with you. But probably it would get to the papers somehow, there'd be a leak somewhere and how they'd eat it up. A regular hell of a mess. The family, Erma, the fellows at the club, everybody at the office, everybody everywhere—you might have to resign your job. It might be too much for you. Erma would stick if only because she'd enjoy telling them to go soak their head. That would be fat too. "Mrs. Sidney, Loyal to Husband in Spite of Grisly Love Nest, Tells World to Soak Its Head." Oh it would be a mess, but it would probably be the safest way. If Erma held out you might be able to keep your job.

If she didn't you might as well kill yourself too. Ah, that's what you're afraid to think about! Looking at it honestly, though, that's what it amounts to. Your job gone, the whole ugly mess opened up, Erma and Dick cut loose, you'd be sorry you hadn't. It wouldn't be too late, you could do that any time, if only you could trust yourself. This would be the time, this way it would be simple and complete. Only you wouldn't like to do it here; you wouldn't like to be found lying in the same room with her, beside her; maybe even you would fall so you would be touching her. Not ever to touch her again, not ever to have her touch you, how good, how sweet it would be to say that and know it was true! Not to lie against her, dead, either, nor near her, nor anywhere within reach of her. In another room you could do it if you could do it at all. There isn't anything so terrible about it. It might be simple and easy—just put the barrel against your temple or in your mouth pointing upwards and pull the trigger. Maybe that's why you've avoided thinking about it, because it would be simple and easy. Then no one would ask you any questions, no one would bother you, there'd be no decisions to make, you wouldn't have to try to figure it all out and bellyache around, you'd be afraid of nothing.

You've thought of it before, several times, but not like this. Once years ago when you lost Jane—what a funny way to put it.

What are you going to do with the gun? If you could just leave it there, put it down and leave it there—but of course you can't. They have a number on them somewhere, it would be traced. It will be a problem to get rid of it. You wouldn't dare take it home and put it back in the bag, that would be stupid. If only you had time, you could go on a ferryboat and throw it in the river. Or you could throw it in from a pier. But you want to get to Jane's house as quick as you can, and anyway, someone might see you. It's incredible how difficult it is to do a simple thing like that without someone seeing you. You might hide it somewhere in Jane's house; there's no danger of their searching there, no matter what happens. Why couldn't you wrap it in a newspaper and leave it on the subway train? Good lord no. You've got to decide it now, definitely. Throw it in the river. When you get off the subway at Fourteenth Street go straight to a pier and throw it in. It won't take more than ten minutes.

Why don't people do that with revolvers? It would be pretty

hard to convict a man of shooting someone if you couldn't show he'd ever had a gun or what he did with it or anything about it. Probably because they lose their heads.

What if they arrest you, how are you going to act? The thing to do is send for a lawyer and not say anything till he comes, not a single word, no matter how harmless it seems. Send for Dick and tell him to bring a lawyer, ask him to bring Stetson, he's the best of that bunch. What will you tell Stetson? You won't dare tell him anything; all about the last two years, yes, but not that there's been any difficulty. Shall you tell him about Grace? What if you don't, and he finds out and questions her? How much does she know? Then he'll suspect everything you tell him. That's a fine how-do-you-do, you've got to be as careful what you say to your own lawyer as if he were after you too. For the Dick part of it, you'll have to leave it to Dick; you'll have to see Dick alone first and put it up to him. Maybe it would be best to tell Stetson everything, the whole works. Impossible. You couldn't do it. Even if you desperately tried there'd be no words for it, you'd sound like a crazy man. You can see Stetson sitting there as if he were doing the chair a favor, his glasses a little crooked, his nostrils wriggling nervously, the corner of a pale blue handkerchief peeping just so from his breast pocket—"Yes. Yes. Yes. What did you do that for?"

You've never shot any kind of firearm to amount to anything, except that little twenty-two rifle you used to hunt rabbits with. It was never much fun; you couldn't bear to get your hands bloody. Red Adams used to string them on his belt by the hind legs, so that his overalls had a ring of sticky blood around the knees. Jane would always help you skin them and hang them up on the back porch to freeze. She's never been squeamish about anything. If only there's nobody there with her! If once you get it over, and get out, and get to her house and find her there sitting in the back room reading, as she often is, you'll be safe. What about the maid? Leave it to her, she'll attend to it somehow. She'll talk of it as calmly as if you had come to ask her to help you skin rabbits.

Suicide's a funny thing. You're afraid to think of it, but once you do think of it there's nothing to be afraid of. It would be different if you thought of yourself as lying there dead and still had to be there, a part of you still alive, and look at yourself, with blood on you, and realize you were no longer breathing and that you would never again walk or talk or put on your clothes or take a drink of water or in any way move. That would be horrible. If it were like that nobody could stand it; you'd have to pretend you were never going to die, and everybody would really begin to believe it instead of just playing at it, the way they do now. As it is, they lie about it, but it isn't hard to see they're lying, and they know it too. The way it works, there's nothing to be afraid of. You stand there in the bedroom, in the middle of the room, and put the barrel in your mouth and point it up towards the top of your head, and there's nothing wrong with you; you can do whatever you damn please, you can take it out again and go and eat your supper, or you can just stand there and watch yourself and see how you feel, you can do anything you want to. Or you can pull the trigger, just simply press your finger down, that's all, finish. Ha, nothing matters then! Right from that instant, which never really comes, because as far as you are concerned it's over before it begins. You could even hit against the bed as you fell, and bust your nose or knock your teeth out, and you'd never know it. There's nothing in that to be scared of; you pass, instantly, from complete freedom to complete oblivion. It's not so easy to think of yourself lying there afterwards, but it isn't easy to think of her lying there either, or anyone else.

You haven't seen many dead people: your father and mother and two or three others. There wasn't much to it, but then they were all dressed up and fixed in the coffin and naturally you'd expect to see a dead body in a coffin, it would shock you more if you saw a live one. You've never seen a dead person just lying anywhere, bent or twisted, with ordinary clothes on, bruised or with a wound, maybe with blood on her. You've never seen anyone die, even peacefully in bed. Except the man who fainted and was carried out one day in the grandstand at the ball park; but that was nothing, you didn't know until you saw it in the paper, the next morning, that he had died of heart failure. When Larry used to tell about the war, you would feel a little sick and wonder how any man could live through it and not go insane.

That's what you were afraid of yourself last summer when you tried to break it off and went up to Maine alone. Especially the night you sat on the boat by the edge of the lake—that was another time you thought of suicide. When you came back Dick said you looked like a dope fiend; Erma thought you ought to go abroad for a year and Jane wanted you to get psychoanalyzed. Yes, or do morning exercises or take an aspirin, you said; and came here the first night and found her sewing on buttons and drinking lemonade. It was a hot night and she was sitting there with both windows wide open and nothing on but that purple negligee she bought at Macy's, with feathers on it. She looked up and said, "Hello, you should have sent me a telegram, I might not have been home." That hard, hateful assurance, like a slow disease that knows there's no medicine.

She'll be sitting in the same chair, now, when you go in. She'll look up the same way, nothing will ever make her look any different. You will close the door behind you, and deliberately take the revolver from your pocket and take off your scarf and wrap around it. What will she do? She'll sit and watch you. Will she be startled or frightened; will she cry out or plead with you or otherwise finally admit your existence as a force, needing to be considered and allowed for? She won't believe in it. At the end you cannot taunt her, you cannot make her tremble, you cannot see the health of fear in her eyes. Useless to fling any more words into that ditch.

She might, though, she might scream. You don't know what's in your face; you are doing something she thinks is not in you, and if your face gives it away she might scream and shout for help. Ah, if she does! You'd like to hear that once. But then you might fail. It would be better to show nothing, just go in as usual and say you're tired, cross over with your coat still on and say it's too warm, you want to open the window a little. Then, when you're back of her chair where she can't see you, you can turn suddenly and shoot her from behind, quite close. But don't forget the scarf, and don't forget to pull the shade down if it happens to be up. You ought to cross the windows first anyway, to make sure they're closed tight and the shades are down. She'll never know what happened. She'll just fall over in her chair, crumple up, slide down onto the floor maybe....

Don't do that, you fool! God oh god! Don't do that! You pitiful sneaking coward, she's right, she knows you, she's safe.

You've figured it all out, haven't you? You're insane well enough. Calm and cool and clever you calculate your chances. Battling Bill. Oh no, you won't lose your head; you're going to handle this thing right. You're going to bust statues and throw the revolver in the river, and fix an alibi by going to Jane's house, and ring the bell, and give the maid your coat and hat—really you're magnificent, it's a masterpiece. You're going to Idaho and grow a beard so no one will ever know who Mr. Lewis is. You're going to get Richard M. Carr to be an accomplice to a murder, just as a little personal favor. Come, come, come fool, can't you do better than that? These are all pretty good, but come now, you must have something really fine, of the very best, artfully concealed. Oh yes, you're going to kill yourself. First you're going to kill yourself and then you're going to Jane's house and send for a lawyer and grow a beard, and live happily forever after.

Leave here. Go back home. Go back home and go to bed. Like last night, when Erma came and knocked at your door, for the first time in months. If she does it again, kill her. Why not kill everybody? Erma and Dick and Larry and Victor and—

Easy, easy. Do you know what you were about to say?

Anyway, you might as well get out of here. You almost pushed yourself into it, but a miss is as good as a mile. And there's no use starting on a new lie, you know you won't leave without seeing her, if only to make sure she's there and see how easy it would have been. Tell it to her all over again; it really does make her a little bit uncomfortable, though she pretends not to notice it. After all she's not made of iron. No; rubber, smelly like rubber; not the same smell, but makes you think of it. She ought to use more perfume or bathe oftener or something—though the lord knows she spends enough time splashing around in the bathroom.

All right. Go on up. Go on and get it over with and go home and go to bed.

You might have known you'd knock that damn lamp off.

# I

*He reached down, and quickly and precisely picked up the lamp and set it back in its niche, trying to make the shade hang straight; it slipped awry again, and again he straightened it. He stood there, at the top of the first flight:*

*"Yes, it's me, Mrs. Jordan," he called down. "Knocked the lamp off again."*

*He was amazed that his voice sounded composed, perfectly natural. To hear it thus made everything seem different; the hall appeared warm and friendly; the little lamp even seemed to be smiling at him with sympathy and understanding. His irritation at Mrs. Jordan was gone; he was pleased that she was there and had heard him and that he could call to her.*

*Her voice came:*

*"Oh—I thought maybe it was someone to see Miss Boyle. If you break it you'll have to pay for it."*

*Once he had started to count the number of times she said that, but long since had lost track. He had on occasion been tempted to smash it deliberately, but now he felt well-disposed toward it and wished it no harm.*

*He stood irresolute, drooping, without impulse. A door in the basement opened noisily, then banged shut; Mrs. Jordan had returned to her room. Silence. Still he stood—the idea of movement was hateful—he felt physically exhausted, and completely indifferent to all things. He told himself, you might as well be a dead leaf hanging on a tree, blown in the wind now, and now hanging still and dead....*

## IX

Do other people feel like this? If they do why do they live? A dead leaf blown in the wind. It isn't so much the helplessness; you could stand it to feel yourself pushed and pulled, here and there, against all protests, if only you knew what was doing it and why. You called yourself a weakling and a coward because you let Lucy go, but that was silly. Those are just words made up by somebody who wanted to pretend that he knew what was pushing him. All words are like that except the ones you can touch and eat and drink. How can you disapprove of anything you don't understand? That's the last refuge of ignorance, that pitiful attempt to give yourself a moral value by making up words to compare yourself with omniscience. If the dead leaf, or a live one either, put on such airs, wouldn't you give it the horse laugh though!

Don't flatter yourself; you're neither a weakling nor a coward; there's not that much significance in all your vain and petty flutterings. Maybe Dick's not so dumb after all; maybe the reason he's not interested in the meaning of anything is because he knows somehow, though he couldn't say it and wouldn't bother to if he could, that there isn't any; at least none that he or you or anybody knows anything about. Erma too. No, not the same way. She'll talk about meanings, she likes to play with them, but at bottom she's no more interested in them than Dick is. Let one of them get in her way once....

Like the time in Cleveland that old camel fell in love with her. You never could understand anyone falling in love with her, but there have been plenty who have done it. Hoskinson, his name was, lived there all his life and owned two or three country banks and had a wife who thought he was a mixture of Leander and J. P. Morgan. He wasn't really old, but he looked ancient and dried up as if he were trying to see how long he could go without taking on water. When he moved you expected to hear him squeak.

Summoned on the telephone, you went one afternoon straight from the office to Wooton Avenue, and when you got there Erma handed you a letter to read, It was from Mrs. Hoskinson, and it said in effect that if Erma didn't let her beloved husband alone the consequences would be extremely unpleasant. She announced that she would call on Erma the following afternoon.

"She's apt to be here any minute," Erma said, "and I don't want to see her. Will you talk to her? I could have sent for Tom Hall, but lawyers always ask so many questions."

"Why not refuse to see her?"

"It wouldn't do any good, she'd camp on the doorstep." You got your instructions. Miss Carr was not interested in the domestic or emotional life of Mrs. Hoskinson. If Mr. Hoskinson should again offer to amuse her by spending an evening playing Debussy on her Louis Seize Steinway, Miss Carr would gratefully accept, and her unconcern as to Mrs. Hoskinson's reactions would be effortless and complete.

The bell rang; the lady was announced and shown into the library; you joined her there and, representing yourself as Miss Carr's legal adviser, in pursuance of your instructions, informed her that after full and careful consideration the decision had been reached that she could go to hell. It was very unpleasant. Mrs. Hoskinson first was furious and threatening; then she wept and implored, pleaded with you to save her husband for her. You were touched, genuinely sorry for her, and when she was finally got out of the house you sought Erma, angry and indignant that you had been let in for such a thing. You made a heated speech, throughout which Erma smiled.

"Why should I make a sacrifice for her, just because she happens to be uncivilized?" she demanded. "I don't want her precious husband, but sometimes he's amusing. If I wanted him, of course, I'd take him. Bill darling, don't tell me I've got to preserve the home."

"I'm not telling you you've got to do anything. It's just a matter of decent human feeling. The woman is really suffering, she's unhappy."

"You're being stupid, you don't realize what you're saying," Erma declared. "Do you mean we shouldn't take something we want if it makes someone else suffer?"

"Yes. Unless we need it very badly, unless the want is vital."

She smiled. "Then you ought to be ashamed of yourself. Your salary has been raised to fifteen thousand, hasn't it? And you say yourself that the men in the mills are underpaid. Whereas I'm making only one woman suffer—by letting Hosky play to me, which he does extremely well. Besides, I'm taking nothing from his wife—do you happen to know that her favorite phonograph record is Drink to Me Only with Thine Eyes?"

"Come on, he sends you flowers every day and writes you ten-page letters with poetry in them and follows you around like a love-sick camel. And don't you tell Dick that I think the men are underpaid, or I won't have any salary at all."

Something disagreeable might have happened, for Hoskinson's attentions became more pronounced and continuous than ever, and his wife was finally driven to threaten, formally and legally, a suit for alienation of affection—if Erma had not suddenly decided to go to Europe.

That was in November, two years after Lucy had left. You

had never heard from her or written to her. In your room was her photograph; for a long time it stood open on your chiffonier, where you saw it every time you brushed your hair or put on your necktie; then, one day, just after you got back from your visit home when you told Jane all about it, you took the photograph down and put it away in a drawer. It's probably still around somewhere.

Throughout those two years it was obvious that everyone, including Dick, expected momentarily to hear that you and Erma were engaged. You yourself wouldn't have been surprised if some morning at breakfast you had found an item on the society page of the *Plain Dealer*: "Miss Erma Carr announces her engagement to Mr. William Barton Sidney." It was of course possible that she would notify you first, depending on whether, at the moment of decision, you happened to be handy. Would you have submitted to that insolent connubial rape? Indeed, indeed you would, though at the time, put as a hypothesis, you would have rejected it indignantly. Much easier to appraise an attitude after time has taken the peeling off.

You did in fact find information in the society column one morning, but it was to the effect that Miss Carr would leave shortly for an extended stay abroad. All day at the office you expected to hear from her, and when at five o'clock no word had come and you telephoned to Wooton Avenue you were told that she was not at home. The following morning she phoned to ask you to lunch.

"Is Hoskinson going on the same boat?" you asked politely, after she had joined you at the corner table at Winkler's.

She made a grimace. "Don't be nasty. As a matter of fact, I was mostly joking when I told Carrie Lawson I was going to Europe, but when I saw it in print it looked so sensible that I began to pack at once. I wonder if I'm more or less running away from Hosky—no, he's not important enough. I'd be much more apt to run away from you. Do you know, you're getting more attractive and dangerous-looking every day. A Lord Byron who has exchanged his limp for a modern American business training. If I met you on the rue Royale…"

"How long are you going to stay?"

"A winter, a month, ten years! Why don't you come over next summer? Meet me in Brittany or Norway or somewhere. You ought to have a real vacation anyway. We could stay over there forever, and you could run back once a year to attend the stockholders' meeting."

You were puzzled and irritated. Was this a proposal of marriage, or was it a polite hint that she would like to change her business arrangements, or was it merely a cat amusing itself by entangling a ball of yarn?

"By the way," you said, "now that you're going away maybe you'd prefer to turn your proxy over to Dick."

"I think," she said solemnly, "I'll transfer it to Mr. Hoskinson," and then laughed gaily as you felt the color mounting to your face.

You said with dignity:

"Seriously, I think it would be a good idea. You don't know how long you'll be gone, and after all who am I? I'm in an anomalous position. You can be sure that Dick doesn't relish having a mere employee dressed up like an equal."

"Has he been nasty?" she asked quickly.

"Lord no. I'm not complaining. It's just that there doesn't seem to be much sense in it, and naturally I feel a little ridiculous."

"You don't need to. You shouldn't." She pushed her plate a little aside and leaned forward, and her grey-mottled blue eyes almost lost their constant mockery as they looked directly into yours. "Bill dear," she said, "if you make me get serious I'll never forgive you. No one but you could do it. One reason I like you is that you understand things without talking about them, so it shouldn't be necessary for me to tell you that I trust you in certain essential ways more than any other person. As for the proxy, keep it if you please." She hesitated, then went on, "I didn't intend to mention it, but the other day Tom Hall insisted that I make a will, and if I fall off an Alp or drink myself to death you'll be able to celebrate by buying a yacht."

You've always been curious about that will. What exactly did it say? Surely not the whole to you; yet with Erma you can't tell. There was no one else but Dick, and she wasn't apt to swell him up. The whole thing! Under certain circumstances, then, you could have given Dick something to think about. Was it changed later when she married Pierre? Perhaps, no telling; if so, has it again been changed to you? What the deuce, once that would have been worth thinking about....

A week later she left, on an evening train, with the whole bunch at the station to see her off. She had been taken by the whim that you should accompany her as far as Erie; either a whim, or she considered that the gesture would somewhat ease the embarrassment of your position as an abandoned swain. Tacit, oh carefully tacit, that was. When the train paused at Erie, long after midnight, you kissed her hand, then on command her lips, briefly and lightly, and swung down onto the platform to make your way to a hotel bed and there horizontally pass the hours until time for the morning train back to Cleveland.

It was more than a year before you got a letter from her, a note rather, and then another year to the next. When she got married she didn't write you about it at all; you learned of it from a letter to Dick. Not much of a swain, but sufficiently abandoned.

If there really is no such thing as time, if it is merely a system of punctuation marks men have devised to make life seem real, your last three years in Cleveland, with Erma gone, Lucy a memory, and your business career a stale joke, a monotonous sequence of pale and feeble gestures—those years were not there at all. The calendars were fiction and their days a mirage. You went to New York twice to visit Jane—and, vaguely, Margaret and Rose. You spent a summer week with your mother, to the discomfort of both. Larry, ready for college, came and wandered around Cleveland for a month, sleeping in the room next to yours at the club and refusing most of your offers of entertainment; graciously and sensibly, for while you were willing to pretend a fond intimacy which did not exist, he reasonably saw no point in it.

It is amusing to speculate on the probabilities in Pearl Street if you had not had that piece of paper signed by Erma in your safe deposit box. You might have found yourself looking for a job; on the other hand it's quite possible that necessity would have quickened your resources and discovered unrealized capacities. Unlikely; but Dick, relieved of the annual unpleasantness, however nominal, of an agreement with your equal authority regarding the membership of the directorate and other problems, might have been disposed to find in you parts not entirely negligible. Though that's not fair either; why must you constantly pretend that Dick tried to choke you off?

He was very funny about it, in a way dumb, as transparent as a horse pretending it's lame and then leaping on four good legs on a sudden impulse or a need for action. Now and then, he would consult you on some minor point regarding which you could not possibly have an intelligent opinion, and the next day make some important decision without even informing you that it was being made. You did once, somewhat to your own surprise, assert the reality of your power—the time that he proposed to put Charlie Harper on the Board and you firmly declined to acquiesce, on the ground that Erma violently disliked him and would not want him under any circumstances. It was well that Dick didn't regard it as very important.

One day he said to you:

"What do you think of this New York thing? We might as well decide it. I was thinking last night—I say yes, at once. Gustafson says that England alone will place half a billion in six months. If we handle it right, and if those idiots keep on fighting a year or two, there'll be no limit—hell, anything's possible. I'm uncomfortable every minute I'm away from those boatloads of easy money, damn it, I itch. What do you think?"

"I think I'll go home and pack up," you laughed.

The next day you and Schwartz went to New York to find offices, and paid a fortune in premiums to vacate leases. Within six weeks the entire organization, sales and administrative, was moved and installed. Exhausted by your labors, you were nevertheless stimulated and refreshed by the interest of the new activities and the new scene. The tempo everywhere was quickened; not only was there the change to the greatest of all modern arenas, but also there was the feverish excitement reflected from the battlefields three thousand miles away, where stupidity and greed were consuming in ten minutes all that the Carr Corporation, with its mines and furnaces and factories and thousands of men, could produce in a month. The most superb and profitable market to be imagined, beyond the grandest dream of optimism; and American business, of which the Carr Corporation was a not inconsiderable unit, justified its claim to alert efficiency by grasping every opportunity and squeezing it dry. Dazed and feebly trying to orient yourself in the strange madhouse, you helped a bit here and there, but for the most part remained an open-mouthed spectator, while

Dick, for instance, plunged into the boiling middle of it, his mouth shut but his eyes open, grabbing with both hands. You reflected that he was making himself and his sister two of the richest persons in America, but certainly it never occurred to him; he was much too busy to think about it.

Then Larry came, was welcomed graciously by Dick, and sent off to the Carrton plant, and you began to feel a solidity in life; you were catching hold of an edge here and there. Above all, one particular edge.

On arriving in New York you had suggested that Jane and Margaret and Rose leave the little flat in Sullivan Street and set up a household for you, in any part of the city they might select. This was your most cherished gesture and the thought of it warmed you for months. Their income was scanty, for half the interest on the capital realized from the sale of the drug store went to your mother; Jane's salary as a staff writer on the *New World* was equally meager; and, speaking casually of your twenty thousand a year, you tried to keep exultation from your voice as you suggested a joint household to be entirely supported by you. Never, you told yourself, never could any man's dream be more perfectly realized. The shortcomings of Margaret and Rose were merely the necessary flaw for perfection. There would be two servants, a maid and a cook, you said, leaving Jane free for her work and Margaret and Rose for school; separate large rooms for everyone, much nicer than their tiny flat....

Jane said no. The others were more than willing, but she vetoed it flatly. She said that you might want to get married, that you should get married, and that you should assume no such encumbrance. You protested that you were only thirty-one, and that you wanted never to get married, anyway. No, she wouldn't do it. You remained in your little two-room suite at the Garwood.

You were a great deal with her, more than at any period

before or since. You took her to plays and concerts, subscribed
to the opera, and persuaded her to use the accounts you
opened at two or three of the stores. What a keen pleasure it
was to feel that, at last, you were repaying her for all that she
had done! Granted that money couldn't really do it, still it was
fun, the best fun you've ever had. You'd get a bill from Altman's,
for some gloves maybe, and stockings and a nightgown, and the
next time you were with her you'd take it from your pocket and
say with mock irritation:

"You'd better check this up, and where the devil do all the
stockings go to?"

She would look at it:

"The stockings were for Margaret, and Rose bought the nightgown without telling me, and I won the gloves from you anyhow
on that bet about the Panama Canal."

"All right," you would say, "I won't ask Margaret and Rose
about it because I'd hate to catch you in a lie."

When the 1915 Christmas bonus was paid, a whole year's
salary extra, in a lump, you bought her a Packard roadster and
drove it down to Sullivan Street yourself. Margaret and Rose
smothered you with embraces while Jane stood and looked at
you; she appeared rather serious, you thought, as you hoped
that what you felt in your eyes were not tears.

"But my dear," she said, "it's much too grand. We can't afford
to keep it, can we? You're a darling, and I don't wonder the
girls want to eat you up, but you shouldn't have done it."

You struck a pose:

"My dear Miss Sidney, a mere nothing. I wanted to get you a
Pullman sleeping-car, but they'd just sold the last one. And
arrangements have already been made with the Sullivan Garage
to send the bill to Fifty Broadway, the first of each and every
month."

You had her get in and sit beside you, and showed her the gears and brakes and the mysteries of the dashboard.

"Saturday afternoon we'll run her uptown and I'll give you your first lesson," you said.

She turned suddenly and put her arms close around your neck and kissed you on the mouth. That was the only time she has ever done that; curious that it should have been about an automobile; it doesn't seem like her. Perhaps it wasn't; maybe it was just something she happened to feel....

You met a lot of her friends—a strange assortment, there were none you ever really liked. Except young Cruikshanks, then just a boy, writing verses on the back of menus and grandly offering them to the restaurant manager as payment for his meal. You thought Margaret was in love with him. And the girl with copper hair who was arrested in the strike out in Jersey and Jane got you to furnish bail for her. She was a Russian or something. You were irritated most by the fellow with the dirty grey moustache, a professor at Columbia, who used to sit around and make wisecracks about women. What did Jane see in him? She said he was amusing and instructive because he was a decadent satyr, and Victor said, not decadent, impotent.

You liked Victor at first; no use denying it, you thought him agreeable and likable. He seemed to you more normal and balanced than anyone else in that crowd.

You contemplated elaborate plans for the spring and summer. You would rent a place somewhere in the country or at the seashore, a modest place not too far out, and there install the family. You and Jane could commute together, using the Packard morning and evening to the railroad station, and at the end of school Margaret and Rose could tell the little flat goodbye until autumn. Jane could have all the funny friends she wanted, though for your part you could do just as well without them. By the middle of February you were already making inquiries as to localities and getting lists from renting agents.

Jane didn't seem very enthusiastic about it. Twice you wanted her to spend a Sunday looking at places with you, and each time she had something else to do. Then she objected that it couldn't be done anyway until the girls were out of school at the end of June, as she couldn't leave them in town alone, and when you suggested that they also might commute that was held to be impractical. You felt that there was beginning to be something queer about Jane; she was the last person in the world to temporize. She was being demoralized by her funny friends.

One Saturday in May, lunching with her downtown, you insisted that she drive with you the following morning to look at a house somewhere north of White Plains which you had been told of by one of the men in the office.

"There are nine rooms, two baths, everything modern, and it's at the edge of a wood on top of a hill overlooking one of the reservoirs," you told her. "Sounds like the very thing we want. Completely furnished, four bedrooms, and a room over the garage for a maid or a couple. I called up the agent and he's holding it for us; I told him we'd be out before noon—"

Something in her face stopped you. Something in her eyes made you feel suddenly silly and unreal, as if you had been caught offering a stick of candy to a queen on her throne.

"I think you'd like it," you said lamely, feeling a fear expand in your heart.

"I know I would," said Jane warmly, too warmly. "It sounds perfect. I'd love it."

"Well—"

"But it's impossible. I'm going to be married. I'm telling you first, as we decided only a week ago, and it's going to be a secret for a little while. Even the girls don't know." She laughed, a short deep little laugh. "When I refused your offer to set up housekeeping because you ought to get married, I didn't guess I'd crowd in ahead of you. Maybe you were just being polite and waiting for me to go first because I'm older."

"I thought—I thought—" you stammered.

You stopped. You couldn't say that.

"Who is it?"

"As if you didn't know," she smiled.

Good god, she was being kittenish about it.

"I don't know," you said. "Who is it?"

"Victor, of course. You really didn't know? You must have. I've been as silly as a schoolgirl."

She laughed again; why did she have to sit there and laugh like a simpleton? Then instantly she was serious; she looked at you gravely:

"I'm so happy, Bill, but don't think I haven't thought of you. I know this interferes with your plans for the summer, and I suppose it's ungrateful, you've been so generous—"

She made quite a speech about your generosity.

You lost your head and almost made a scene there in the restaurant. Your feeling that you had been betrayed was surely not entirely unreasonable. This was the twentieth century and you claimed no patriarchal rights, but after all you were her brother, had been granted all the privileges and prerogatives and expectations of a brother, and certainly consultation on the choice of a husband was one of them. She might have asked your advice if only to ignore it. You pretended to no power of veto, but by heaven, if you had it you would certainly use it on Victor Knowlton—a half-baked writer and lecturer, coarse-grained, opinionated, most of his success due to his questionable methods of persuading presidents of women's clubs that it was worth five hundred dollars to hear him spout for an hour about nothing. You had heard curious tales about him which had amused you at the time, but which, remembered now, convinced you that he was no man to marry your sister.

Jane, at first apparently amazed at your violence, assumed a patient and soothing forbearance which infuriated you. She offered no defense; if this petulant child has bruised himself, she seemed to say, I shall not aggravate the wound, I must humor him, poor kid. It was maddening.

"Very well," you exclaimed, "if you will have it, yes, that's what I mean. No man is expected to be a saint, but neither should he be a promiscuous pig, if he expects a decent woman to marry him."

"I don't think I need defend Victor against the charge of being a promiscuous pig," said Jane slowly. "That's a little strong isn't it? Anyway it's his own affair, just as my own checkered past is mine. And from your own standard you must admit it's decent of him to want to marry me after having had me for nearly a year. Of course it's true that I've argued against it, but now that we've decided to have children—"

You stared at her. This couldn't possibly be your sister, your dear Jane. This was some mocking harlot....

You wanted to yell at her, shout some insult at her, but you felt suddenly weak, done in, and frightened. You felt also that you were incapable of movement, which was just as well, for you felt a desire to lay your hands on her, choke her perhaps, or strike her in the face, not hard enough to leave a mark, but enough to move her, to make her feel your outraged virility.... She deserved it. Had she not encouraged you to believe that she felt about the family as you did, that it was the closest and most important of all human relations; had she not permitted you to spend considerable sums of money on her and the girls which you could very well have used for other purposes; had she not treacherously pretended to a complete confidence and intimacy, all the while—nearly a year, she said—withholding from you her vulgar—

Discussing, probably, with him, her generous brother....

Well, it s all over, that's that, you told yourself, standing on the narrow Fulton Street sidewalk, after she had parted from you at the restaurant door and hurried off to the subway. Nothing tragic, of course, but deeply annoying and irritating—and revealing a hard selfishness, along with other weaknesses and impurities, where you would least expect to find them. An experience presumably shared by all brothers who have some regard for their natural obligations and try to do the right thing.

You wandered aimlessly up Broadway. You might as well telephone that agent that you wouldn't go up there tomorrow; what the devil could you do with a house on top of a hill with four bedrooms? What was there to do anywhere, with anything?

Monday there was a letter from her, suggesting that you get the Packard, or send for it, saying that as it had really been meant for the four of you she couldn't very well keep it any longer, especially in view of your dislike for Victor, which she ardently hoped would disappear when you knew him better; and anyway, he already had a little touring car and there was no sense in owning two. You replied briefly that the roadster was hers; she could do as she liked with it, give it to Margaret and Rose or sell it for junk, it was none of your business.

You had the idea that even if she had told the truth regarding the past year, marriage need not be inevitable, with its finality and permanency. She would tire of him, or he of her, and then a generous brother with a sense of responsibility and money enough to buy motor cars and rent summer homes would be again welcomed and appreciated. You would see her once more and put it up to her: she didn't like the idea of marriage, she had argued against it, then don't do it. There may be no children. It would be easy to persuade her that it would at least be more sensible to wait....

You were still turning it over in your mind when a few days later, in the morning mail, that thing came saying that they were married. It was like them not to use a plain dignified engraved announcement. It was on some kind of art paper, purple or blue, and the lettering was so cockeyed you could hardly read it: something about Jane Sidney and Victor Knowlton, having sacrificed to the gods at the City Hall on May twenty-first, would be legally at home....

Any man who expects to get anything from a woman is a fool, or if he does it's just an accident. No matter who she is, she takes what she wants, and a fat lot she cares about you. Essentially they're barbarians, animals, they'll tear you to pieces in an instant and think nothing of it, like a jackal, and then lie down and stretch and lick themselves, and expect to be patted by the next one that comes along. It's too bad they don't do it literally, devour you, then it could happen only once. Erma would agree with you all right; she's at least honest about it. Mrs. Davis didn't hurt you any maybe; she used you; what did she give you? A son; a hell of a favor that was, he ate a dozen dinners at your expense and made an ass of you with that joke of a statue —though he may not have meant it—and he's spent over seven thousand dollars of your money hanging around Paris and Rome probably cracking more jokes about rich boobs who don't know anything about art.

Lucy—Lucy wasn't a woman, she was Lucy. It would have been the same with her—no. No! That was like a raindrop that never falls from the cloud—is whirled upward instead, to float above the atmosphere eternally, finding no home; or a flower bud, congealed still folded, preserved in a crystal, lifeless without having lived.

The most savage and insolent feast though was that of little Millicent, in that room with the afternoon sun blazing at the window, long ago, as she went silently back and forth collecting things from your closet and dresser and piling them on a chair, and finally turned and came towards you....

Abandoned, bitter, with nothing anywhere in reach to hold onto, you were not surprised that the old familiar fantasy returned; you accepted it, and felt her hands again for the first time in many months, the night after Jane left you standing in front of the restaurant.

**J**

He turned and walked over the strip of dingy carpet to the foot of the second flight of stairs. Listlessly, almost automatically, he moved; it would seem that purely by chance did he turn this way and not that. His hand slid along the rail and did not leave it, though the hall's light was ample to see the way.

Above was semi-darkness, drifting down, almost to the foot of the stairs like a threatening fog. He hesitated before it, dully, enveloped in silence. Nothing could be more ordinary or familiar to him, yet he hesitated, feeling a strange new quality in the dim dreariness.

That was the time to fight it, he told himself, so plainly that he thought it was muttered words, though his lips did not move.

Then you might have beaten it and come free.

# X

It came and went, capriciously; sometimes overwhelming you with a sudden fierceness sweeping aside all thought of resistance, and again, though invited and welcomed by you, approaching timidly and cautiously, now advancing now receding, hiding in the corners of your fancy, mistrustful and shy of capture.

It would rarely come more than once in a day or night, though there were times—for instance, that evening after Erma came to New York. That was startlingly vivid, twice, though it's hard to see how it could have had anything to do with Erma, unless it was that she reminded you of the old days in Cleveland when you experienced it so often that it was like lacing up your shoes or buttoning your trousers.

Erma would have loved being told that the first effect of her return was to sharpen your memory of little Millicent!

At that she wouldn't care a hang. It would amuse her. Has there ever been anyone about whom she cared that way? Lord no. You never saw Pierre, but you've heard her talk about him. She would yawn and say something clever about a psychical intrusion, as she did the time she found that violinist wearing rose petals in a silk belt around his waist under his shirt, the damn fool. It was like her to tell you about that, with no apology except to say that it was too good to keep.

If you had known her as well as you do now, what would you have done that morning when she informed you the time had come? It is difficult to remember how much you did then know. Probably it wouldn't have mattered, for you were ready to grab at anything; if she had happened to postpone her decision another week or two you might have followed Larry to France and got your head shot off.

Jane had been married nearly a year; you had decided to tolerate Victor, but you saw them infrequently, partly because you felt that Margaret and Rose were trying to use you for a good thing and you didn't intend to stand for it. Especially Rose. Jane, trying to manage a baby and a job at the same time, was too busy to notice it.

You sat there that night in Erma's elaborate bedroom, wondering what was up. It was her first big dinner and dance at the house on Riverside Drive, and had been marvelously successful; she could do that sort of thing so easily, almost without thought. You supposed that she would tire of it in a year, or at least as soon as the war was over; she would probably return to Europe. Why had she asked you to stay after the mob had left? If she wanted to see you alone why couldn't she have made it last night or tomorrow? What did she want anyway?

The door from her dressing-room opened, and she entered, fresh and charming with no trace of the night's fatigue, wearing a soft yellow negligee, just the color of her hair, and slippers the same, with her white ankles showing beneath the hem as she crossed to you. As if she had done it a thousand times before, she seated herself on your lap, looked directly at you, her eyes bright and soft and intense, and stroked your cheek with her hand.

"Poor Bill, you're tired," she said.

You were somewhat disconcerted. During the four months that had passed since her return she had been most friendly, but had given no indication of an ungovernable longing for your person. She had once or twice observed casually that she must some time have a long business talk with you, but her present costume and position seemed ill-adapted to that purpose.

Through the stuff of your trousers you could feel plainly that the negligee was all.

"Not so very," you said.

"Neither am I," she replied, "put your arm around me." You held her close, at first mechanically, like a conscientious proxy; then, approaching excitement, on your own account.

"Kiss me," she whispered, "your arms are so good!" You could feel her hand at the back of your head, the spread fingers pressed hard against you, beneath the hair.

Where the deuce did she get those pajamas? Had they been Pierre's? They were right there in her dressing-room, though she had moved to that house only a week before—and seemed new. A marvelous soft white thick silk. She declared she had bought them that very day, and it is quite possible. At any rate you almost felt tender toward her for that whiteness, having always detested colored pajamas.

A strange night that was. Like watching yourself from the top of a mountain, too far away to see clearly....

In the morning it astonished you that she arose when you did and insisted that you have fruit and coffee with her; and there, at the breakfast table, she announced her opinion that it would be a good idea to get married. You were already so confused by the sudden shift in status, and so tired and sleepy, that at first you regarded this idea as an additional and unnecessary complication.

"Since we've known each other over twelve years," you said, "that suggestion, at this precise moment, is open to a highly vulgar construction."

"Not unflattering to you," she replied. Her eyes and voice were clear; she looked thoroughly rested and refreshed.

"I can't think why you propose it." You drew yourself another cup of coffee from the enormous silver percolator. "Already

I'm completely your slave and likely to be so forever. I don't forget that a long time ago, before I knew you very well, I made the mistake of believing that you were in love with me."

"How funny for you and me to be talking of love," she observed.

"After the derision we've heaped on it. Yes."

"That was just conversation. I mean it's so unnecessary, it won't get us anywhere. We already know everything that counts between us, we know a lot more than we'd be willing to admit. We understand each other."

"I'm damned if I understand why you want to marry me."

"Oh. Well. Ask the flower why it opens to the bee, or if you prefer, the lady-salmon why she swims a thousand miles to that particular creek. If she's properly brought up she'll tell you, but it won't be true."

"More conversation," you said drily. "Ordinarily I'm ready to play, but you seem to be making all the rules. What do you want me around for? As your trusted adviser it looks to me as if you're making a bad bargain."

"Council of perfection." She lit a cigarette and was lost in smoke. "Show me a better one. I'm tired of being *Veuve Basset*. I want to invest in a husband."

"By god you're frank about it."

"You ask why, and you insist. Perhaps I'm still curious about you, which would be a triumph. I watched you once fastidiously refuse a prize that most men would have given an eye for. Or, maybe, I merely want a screen inside my bedroom door, in case the wind blows it open....Heavens, there is no why. What if tonight at dinner the oyster on your fork suddenly twists itself upright to glare at you and demand, why am I selected for this honor?"

You lifted your coffee cup, whipped into silence by her smiling brutality; and doubtless you looked whipped, for she pushed back her chair and came around the table and kissed you on top of the head.

"Bill dear, I do want to be your wife," she said.

All day long at the office, and the night and day following, you pretended to consider what you were going to do, knowing all the time that it was already decided.

You had supposed that she would want a starched and gaudy wedding, now that she had entered for the big show in the metropolis, and were relieved when she said it was too much bother, that was for peasants and titled sheep. On a fine October morning, less than a month after the breakfast betrothal, in a dark little parsonage parlor somewhere in South Jersey, with its funny curtained window overlooking a white church across a bit of green lawn, with Dick and Nina Endicott as witnesses, Erma made her marital investment. You and she went on with the car and chauffeur into Virginia, and later clear to the gulf, while Dick and Nina returned to New York by train.

Unquestionably there is something in you that has always kept Erma just this side of satiety; of satisfaction too, but that is something her restless appetite will find nowhere unless in the grave. A dozen times you have been convinced that at last she had cut loose, that finally she had done with poking around inside you and had abandoned you to fate and the weather, only to find her back and at it again, after a more or less prolonged interval, like a pertinacious terrier suspecting one more rat in that exasperating hole. Piqued, she enjoys her defeat and proclaims it to you, a trick which at first caused you some uneasiness, for she is clever enough to know that the words you do not pronounce are the ones to listen for. You too have pretended to listen for them, but that's a little joke everyone plays on himself. Never fear, they'll stay where they belong, they're more afraid of you than you are of them.

The first interval, at least the first you were aware of, came soon after the end of the war—the spring following the armistice, when New York was still full of returned captains and colonels being painfully and violently deflated. That fellow who worked for months sorting out reports and making summaries for you had commanded a regiment at Chateau-Thierry. He was a nice chap, but so dumb you had to send him back to Nicholson for replacement. Later he went out to Carrton, with Larry; only Larry came back before long and began to surprise all of you.

It was Larry who introduced Major Barth to you and Erma; brought him out one evening for bridge. There was nothing impressive about him, except his size—almost massive, well-proportioned, with a little blond moustache that looked like a pair of tiny pale commas pasted couchant, pointing outwards, against his youthful pink skin. You would not have noticed him at all, among the crowd, but for the subsequent comedy.

The big handsome major began to be much in evidence, but still you took no notice; Erma's volatile and brief fancies in the matter of dinner guests and dancing partners were an old story to you. It was a departure when she phoned you one afternoon to ask you to dine at the club; and when the request was repeated several times in a week you wondered mildly whether the cook had broken his leg or was merely off on a spree. Then, returning home one evening at nearly midnight, on mounting to your rooms on the third floor you saw light through the keyhole as you passed Erma's room on the floor below, though John had told you that she was out and would not return until late. Perhaps it was her maid—you started to knock—perhaps it wasn't—you shrugged your shoulders and went up to bed.

In the morning you arose rather later than usual, and you were in the breakfast room with your emptied coffee cup before you, just ready to fold up the *Times* and throw it aside when you heard footsteps at the door and looked up to see Major Barth enter, twinkling and ruddy. His hesitation at sight of you was so momentary that it was scarcely perceptible.

"Good morning," he said pleasantly; and added something about supposing you had gone to the office and wishing he had one to go to, as he passed behind your chair to reach the bell button. Stupidly disconcerted, you mumbled that you had slept poorly and must now hurry off; John appeared; with desperate politeness you pushed the *Times* across the table to your guest and hastily departed, hearing behind you enthusiastic references to orange juice, bacon and eggs, fried potatoes, apple jelly.…

It so happened that that evening you and Erma were dining out, somewhere the other side of the park, As usual she came to your room and tied your cravat; she still does, now and then; that's one of her thousand unlikely gestures that there's no accounting for. She hummed the air of *una furtiva lagrima* as she stood close in front of you neatly arranging the ends of the bow.

"We'll hear Caruso do that tonight," she said, "provided they don't go to sleep over the coffee."

"Yes." You turned and picked up your vest. "Will the major be along?"

She sat on the arm of your reading chair and looked at you, appreciatively, and at your question there was a flicker in her eyes, not amusement, just that flicker of nervous life without any human meaning. Then she smiled.

"Tim interrupted your breakfast, didn't he?"

"No! Not Tim! Don't tell me that rhinoceros is named Tim!"

"Timothy," she declared. "I'm sorry he walked in on you like an unexpected mountain—I should have told you."

In front of the mirror, with your back to her, you arranged your coat.

"And is he—that is—are we adopting him?" you inquired.

She was silent. Then she said:

"Sometimes you frighten me, Bill. You feel things too well, much too well for a man. How long have we been married, a year and a half? Yes, eighteen months. We've had dozens of house guests, some under rather peculiar circumstances, like the Hungarian boy last winter, and you've never lifted an eyelid. But you feel Tim at once; you're much too clever."

You were now dressed, and stood by the chair looking down at her, your hands in your pockets.

"He slept with you last night," you said.

"Yes," she replied.

"And I am supposed to breakfast with him and discuss yesterday's market? My god, Erma, after all we're not caterpillars. I think I know the kind of bargain we've made; I'm not likely to try sermons about chastity and fidelity on you. This is a made-up speech; I thought it out at the office this afternoon. That's how close you and I are to things like that. I slept like a top last night. I'm not pretending any personal torment, but when that jackass walked in on me this morning I felt like an embarrassed worm. What do you want me to do? Shall I go and live at the club? Do you want a divorce?"

"Come on," said Erma, "we'll be late."

It petered out to no conclusion as you sat side by side on the soft limousine cushions, rolling down the Drive, crosstown and through the park. Certainly, she said, she did not want a divorce; and what earthly reason was there for you to move to the club or anywhere else? These problems obviously arose from feelings within you which were entirely foreign to her repertory, she added. She had not sufficiently realized that your rare perception would find in the major's breakfast presence any greater significance than in that of any other overnight guest. As a matter of fact, she had not much cared for so emphatic an intimacy with him; it had been unavoidable because he was at present so poor that he was living in a dingy little furnished room down on Seventh Avenue. He had hinted that a position with the Carr Corporation would be acceptable, but really it was impossible; he was much too dumb to wish off on you and Dick.

Something like that it went. The central question, were you to be expected to share the morning *Times* with gentlemen who had spent the night in your wife's bedroom, remained unanswered. Your mind was already using the plural, gentlemen, for you saw clearly that the major was but the inconsequential founder of an amorous dynasty.

As the years have passed Erma has become progressively more callous to your rare perception....

At that she knows you better than anyone except Jane. She knows profoundly what she can count on with you, she always has; it was amazing how sure she was when Dick and the whole Board, the whole bunch except Schwartz, were ready to throw you out on your head. For that matter the entire affair was amazing, like a Fourteenth Street melodrama in tails; and but for Erma, Jackson would have got away with it and you would have been the conquered villain.

How Jackson got that dope from the Adams National, and how he worked through Mrs. Halloway to get the inside agreement with the Bethlehem crowd into the papers without any of the usual wire-pulling came out later, but you knew none of that then and had no way of getting at it. You couldn't blame Dick, nor any of them, for it was strictly up to you. There were no other copies in New York, no one else had access to it, you were known to be on friendly terms with Halloway. No wonder Jackson grinned at you that morning in the elevator.

You decided that you must tell Erma all about it, give her all the facts, carefully and completely, and went home early that afternoon, hoping that she would have returned since your telephone message. Larry came into your office just before you left.

"We're hearing a thousand crazy rumors down on the twentieth floor," he said. "A lot of bunk. Jackson comes through looking like a hyena that's just found a whole graveyard, the big stiff. It's none of my business, but I just wanted you to know we're for you—"

You thanked him and reassured him, not very successfully, thinking that perhaps you were leaving that office for the last time, that pleasant luxurious room with your name in dignified gold letters on the door.

At home, in the hall, a servant told you that Erma was in her room and wanted to see you at once.

When you knocked and entered she was there curled up in the purple chair, her bare feet (which you had once thought an affectation) on the velvet cushion, perfect and white-glowing in the dim light, the smoke a blue spiral from the cigarette between her fingers; she did not move as you came in, except her eyes. On another chair, facing her, nearer the window, with a teacup in his hand, sat Dick.

"Hello," said Erma. "From what Dick tells me I should have thought you'd be on a boat for Africa by now, armed to the teeth."

Dick muttered something about "unexpected" and "unpleasant" and put his teacup down, and then turned to you and demanded to know how you had learned he was there.

"I didn't," you said. "If I had I'd have waited for you to leave." You turned towards the door.

"No," said Erma, "don't run away. Sit down and have a cup of tea and hear Dick's funny story. I haven't been so thrilled in years." She flung at him one of those sharp little smiles which, turned on you, always made you feel like pinching her. "After all, Bill lives here, you know. This is his home."

"All right, we've had it out, I'm not here to prove to him what he already knows. I've told you just how it stands, he denies it, just denies it like a damn fool, though it's as plain as the nose on his face. I'm telling you he's disloyal and crooked and he's got to get out. Why waste time beefing about it?"

"Goodness, how positive you are," said Erma. "And how moral."

"Moral, hell. I don't reproach him, I think he's crazy, unless he got a million for it. I've told you I didn't want to believe it, I didn't believe it, until it was impossible not to. Anyway I didn't come here to argue about it, I came to tell you what has to be done. We could have gone ahead at the meeting yesterday, they were all for it, but I thought it was only decent to tell you about it first."

"Thanks." Erma had poured you a cup of tea and broken a lump of sugar in two so as to give you one and a half. You took it and sat down again, feeling a detached admiration for the vigor of Dick's assault. Until this morning he had remained unconvinced; now, having decided, with characteristic energy he struck at once. You were through with worrying about it; the whole outfit could go to hell; as for Jackson, who had certainly framed it, he was too clever for you. In another month you would have had the goods on him—how had he found out?

"This is really sad," Erma drawled, "but so piquant and exciting. Bill has some kind of a paper in a private safe about a secret agreement on a government contract, and he goes to your bitterest enemies and offers to have it printed in a newspaper so the government will have to repudiate it and give the contract—now come, Dick, you don't really believe that."

"I've told you, the proofs—"

"Oh your proofs! Some day some man is going to prove that drowning is good for a headache and you'll all run and jump in the ocean. Good heavens, don't you think I know whether I'm married to a treacherous little rat? Of course he might have been drunk—or trying to prove something. Were you, Bill? Did you? You don't need to answer, I see it in your face. Dick darling, the next time you want to get dramatic and unearth a dark and malignant plot select your villain with some regard to plausibility; don't pick on poor Bill."

"I'm not picking on him. You're so damn clever." Dick plainly restrained himself with difficulty. "There's no use arguing about it." He turned savagely to you. "Are you going to resign and get out, or not?"

"He is not," said Erma.

"Then we'll kick him out."

"No you won't."

"The hell we won't. He goes tomorrow. Come down and try arguing with the Board about it and see how far you get."

"I don't intend to argue; I'm not interested in Boards. I'm quite ignorant about them, but I know I own half of the company, and I know in a general way what that means, and Bill isn't going to resign and he won't be kicked out. Or if he is I'll find a new interest in life and we'll see if I'm clever or not."

Dick was on his feet, glaring at her, nearer explosion than you had ever seen him. You watched him, fascinated; if he really did blow up Vesuvius would be nowhere.

"I'm really sorry for you, Dick," said Erma coolly, "I don't enjoy putting a ring in your nose, it's rather painful."

As she said it he charged at the door; as he opened it, he flung the words at her, "You goddam little fool!" and was gone. The door remained open after him; you crossed over and closed it and then came back and stood in front of your wife.

"The most amusing part of it," you observed, "is that neither of you cares a hang about the bone you're picking. Nevertheless I'm grateful to you, really grateful, for the whole thing is a frame-up and this gives me a chance to prove it."

"Not Dick?"

"Lord no. A buzzard named Jackson. Now I'll get him."

You hoped she would ask for details, but she wasn't interested. With Dick's nose ringed the rest bored her.

The Jackson business left a bad taste in your mouth; even at the moment of triumph it was repugnant to you, and probably you would never have gone through with it but for the necessity of justifying Erma and yourself. When the exposure finally came you felt no glory in it, though you were praised and congratulated on all sides; the Board pompously voted a formal apology and commendation; Dick was completely got, the only time you have ever seen him with all banners down. He sent Erma a carload of orchids, with a note, "You are damn clever—so is Bill," and he carried you off to dinner and insisted that you tell the whole story from the beginning, since the Cleveland episode ten years before; how you had suspected Jackson on sight, how with Schwartz's help you had first connected him with the Pittsburgh crowd, but without any proof to offer, how you had gradually hemmed him in until he was left almost powerless, and how at the end, finding that the trap was about ready to spring, he had desperately got the Bethlehem copy through Mrs. Halloway, and tried to get you out of the way and put himself right with Farrell at the same time.

Dick looked at you speculatively:

"So you knew from the first he was double-crossing us."

"Well—I felt it."

"Damned uncomfortable faculty. I expect what you feel about me wouldn't look well in the annual report."

"We'd have a new president in twenty-four hours," you grinned.

"Which reminds me," said Dick, "how would you like to be vice? Next to old Powell, we'll have to leave him First. You must be fed up with that nineteenth floor; we can put Lawson in as Treasurer."

You shook your head. "Unless you want the place for Lawson."

"Hell no. I'm talking straight."

"All right; I don't want it. I'm already plenty close enough; I'm talking straight too."

The phrase came back to you a year later, one evening as you were strolling idly, alone, down the avenue. Yes, you were close enough, too close, to everything; you were almost suffocated by the embrace of alien things and people. Jane, with her husband and four-year-old son and the new baby—what was that house to you? Why did you ever go there? And why did you bury yourself every day in that damn office—all those monkeys running around yelling at each other about nothing—all those senseless endless rows of figures, eight million four hundred and sixteen thousand nine hundred and twelve last year it was seven million sixty-three thousand five hundred eighty-four—absolute insanity. They called that the world of action, building bridges across rivers so that people could hopefully exchange the boredom of one side for the inanity of the other. Worst of all was your own home, rather your wife's, where nothing belonged to you and there was no friendliness; where Erma's cold soul penetrated into every room and every corner, and even the servants, perfectly trained, were also perfectly insulated.

Yes, it was all insufferably close, and you could see no escape. Larry had left that afternoon; chucked the whole thing overboard and gone west; perhaps just another young hopeful crossing one of their bridges. Why not follow him? It couldn't be any worse than this.

You had crossed over to Broadway, and were wandering

around looking at the theatre signs, thinking you might try a show, when you suddenly remembered that you were expected at home for dancing; you hailed a taxi....

It was a year after that, a little more than a year, for it was the second autumn after Larry went to Idaho, that you moved to Park Avenue. You had been married five years!

"I've never lived in anything between a hotel room and a house," said Erma. "The word apartment has always sounded stuffy to me. If we don't like it we can probably sell without much loss."

"I think we may scrape along somehow," you remarked drily, "with nineteen rooms and eight baths."

The arrangement was ideal, with your rooms on the upper floor, at the rear; and the night you first slept there you complacently accepted Erma's suggestion that all the knocking should be at your door. It had already been so, in effect, for two years; this merely formalized it. If it was an indignity there was nothing personal in it and you had long since ceased to feel it. Rather you were relieved that it was possible to make such easy terms with her.

She must have spent close to half a million furnishing that apartment. More than ten years of your salary. You figured it up with her once, but that was before the hangings had come over from Italy and the pictures and stuff she bought later in London. My god what for? She hadn't gone in for the big show after all; there were too many rules to suit her. You never knew who you might find when you went home to dinner—anybody from that French duke with his cross-eyed wife down to some bolshevik professor. A whole tableful. Then for a month at a stretch you'd dine at the club, preferring that to a solitaire meal at home, while she would be off god knows where, chasing restlessly after something which she never found.

Nor did you; you weren't even looking for anything. Though

you did one evening see something that stopped you and set
you staring, standing there in the middle of the sidewalk, with
your eyes blinking in the whirling snow. After a too ample
dinner at the club you had gone out for a brisk walk in the
winter night and, striding along Fifty-seventh Street, suddenly
in front of Carnegie Hall a name on a poster caught your eye:
Lucy Crofts. It was a large poster, and her name was in enormous black letters. You approached, and read it through, twice
—eminent pianist, European triumphs, first American recital....

The date was in the following week.

Twelve years ago, you thought, it seems incredible. She's
nearly thirty. Over thirty. Those braids of hair, that loose torrent of hair all around her. She's had lovers, she has kissed men
and held them in her arms, men have got up from her and
yawned and said my god I'm hungry....

Lucy, Lucy.

Yes, call her now. If you could get her back as she was—you
don't want much, do you? Let her come in now and run up
the stairs to you, and you can take her up and introduce her,
politely—Lucy, this is—

# K

He was moving up the second flight, into the semi-darkness, slowly and wearily. He paused and listened, glancing upward; there was no sound and all he could see was the dim shape of the projection of the wall at the next landing and a corner of the door opposite—the rear door, which was rarely used.

Involuntarily—a habitual gesture performed without aware-ness—his left hand went into his trousers pocket and came out holding a ring with two keys on it, and still involuntarily his fingers selected one of the keys and turned it to the correct position for insertion in the keyhole. His right hand remained tight on the rail, as if without that support equilibrium would desert him and he would tumble backward like a puppet severed from its string.

He felt the key in his hand and looked down at it, wondering how it had got there.

# XI

Lucy, permit me, this is you, this is your understudy. Congratulate me, my dear.

That evening at the recital the expectation was dead before you saw her. You arrived early, to be sure of not missing her entrance, and the two sturdy matrons on your right told each other all you didn't care to know. One of them had heard her play in Vienna and had later met her in Cannes; the other had known her husband, who had left his estates in Bavaria to be with her on her American tour. Never had there been so devoted a husband, she declared. And so on. By the time she made her appearance nothing was left of this international artist to connect her with Ohio meadows and Cleveland nights.

She was very beautiful, superbly dressed, perfectly composed, completely charming. The audience loved her at once. You were thrilled for a moment as she stood at ease, graciously inclining her head to the applause; then as she sat down and began to play you felt bored and indifferent. This trained woman playing Mozkowski to a full house—what a place to come to, to find Lucy!

After the first intermission you did not return.

The one other time you saw her, that evening in Paris at the Meurice, you were positively frightened. Erma recognized her across the lobby and insisted on going over to her. You held her back, actually held her forcibly by the arm.

"It will be amusing," she insisted. "Come, she may even fall on your shoulder and weep. Heavens she's magnificent! She doesn't look much like your little country shepherdess, does

she, Bill? I understand she can't play much, but all the critics
rave about her so she'll smile at them."

You were ridiculously relieved that Lucy and her companions had disappeared through the revolving door into the rue
du Mont-Tabor.

The year in Europe was fun. You went for three months,
then extended it to six, and then to a year. Erma insisted; she
also insisted that she be permitted to foot all the bills, which
was just as well, since the suite at the Meurice, for instance,
was two thousand francs a day. Good lord how she can spend
money! At Algiers she practically gave away that Minerva because it had skidded on a narrow road in the Atlas Mountains
and she said she would never feel comfortable in it again.

Yes, it was fun, but a dry remote fun with no juice in it.

None of those places was as good as the promise of its name.
What joy you might have found in Paris, for example, if you
could have seen it as a youth, with Jane! Or the drive from
Perpignan to Port Vendres, through the little fishing villages
and past the red and blue cottages among the vineyards on the
terraced hills. Or that inn, on the road to Bou-Saada, with the
little black table in the tiled alcove and the purple hens clacking
outside the window under the almond tree, waiting for crumbs....

"I think you should see Germany," said Erma one evening in
the hotel garden at Vienna. "At least Munich and Nurnberg.
It's another month before the year is up, and anyway what's the
difference if it's two years, or ten?"

"None whatever," you agreed, "Lawson's signature on a
voucher is just as properly illegible as mine. All the same I'm
going back when the year's up."

It was arranged that you should go on to Munich alone,
leaving Erma at Vienna, the reason given being that—no matter
what, the real reason joined you that evening for dinner and

the opera, as he had for some evenings past. He was a silent and melancholy Norwegian who had come to the Austrian capital to study psychoanalysis, and you reflected with amusement that he would learn damn little about inhibitions from Erma.

You wandered around Nurnberg a few days, wondering what the devil you were there for, and then went on to Munich for no discoverable reason save that you had a railroad ticket.

That was the best laugh you've ever given yourself. It is strange that you didn't feel uncomfortable about it, for certainly you were sufficiently ridiculous. You made the decision one morning in your hotel room, after solemn deliberation: you would find out what a prostitute was like. You accepted the advances of one, that evening in a beer garden, and were taken by her to a clean and modest little room up three flights of narrow wooden stairs, in a side street, near a railroad station.

She slipped off her dress, and then, stopped by a question you asked about some German word, sat down on the edge of the bed with her fat thighs and knees extending like massive pillars from the lace edge of her pink underwear, and her fat bare arms crossed on her adequate bosom. You sat on a wooden chair directly in front of her with your hat on your knees.

She roared with laughter at your question and explained to you that one didn't say that in German. This led to another question, and another. She suggested a bottle of beer; it was sent for, and brought, and drunk, while the lesson in German went on enthusiastically. About the only sentence of hers which you understood was when she said that the only way to learn German was to live with a German woman, men didn't know how to teach anything.

There was a second bottle of beer. Suddenly she glanced at the clock on the table and observed that time was up. You arose, handed her some thousands of degraded marks, and departed, hearing behind you, as you descended the narrow stairs, a rollicking guttural song.

In the taxi on your way back to the hotel, and up in your room undressing, you laughed aloud; you hadn't seen or heard of anything so funny in years. Wouldn't Erma enjoy it! Or would she? Yes. You laughed again. A prize bit of erotica; there was so much of her, and you took so little! It was admirable of her to treat it as a matter of course. What was it she said with a grin as you went out—a phrase you didn't know.

It was a day or two later that a telegram came from Erma saying that she had decided to go to Spain for a few months. You wired that you were preparing to return to the States, and departed that evening for Southampton via London.

The months in New York, stretching to over a year, with Erma away, showed to your astonishment her importance as your only surviving bond with life. You missed her amazingly; every day there was something you wanted to tell her about; you wanted her with you at the theatre, sitting there beside you with that deceptive disciplined stillness; you wanted to go home to her from the office, even if only to be greeted by—well, as she had greeted you one autumn afternoon, for instance:

"For god's sake, Bill, why don't you, just once, come home drunk riding an ostrich—or not at all?"

The discomfort of an interrupted habit, you told yourself; but she was no old shoe. You began to respect yourself for having married her, for apparently you had not after all merely prostituted yourself to a paper in your safe deposit box; and at least it could be said that she had treated you as she had treated no other man. So when her cablegram came from Scotland you were pleasantly excited by the task of scurrying to and fro for servants, finding John and persuading him to return, getting rugs and silver from storage, having the apartment renovated and arranged so that it would call from her one of those rare appreciative smiles.

On the pier you met her, alone by her wish; she kissed you facetiously, then meaningly, and declared that there was not a man in the world to compare with you except the Spanish soldier who had examined her passport on the border north of Figueras. Surrounded by an ocean of trunks and boxes and bags, you sat and amusedly heard her explain to an astonished customs inspector that since every article contained therein was dutiable, she hadn't bothered to make out a declaration.

Within a month you wished she were back in Scotland, or somewhere out of sight of land, eastbound on the Mediterranean perhaps—or for that matter at the bottom of it. Incredulously you recalled that you had seemed to long for her return.

The following summer it was that at her suggestion you went to Idaho, to Larry's ranch, where again you were close to Jane by the memory of her footsteps of the year before. A desert and mountain idyll that ended by your tiptoeing in your bare feet down an icy hall in the middle of the night, to hear Erma get slapped by your brother, presumably in the face, though in the darkness it might have been merely an arm or shoulder. How many times since have you looked at her and failed utterly in your effort to imagine a slap, an honest resounding slap, landed on that proud ironic lovely face! Certainly, Larry or any man could not have done it in daylight.

Earlier was that day when, lying on your back in the bright sunshine, by an insane trick of your fancy little Millicent suddenly became Jane....

When you got back to New York you found the revolver in your bag.

That winter Erma suddenly took it into her head to give Margaret and Rose a lift. She and Jane have always been funny together—in a way they genuinely like each other, but from the first they've always backed off a bit, as much as to say, you may be all right but just keep off my grass if you don't mind. She didn't get far with Margaret either—Margaret's a strange kid and a good deal of a damn fool, thinking she's in love because Doctor Oehmsen has articles in the *American Science Journal*, or whatever its name is, and takes long walks with her and explains what electrons are or what he thinks they are. Presumably she has slept with him, so had Jane with Victor; your sisters seem to have a faculty for driving without a permit. Except Rose. At Erma's first gesture didn't she jump though! Erma soon got fed up with her clever tricks, but Rose held on till she got what she wanted.

At first you thought she was after Dick, and maybe she was, but if so she soon found that Mary Bellowes was ahead of her. Mary Alaire Carew Bellowes—it looked very imposing on the announcement, almost as imposing as one of her grand entrances into a drawing-room. Instantly and admirably Erma was on to her the first time Dick brought her around.

"Pure bitch," she whispered to you as you lit her cigarette.

"Pure *bitch* or *pure* bitch?" you whispered back.

"Both—so much the worse," she replied aloud.

Later, after they had gone, you told Erma that Dick deserved better, and that as an older sister it was up to her to save him from so unpleasant a fate. She replied that that remark was your record for stupidity, that if she poisoned la Bellowes that night, Dick, having apparently decided to get married, would find another just like her in a week, and that no nice woman should be wasted on him anyway.

"But what will happen?" you demanded.

"She'll spend his money, which must have accumulated frightfully by this time, within a year he'll drag her around the room and tear her clothes off, and the next time he goes to vote and they ask him if he's married he'll say no and get sent to jail for perjury."

The wedding was as different as possible from your and Erma's rustic nuptials; no Jersey parsonage for Mary Alaire Carew Bellowes. You were best man, and when at a solemn moment Erma made a grimace and winked at you, you almost dropped the ring. They took a mansion on Long Island and four or five floors on the Avenue, and for the first time Dick began to take an interest in the private ledger. But even her furious assaults could not greatly disturb the serenity of those colossal columns; and they were restored again to assured security within the year, when Dick declared to you one day at lunch:

"By god, Bill, every woman alive ought to be locked up in a little room and fed through a hole in the wall."

You decided that it was not a propitious moment for sounding him on a proposal that had occurred to you that morning. Only a few weeks previously you had returned from Ohio, from your mother's funeral, and to your surprise Larry had not only accepted Jane's invitation to come to New York for a visit, but had apparently settled down for an extended stay, having moved recently from Jane's house to a couple of rooms on Twelfth Street. He had told you nothing of his intentions, but you thought it just possible that five years of Idaho had been enough for him and that he might welcome another chance at the career he had once started so well and abandoned in disgust. You decided to ask Dick whether Larry was wanted and if so on what terms.

This project was temporarily set aside by the sudden appearance from nowhere of Mrs. Davis and your son. Your son Paul. For all the reality there is in them, those words might as well be your neighbor Mars or your great-grandfather Adam; and yet, during that brief episode, he did succeed in leaving his mark on

you, with what must have been unconscious sarcasm—he wasn't
as acute as all that. It's unbelievable that that was only two
years ago; it seems a wild distortion of fact to say that the passage of time since you sat there in Paul's studio has been the
same as, for instance, that between your return from Europe
and the trip to Idaho. Measuring time by clocks is a joke like all
the other arithmetic. Two years ago! If you could go back....

You thought the shoulders and chest and upper arms should
show, but Paul would barely allow you a neck; he insisted that
your head should emerge from a rugged column of unpolished
marble. He gave many complicated reasons, none of which
appeared to you to demolish the fact that you were paying for it
and might therefore be permitted to have what you wanted;
however, he had his way. Day after day you went directly after
lunch to the bare little room overlooking the dirty little West
Side street, and sat there and let your mind wander, jumping
crazily from boyhood to yesterday and back again, while Paul
worked away, sometimes whistling, sometimes with a cigarette
in his mouth, always gay and intent. No one knew anything
about it. You wondered what you would do with the darned
thing when it was finished. Put it in a gallery; sure; stick it
under your arm and go up Fifth Avenue stopping at each
dealer's to ask if he didn't want a nice statue of a modern lieu-
tenant of industry for his window. You couldn't very well display it at home or at the office. You realized with surprised and
mildly irritated amusement that it was in fact a problem, of
which the only possible solution was to sneak it home secretly
and hide it in a closet.

One day Paul said:

"The Greenwich Galleries over on Eighth Street would like
to have this for a month or so, if you don't mind; they're going
to have a little show of modern American sculpture."

"When?"

"Around the first of April."

It was arranged, with the proviso that your name should appear neither in the catalogue nor on the card. Before the end of March it was finished and delivered; and Paul, with several hundred dollars of your money in his pocket and an account opened for him in a Paris bank, was gone. No sort of intimacy had developed between you; he was too shrewd and intelligent not to attempt to conceal how utterly you were to him merely a lucky find for which he owed gratitude to a smiling providence and a devoted mother; and the more you were with him the more removed you felt from that careless and cocksure beggar whose every attitude and word contradicted all the values for which you had sacrificed yourself.

Twice you visited the Eighth Street galleries to see your head and face in marble publicly displayed, and to watch others looking at it, while pretending your attention was elsewhere. It had been given a prominent position on a center table in the large front room. You thought it rather a good likeness, and unquestionably it was arresting and effective, with the large well-moulded head, tilted slightly backward and to one side, flowing gracefully out of the rough and jagged column. You both feared and hoped that someone would recognize you as the original.

Then the confounded idiots, forgetting entirely the careful instruction, given them by Paul, that it was to be kept there until you called for it, on the very day the show ended had it delivered to your address on Park Avenue. When you got home from the office there it was in the middle of the big table in the library, with a wreath of ferns and red roses around its brow and a circlet of yellow daisies hanging from its neck. Erma, having apparently just finished this decorative effort, was seated at the piano; you heard her strumming as you came down the hall; and when you entered she crashed into the Polonaise Militaire.

You tried to laugh, but it was too much for you. You struggled to hide from her the fury that was rising in you, but it was too late, she was looking at you, and suddenly she left the piano and came towards you, towards the table.

"I tried to fix it up as nice as I could," she said, reaching over and pretending to adjust the daisy necklace. "There have already been three men after it for the Hall of Fame, but John and I chased them. Bill dear, it's marvelous—that indomitable will, that gallant fling of the head—I've decided to call it William the Conqueror."

You turned and left the room, and the house; got a taxi and went to the Club, and spent the night there.

By the following afternoon you felt better about it, especially about Erma. She might be cruel and pitiless, even malicious, but she was right. She had taken the only possible intelligent attitude toward the damn thing. Still you felt a little shaky when on arriving home and learning that she was alone in her rooms you went to the end of the hall and knocked on the door.

You entered, calling out:

"Vive William the Conqueror!"

She chose to be semi-serious about it, after you had explained its origin and reason of being and she had poured you a cup of tea.

"Your young sculptor is either very stupid or a first-rate satirist," she said. "I'm sorry he's gone; why didn't you bring him to see me? He made gorgeous fun of you, Bill. It saddens me. You are the one man who I would have said couldn't be fooled like that. Do you remember the granite Gaspard de

Coligny on the rue de Rivoli, behind the iron fence? Beside
every statue of a man folding his arms and looking masterful
should be placed another of him in a dentist's anteroom, or
being seasick, or itching with love."

"There are masterful men," you observed.

"None with a sense of humor," she replied, "and the others
only when the forces that confront them happen to be inferior.
Of course you aren't masterful at all, there's never been a
minute in your life when you haven't been ready to run if somebody made a face at you. That's why William the Conqueror is
so magnificently funny. Elizabethan. 'In action how like a god!'
No, that was apprehension. All the better. And I thought you
really did have a sense of humor, and you sat there day after
day and let him do that to you!"

You wanted to say, casually, well, he is my son and I was
willing he should amuse himself. That would have brought her
up. She who was never startled or surprised would have opened
her eyes a little on hearing that you had a son of that age and
quality. You did very nearly say it, but instead took a second cup
of tea and listened to her further analysis of your character.

That evening William the Conqueror was stowed away in a
corner of your dressing-room.

You've never told yourself the truth about it, deep down. It
seems perfectly simple: there it is, the marble head and face of
a man who looks like you but who obviously is not you at all.
You as you might be with Dick's will and Jane's serene confidence. Well, it isn't you, that's all there is to it, merely a piece of
marble disfigured by falsehood, only a little more subtle than if
it had a hooked nose or a double chin. But it's exasperating
that, no matter how many times you repeat it, you never quite
believe it. What the hell, what does it signify, what's the difference? Why do you try to kid yourself? Have you got a sneaking

notion that your son, being a genius, penetrated to a truth perceived by none other? Jackass! Masterful jackass. Call yourself names and joke about it all you want to, some such idiotic idea is buried somewhere in your guts and keeps gnawing at you....

You put it away in a corner, but not, observe, out of sight. Not boldly on a table—but not in a closet either. Sometimes, undressing, it would amuse you to call out, "Here, old top, make yourself useful," and throw your shirt or underwear over its polished brow.

You couldn't resist the impulse to show it to Jane, swearing her first to secrecy. You pulled it out near the light and introduced it derisively as William the Conqueror, explaining that it had been christened by Erma. She looked at it from all sides and then sat down on the floor in front of it and looked up at you.

"It's extremely good," she said, "but it isn't you."

"No? Why not?"

"It's too—" she hesitated. "It's too stupid. It's what you would be like if you went around bumping people off of sidewalks."

Doubtless Gaspard de Coligny did so.

That was the evening of your birthday party—your fortieth birthday—another of Erma's unlikely gestures. Lord, families are jokes—look at that bunch around that table! Jane and Erma, Larry and Rose, Margaret and Dick, Victor and Mary. Mary Alaire Carew Bellowes Carr was the finishing touch. She could hardly eat her soup on account of a sore arm, said she had fallen off of a horse. "Probably Dick pushed her off," you heard Erma say to Rose. Victor and Erma got into an argument about bringing up children and she was much too nimble for him, made him so mad he couldn't eat.

"At least they have a better chance than the ones that are

scraped out!" he yelled at her. Mary looked shocked and Rose giggled; Erma smiled sweetly at him and said:

"That's not personal, is it? I'm sterile, you know."

Which was a lie; she could have had a dozen if she'd wanted to. Not that you made a point of it.

There they were, seated around you, your world, gathered there in honor of your birthday, the oldest and fondest faces you knew after forty years; If there was happiness and security and love for you anywhere, here it was. Here it was! Larry had rejected you with scorn and severed whatever bond had been between you. Jane had deceived you and cut loose with a laugh. Dick had been willing, "on proof," to kick you out, and would be again under similar circumstances. You could depend on Erma so long as you amused her; so could a dog. The others didn't count. Was there then no assurance anywhere? People seemed to like it, they laughed and struggled and seemed to like it. With some the explanation was simply that they were brainless idiots, like that nut Simpson who kept the score card of his best game of golf stuck on the wall in front of his desk with a sign above it, *Ad astra per aspera*. Maybe that's it, maybe the only ones who come out all right are those who have sense enough to go crazy.

Crazy or not, they had something to hold onto. Dick fought downtown all day long, day after day, competitors, fellow directors, lawmakers, nature itself—something, anything, to give a sock in the jaw. He would ride a horse over ditches and fences as if life and honor were both in the balance—only he wouldn't care too much about honor, at least he'd furnish his own definition. No use sneering what for; he's excited about it and he loves it. Jane got a kick out of everything, her children, her job, making wine out of raisins, hurrah for La Follette! Larry hated that office more than you did, but he was more a part of it in two years than you were in twenty. That summer in Idaho he rode forty miles and back in the mountains to get an old range mare, not worth ten dollars, which had got out of the corral and gone back to the Indian camp where she'd had a colt the spring before. Rose would spend two whole days walking all over town, hunting a new shade of rouge.

But Rose knew what she was about better than most; she's really as lazy as the devil and wouldn't walk across the street unless she was going to get something out of it. She's the only person you've ever seen work Erma successfully, by sheer impudence. She had her way with Margaret too. It was the evening of the birthday party, up in your room, that Jane told you she had that morning had a final interview with Mrs. Oehmsen and arranged definitely that the divorce proceedings should be postponed until autumn, October at the earliest. Rose's wedding was set for the middle of September; so Margaret could be a maid of honor a full month before she became a co-respondent; and Rose, off on a European honeymoon, would be three thousand miles from tabloids.

"How did you persuade her?" you asked.

"I told her that if she didn't promise to wait Margaret would go off to the South Seas, and Dr. Oehmsen would follow her, and she'd lose all her fun."

You reflected that Rose, whom you actively dislike and with whom you had had least to do, was the only member of the family who had got any considerable thing out of you. It was at your wife's house that she had carried on her campaign and captured her husband. Jane and Margaret, nothing; Larry...

That wound had been reopened, but with less loss of blood and negligible pain. One day at lunch you said to Dick:

"By the way, I'm wondering about Larry. He seems to be hanging on here for no particular reason, and it's just possible he's fed up out there and would like to try his hand again at selling a few carloads of bridges. If he should ask me about it I'd like to know what to say. How do you feel about it? Would you want—"

You were stopped by the surprise on Dick's face. He said:

"I'm buying Idaho and Larry's going to run it. Hasn't he told you?"

From the explanation which followed you gathered that shortly after Larry's arrival in New York he had gone to Dick with an ambitious and carefully formulated proposal for buying an enormous tract of land, practically the entire valley in which his present modest ranch was located, and engaging simultaneously in cattle-raising and dry farming on a large scale. Dick had agreed to furnish over half a million cash capital, and the plans were now almost complete. Larry's prolonged stay in New York was for the purpose of concluding arrangements regarding equipment and other details.

"Your kid brother knows how to drive a bargain," Dick grinned. "He had the nerve to suggest that he keep the ownership in his pocket and give me a nice pink and green seven percent mortgage. Seven percent! The chances are probably about eighty to one against us, but he sold me."

You were humiliated and furious that you had been left to learn about it from Dick. Only a few days later, however, dining at Jane's, Larry told you all about it, explaining that he had purposely kept you out of it because he wanted Dick to come in purely as a business proposition, not as a favor to his brother-in-law; and you didn't disclose that Dick had told you.

"I wanted to invite you to take a slice," Larry added, "but it's too risky. If Dick's half-million is blown away in the sand it won't break him, but you've worked for what you've got."

You glanced at him quickly, suspecting irony, but saw none

on his candid face. Doubtless ten years of Erma had made you a little touchy. Well, there's more than one kind of work.

You walked home that night, a good three miles, with pleasant breaths of June air even there on Fifth Avenue, penetrating somehow through the miles of city pavements and smells. It would be peaceful and pleasant now, you reflected, back in the little Ohio town under the maple trees—good lord what a silly idea! That would be worse than this. Anything would be worse than anything else. Soon now Erma would be off again, you didn't know where and you didn't care, only you weren't going with her; Larry would leave for his empire of sand and sagebrush; Jane and the children would pile in that old Stephens, headed for the seashore....

You belonged with none of them. Nowhere.

Erma was not at home when you arrived. You wandered through the silent, vast and impeccable apartment—faience, chinoiserie, Sheraton, Kermanshah, bayeta—what bunk, toys for bored morons. The people who made them were bone-dust. You wanted to break or tear something.

You hated the thought of your bed, but it was at least inviolably yours, and you went to your room to undress. As you removed your coat you observed that the maid's carelessness had left William the Conqueror out of his corner, pushed out away from the wall; there he was with his gallant head facing you, smiling and confident. In a sudden fit of rage you hauled off and gave him a kick, and nearly broke your foot in two.

Painfully you got the shoe off and put the foot in a tub of hot water and sat there looking at the evening paper....

# L

He stopped and stood perfectly still.

The voice came faintly from above, through the closed door at the front of the upper hall, not yet within his eyes' range:

"I can't give you anything but love, baby,
That's the only thing I've plenty of…"

It was thin and colorless and it could scarcely be called a tune. Not a monotone, rather three or four false and mongrel tones, alternating crazily into a petty and exasperating chaos. There was a long pause, and then it came again:

"Happiness, and I guess…"

It stopped.

He trembled violently, then controlled himself with an effort, and remained motionless. The voice sounded once more, more faintly than before:

"I can't give you anything but love, baby,
That's the only thing I've plenty of…"

Then the pause again, longer than before; and then:

"Happiness, and I guess…"

Silence.

So, he thought, she isn't seated, reading; she's moving around doing something, going back and forth from the front to the bedroom; can't hear her footsteps, probably she has on those slippers with the felt soles….

# XII

She always sings it like that; she doesn't know the rest of the words. Except that second *baby*, why the hell doesn't she put that in at least. If you can call it singing. Long ago, back in the old days, long ago, her voice had a thrill in it—maybe it still has—something has, but it can't be her voice.

It did have, though, that first night you heard it again. Not long ago you cursed fate for letting coincidence find her for you, but the wonder is you didn't find her sooner. Over five years she had been here in New York, sometimes perhaps near enough to be seen or heard—on a subway train, or in a department store, or on the street somewhere. Sooner or later…

You got to the theatre after the curtain was up, as usual when with Erma. It was the evening before her departure for the Adirondacks. Soon after the curtain fell, at the close of the first act, you heard a voice directly behind you:

"I guess I left my handkerchief in the ladies' room."

The effect was curious. You didn't recognize it, it didn't even occur to you that you had ever heard it before, but it stirred you amazingly; you were startled and alert; not turning your head, you let some question of Erma's go unanswered and waited breathlessly for it to sound again. A man's baritone had replied to it:

"Shall I lend you mine?"

Then the first voice:

"Yes, I guess you'll have to."

You turned like lightning and looked rudely, directly into her face, and recognized her at once.

If you had had an ounce of brains you would have told Erma
you had a sudden attack of indigestion or dementia praecox or
something and got up immediately and left the theatre. With
the ghost you had made of her growing stronger and more
hateful every year you might have known it was dangerous. Or
perhaps you expected the reality to kill itself and the ghost too?
You did not in fact calculate at all. You sat throughout the intermission listening to the scraps of her voice, and by the end of
the second act, feeling her presence so near, you were in a state
of intense excitement.

"Maybe the woman found it," she had said. "I'll go back after
the second act and see."

When the curtain fell again you mumbled an excuse to Erma
and were out of your seat and at the rear of the orchestra
before the lights were on. She came up the aisle on the arm of
her escort, a tall thin man in a brown suit, and you stood aside
as they passed. Then he went one way and she another, and you
darted after her and touched her on the shoulder.

"I beg your pardon, but aren't you Millicent Moran?" you said.

She turned and looked at you calmly.

"I used to be, but now I'm Mrs. Green," she replied. You saw
by her face that she knew you before her sentence was ended,
but characteristically she finished it before she added in slow
surprise:

"Why, I remember you."

"Battling Bill," you stammered.

"Will Sidney," she said. "It's awfully nice to see you again."

"I'm surprised you knew me."

Seeming to have nothing to reply to this, she stood and
looked at you. You felt suddenly foolish and uncertain, at a loss
what to say, but a wild and profound excitement was racing
through you. You hesitated.

"Maybe we could meet some time and talk over old times," you said. "I have no card with me, but you can find me in the phone book. William B. Sidney."

"That would be nice," she agreed.

"And if I could have your address—"

She gave you her address and phone number and you planted them firmly in your mind. Then she said goodbye and was off, presumably to the ladies' room to find the lost handkerchief.

Throughout the last two acts and intermission you were fearful that she might say something to you there in the seats, forcing you to introduce her to Erma and dragging in the escort, who you supposed was Mr. Green. He was a stiff and thoughtful-looking person, wearing a neat business suit and a high starched collar, hard to place; you guessed him as being something queer, like a newspaper financial writer or an expert on garbage disposal. At all events, you acutely did not want Erma to know anything about it and were greatly relieved when the last curtain fell and you became aware that they were on their way up the aisle towards the exit.

That night you could not sleep. That was nothing unprecedented for you, but the wakefulness had a new character, not the familiar spasmodic jerks from strained artificial quiescence into irritated alertness, and back again, endlessly. No, you were completely and unprotestingly awake.

This chance encounter had brought to a focus all the stray implications of a question that you had dodged for years: what to do with the ghost of little Millicent which more and more dominated your most intimate and secret moments, which was gradually assuming so complete a control of your fancy that there threatened soon to be no reality left except the chair you sat on and the food you ate. It was a most capricious ghost, with a varied and checkered career extending over twenty years. At times long periods had elapsed without a single appearance; at others it was with you almost constantly, if not actively guiding or overpowering your thoughts, at least hovering dimly on the border of consciousness. It had been most assertive and insistent at such times as some source of active interest had been withdrawn from you, as for instance when Lucy went away, or when you lost the companionship of your sisters by Jane's marriage, or when you returned from Europe alone. You lay for hours, recalling and analyzing, objectively and dispassionately, these familiar phenomena.

At times you had hated it. You rejected it as infantile, shameful, unmanly, vile. You felt so but you never thought so, because on those occasions there was such a boiling turmoil of sensations within you, the blood rushed so hotly to your head and your fingertips, that thought was out of the question. If later you tried to think about it you found that with the sensation and the revulsion gone it was too unreal and remote to have any significance. Then it would return—but not necessarily the same. Sometimes it was as pleasant and inoffensive as picking roses in Erma's garden at Whitestone.

Now that you had seen her again, it struck you as amazing that not once in all the years had you thought of trying to find her. Not that you hadn't done it, but that it hadn't even occurred to you. You might easily have traced her. You might have found her five years ago, ten—

What for?

For life! For someone to care about, to quarrel with, to be jealous for, to be tender to—you could snap your fingers at Erma's catty contempt, you could smile at Dick's furious and dominating roar, Jane could bring up her brats and start a free love colony as far as you were concerned....

Bah, you thought, you were vastly exaggerating the importance of this. All men had their fantasies and their pet dreams;

the healthy and sensible thing to do was to take them as they came and let it go at that. As for Millicent, the woman, Mrs. Green, she was assuredly of no significance whatever. She had nothing to do with ghosts. You recalled how she had looked, standing before you in the theatre: her slim, slightly drooping figure in its plain dark dress, her dull light brown hair, combed carelessly with strands escaping here and there at the edges, her level slate-colored unblinking eyes, her pale unnoticeable face. You would have said that whatever passion her blood might have held had been washed out long ago. She was ten years younger than you; thirty now, then. She had a husband; children, probably. She had excited you all right, but that was just the stirring of a memory; you had been a fool not to swallow the impulse to speak to her. She might quite easily make herself a nuisance, writing and telephoning.

You finally got to sleep.

You arose late the next morning, not intending to go to the office, for Erma's departure-days were always crowded with last-minute errands and problems. This time she was bound for the Adirondacks, to spend the summer roughing it in a twenty-room cabin she had bought from the Hatton estate. John and his wife and two maids had gone up the preceding week; four or five other servants took the morning train; Erma was supposed to leave right after lunch in the new Lincoln, with Dorst driving. They finally got off about five, leaving you with a pocketful of memoranda about hats, rugs, dog-biscuit, tennis rackets.

You were expected to follow in a week or so, but you hadn't definitely committed yourself. You supposed you must go somewhere; no use hanging around New York in July and August. In the meantime you took a room at the club.

At the office, the following morning, you rather expected to find one of the pink slips on your desk: "Mrs. Green telephoned; no message." It wasn't there; nor the next day, nor the next. You remembered with amusement your experience with Mrs. Davis in Cleveland; well, at least Mrs. Green would never bring you a son nearly as old as yourself to send off to Europe to have a good time at your expense. Apparently she didn't intend to bring you anything; there was no word from her.

One morning, about a week after Erma's departure, you went from the club directly to Park Avenue and from the drawer of your desk got the leaf torn from the theatre program on which you had scribbled the address and phone number. You called the number at once, from the instrument in your room, and after a prolonged ringing her voice answered, sleepy and muffled.

"I'm sorry if I got you out of bed," you said.

"Yes," she replied, "I don't usually get up till noon."

Would she have dinner with you? Yes. This evening? Yes. Should you call for her at seven? Yes. You hung up, wondering if she had been too sleepy to know what she was saying. Habitually arising at noon didn't sound much like the mother of a family.

Although two or three of the cars, and Foster, had been left behind by Erma and were at your disposal, you thought it best to take a taxi; you decided not to dress, and were glad of it when you got to the dingy little room on Twenty-second Street and found her waiting for you in the same nondescript dress she had worn at the theatre. She had her hat on.

"I wish I'd asked you to make it half-past six," she said. "I only eat breakfast at noon, so I'm always pretty hungry around six o'clock."

It was hot, the first hot night of the summer, and you took her to the Castle, on Thirty-sixth Street, where you could sit by an open window. Your efforts at conversation, which became more desperate as the evening advanced, were fruitless and finally ridiculous. She seemed entirely devoid of opinions even regarding food, but was by no means indifferent to it. You were insufferably bored, and at length exasperated; it was impossible, you thought, that any human being out of the grave could be so utterly colorless and flat. Doubtless she had been the same as a child—the change was in you. You looked at her pale inscrutable face and tried to recall the eager restless hours when you used to await her knock at your door....

Dinner over, you suggested a show or a drive through the park and along the river. Here she had an opinion; she would love the drive. You found an open taxi and went back and forth in it for two hours, until you were dizzy, feeling almost as if you were entertaining a deaf and dumb schoolteacher aunt from the Middle West. When you finally returned to Twenty-second Street you left her at the outer door and sighed with relief that it was over.

And phoned her again within three days, god knows why. It is strange that you did it without feeling any hint of the old uneasy misgiving—naturally and almost gaily indeed, reflecting that you might as well be bored by that funny sphinx as by the blockheads at the club or yourself.

Those first few times with her you did succeed in dragging forth, gradually and bit by bit, many of the details of the twenty years since her mother had hauled her aboard that westbound train. Not that you were especially interested, but there seemed to be nothing else she could talk about at all. They had gone to Indianapolis, she said, where an uncle lived, and there Mrs. Moran had resumed the profession of washerwoman and continued at it for eight years, until Millicent graduated from high school. On the very day of high school commencement Mrs. Moran took to her bed, and died three weeks later, in the middle of the night, with her educated daughter holding her hand and staring at her with dry eyes.

"No, I didn't cry," said Millicent. "I never have cried but once."

She wouldn't say when that was.

She had gone to live with her uncle, and got a job filing papers in a law office. This was not to her liking (too dull, she said!) and she soon gave it up and through her uncle, a floorwalker, got a place at the stocking counter of a large department store. All this was merely preparation for her real career, which began when at the age of twenty-one, three years after her mother's death, she was offered a position at the cigarstand of a big hotel —as she said, the swellest hotel in Indianapolis. You have heard five or six versions of the genesis of that job; probably the one about the assistant hotel manager buying stockings for his wife is most nearly correct. For four years she stood there peddling cigars and cigarettes to the cosmopolitan world of Indianapolis notables, commercial travelers, visiting lecturers and barber-shop customers, until one day Clarence Green, covering Indiana and Illinois for the Rubbalite Company, a middle-aged widower, asked her to become his wife.

They were married at once, and when shortly afterwards he was transferred to eastern territory, came to New York and established themselves in a flat. Here the story became so vague as to be almost incoherent. It appeared that toward the end of the first New York summer she had returned from a week in the country with her friend Grace something or other to find the flat bare, stripped of everything except her personal belongings. At some stage or other there was a divorce and an award of alimony amounting to a hundred and fifty dollars a month.

"He's very prompt with it," she said. "It's never been more than four days behind time."

It appeared also that she had had several offers of marriage in the past three years, one from a very wealthy man who owned a house in the country, but she had decided that the alimony was enough to live on, and it was so nice not to have to

bother about anyone else. You were incredulous about the pro-
posals; she wouldn't tell you any names; she said she didn't want
to compromise anybody. You looked at her critically: why would
any man want to bathe in that stagnant pool?

You were in her room, late at night; you had dined at Arrow-
head Inn and afterwards sat out on the terrace to get the breeze
from the river, waiting till after midnight to return to the city's
hot walls and pavements. She was on the couch—which presumably served also as a bed—propped up against the wall with
the two skinny pillows behind her, and you sat in the rickety
wicker chair.

"I'll probably go up to the Adirondacks the end of the week,"
you said. "My wife is wondering why I stay down here in this
furnace. I haven't told her I met an old college friend."

"How long will you be gone?"

"The rest of the summer probably. I don't usually come back
until after Labor Day. Maybe even later."

"Your wife is very rich, isn't she?"

You nodded. "I'm worth a good deal more than I ever expected to be but I'm a pauper compared with her. When I
remember how I used to cut down on cigarettes so I could buy
candy for you—"

"I still like candy," she said.

"Then I'll have to bring you some, for old times' sake. A
bushel basketful, just to show off."

She was silent. You looked at her and saw that her motionless eyes were regarding you steadily, fixedly, so that you felt
uncomfortable and moved your own eyes aside. A thrill of
expectancy ran through you; you sat perfectly still for what
seemed a long time, glancing at her and away and back again.

"Come here," she said in a low dead voice, without moving;
not moving even her lips, it seemed.

You got up instantly, but without haste, and went and sat on the edge of the couch beside her.

At the first touch of her hand you felt yourself tremble all over; you caught your breath, and something within you struggled to retreat, to get you to your feet and away. But you were already overcome and helpless; indeed, as you see now, you had been at the first sound of her voice that evening in the theatre. It seems insane, and it's a puzzle beyond your unraveling. In all her gestures there is something terrifying and irresistible: the way her skinny calves press against your leg when she sits on your lap, the feel of her feet, neither warm nor cold, but overpowering, when they touch you, above all the thrill when she puts her hands on you. She must have known from the beginning that you were done for; why did she wait so long? She told you afterwards that she felt she must be fair to Mr. Gowan! At times it has almost seemed that she expects you to believe her obscene nonsense....

That first night you didn't stay long; you finally became aware that she was running her hand through your hair and was saying, "It's so late I guess you'd better go."

You felt embarrassed and didn't want to look at her face. Her hand was burning you, though its stroke was now steady and peaceful. You twisted around and got off the couch and onto your feet, glanced at your watch and looked around for your hat.

"You called me Mil," she said.

"Yes."

"When you go out downstairs don't bang the door."

"All right."

"I'll see you again, won't I?"

"Yes, of course. I'll telephone."

She remained on the couch as you let yourself softly out of the room.

You got a taxi on Seventh Avenue, but on arriving at the club didn't feel like going in, to bed. You walked the deserted streets, aimlessly, until the early summer dawn approached. You felt that something profound and inescapable was happening to you, and you could understand neither the thing itself nor the deep discomfort of your feeling about it. The sensation of guilt and uncleanliness was nothing new; that had often come with fantasy and even with Erma; but not as now with a dread and disgust that terrified you. Were you letting yourself in for something so ugly that for once you would not be able to argue yourself into forgiveness? You thought impatiently that such bunk was unjustified and unreasonable; after all a woman was a woman, and hands were hands, and it was damn funny if you were too fastidious to get your shoes soiled a bit.

Your thoughts stammered all around the question of what you were going to do. You would not stay here to lose your summer in taxicab trips to roadhouses ending in a series of adventures like this night. With a shudder you recalled the room: the creaky old wicker chair with jagged straw-ends sticking out of the arms, the cheap worn carpet, the couch-cover stiff with dirt, covered with spots, the ancient and tenacious remains of a crushed chocolate cream on one edge. Of course it wasn't entirely her fault, you can't live at the Sherry–Netherland on a hundred and fifty a month, but she might at least scrape off that chocolate.

You needed to be away for a while anyway. You rejected definitely the Adirondacks. Not only was Erma there, but there would certainly be a gang of the old familiars, and you were fed up with them. If you went to Jane's at the seashore—no, you might stand Victor in small doses, but not as a steady diet. You could go to Idaho—Larry had left two weeks previously, with

Dick's half-million in the corral and his plans of empire complete. You would be in the way, not at all welcome, and what would you do when you got there? All right, then go somewhere alone, anywhere out of this damn town, Quebec, Bar Harbor, Nantucket, take one of the cars and drive along the Maine coast. You were perfectly free to go where you would, you had plenty of money, you had good health and a sound intelligence—it was funny if you couldn't amuse yourself somehow.

Incredulously you became suddenly aware that along with this you were wondering if you could not safely go off with Millicent somewhere without risk of recognition....

It was after dawn when you finally went to your room, relaxed your body in a tub of hot water, ate a sandwich and some coffee, and got to bed just as the day's heat began to creep through the window and the city's clamor started its infernal crescendo.

The next day but one you telephoned. She was sorry, she couldn't see you that evening, she had an engagement. With Mr. Gowan? you asked idiotically. Oh no, she said, with another young man. Tomorrow evening, then. No, she was sorry, tomorrow evening Mr. Gowan was going to take her to a show. You observed that the hot spell was terrible, and she said she didn't mind it a bit.

"Maybe we could make it Friday," she said.

Friday evening it was raining and was much cooler, so you gave up your plan for a drive into the country and took her to a theatre instead. You had seen the play before and didn't care much for it, so you amused yourself by watching her out of the corner of your eye—her silent motionless absorption, her hands folded in her lap, so still that when they moved you almost jumped.

"I believe I could go to a show every night for a year including Sunday," she said after the first act.

"I wouldn't want to if they were no better than this one," you replied.

"I've seen it five times."

"What! Five times!"

"Yes. Not because it's so good, but in the summer time you run out when you go as often as I do."

You were astonished; later you learned that it was her one passion, that she would willingly see any play five times, or ten, anything from the Follies to Ibsen.

You went directly from the theatre to Twenty-second Street. You had decided not to go in, but you went. Entering, you decided you would stick to the wicker chair, but you didn't. At two in the morning you were still there, propped against one of the skinny pillows smoking a cigarette.

"I bought a car the other day," you said. "It will be delivered tomorrow morning. I thought it would be fun for us to drive out of town some of these hot nights."

She sat munching the Dutch chocolates you had brought, with the same old gestures, methodical as some automatic engine of destruction.

"It must have cost a lot of money," she observed. "I don't see why we couldn't use one of your wife's cars, if she has so many."

You explained again the risks which a man of your prominence must avoid.

"I couldn't stay away all night," she declared. "If I did and Mr. Green found out about it…"

You were glad that her concern for her alimony imposed caution upon her too, but you wished she'd stop calling her husband Mr. Green.

"No, we couldn't do that," you agreed, "I meant to drive out in the country for dinner, maybe sometimes have a picnic lunch in the woods somewhere."

Her hand stroked your knee and her eyes closed slightly, as they had a little before, as they have a thousand times since.

"It would be nice to be in the woods with you," she said. "Last summer I used to go with Mr. Gowan out on Long Island. And Mr. Peft had a boat in the Hudson River—that was two years ago."

"You know a lot of men, don't you?"

She chuckled—a low faint rattle that left her shoulder, resting against you, perfectly motionless.

"Wouldn't you like to know though," she said.

"What does Mr. Gowan do?"

You were learning that she had three separate methods of replying to a straight question like that, each sharply distinct from the others, as though she had made formulas of them. This time she chose to be direct.

"He runs taxicabs. He doesn't run them himself—he owns thirty-seven of them—the brown ones with a little bird on the door."

"That's funny."

"Why?"

"Oh nothing, only he didn't look to me like a man who would run a fleet of taxicabs."

"How do you know what he looks like, you've never seen him."

"Sure I have, that night at the theatre."

She turned her head; you felt her chin rubbing against your hair; then she bent down and softly bit your ear.

"That wasn't him," she said.

"You told me it was."

"Well, you shouldn't have asked."

"Who was it then?"

She chuckled again. "It was Mr. Green."

Her husband! Hell, of course not. You gave up, exasperated at her petty infantile obscurantism. Feeling your irritation perhaps, her hand crept up and gently stroked your arm. At first you wanted to move away from it or push it off, but soon your blood quickened...you became quite still....

"Not any more," you said, almost pleading, and put your hand up and covered hers with it.

"It's very late," she sighed.

It was a week or so later, after you had been out several times in the roadster, that you found courage to speak to her about her clothes. You weren't sure how she would take it, and you didn't know what you might be letting yourself in for. But the endless alternation of those two cheap dresses, the dingy brown and the awful polka-dot, was too much for you. And good lord, such hats. You had a high opinion of your own taste—not only was it naturally good, but it had been excellently trained by ten years of Erma. Of course, you thought, there's no occasion to get extravagant about it.

"I've never paid much attention to clothes," she said indifferently. "Even if I had money, it's so much trouble."

You had considered a couple of dresses and hats, but found that one thing led surprisingly to another. Once started, she became almost enthusiastic, particularly about shoes; but even with shoes she never said, yes, I want that. She would admit preferences, always a little grudgingly, but it was left to you to make the definite decision. You wondered how she ever got things bought alone.

The new things were an improvement, but they looked funny on her. Her skin was absolutely without color, the same dead grey all over her face, without any shade of difference between her cheeks and her chin or her ears and her forehead, and she never uses any rouge or lipstick though she constantly

dabs herself with powder that has a strange tint of brown in it.
She must get it in Harlem—only as far as you know she's never
been there. Her face hadn't been so noticeable with those drab
old dresses, but when she put on something with life and color
in it, it was almost startling to look at her.

When you gave her the money to buy some things herself,
underwear and nightgowns, she carefully gave you the exact
change the next day, with the cash slips and price tickets in a
neat pile, added up. She's always been straight about money,
presumably because she doesn't care much about it. You might
have known better when she handed you that bunk about Dick,
though of course that's not the same thing. Nor the alimony
either; there's no finding out anything she wants to hide; you
don't know to this day whether she actually did get alimony
from her husband, nor for that matter whether she was ever
married. Your first suspicion of that came the day up at
Briarcliff when you proposed a trip somewhere, and suggested
central Pennsylvania as a locality where you would run slight
risk of meeting anyone who knew you. When you asked her
about that she seemed not at all concerned.

"But not so long ago you were afraid to stay out overnight,"
you reminded her.

"Yes. Well…it doesn't matter."

"We can stay a week, or two, or a month, just as we like.
What do you say?"

"I think it would be very nice."

All right; that was settled. From the eminence of the Lodge
you looked out across the expanse of woods and meadows to
where a strip of the Hudson was flashing in the distant sunshine, and wondered why the devil you were doing this.

You have continued to wonder to this minute. There's something in it that pushes you along always a little ahead of yourself,

so that you never quite catch up. Like suggesting that trip. Admitting that there's something in it you can't resist, that's no reason for entirely losing your senses. Why couldn't you use her and buy things for her and get some pleasure out of it—no, you had to wallow, you had to try to squirm out of it somehow, you were afraid to be away from her, you must eat with her and sleep with her so that there wouldn't be a single moment she wouldn't be gnawing away at you like a rat.

Already, many a night in that little hotel in the Pennsylvania mountains, as she lay beside you, you felt that if she touched you again it would be unbearable. Once you said:

"For god's sake, Mil—"

She paid no attention to you.

# M

Another step or two and his eyes would be on a level with the floor above, and he would be able to see the light in the crack under the door.

He removed his right hand from the rail and thrust it into his overcoat pocket where it closed once more around the butt of the revolver. His other hand, holding the key, rested against the wall; and as he moved up another step and the hand came suddenly into contact with a nail that had been driven into the plaster he jerked it away nervously, and dropped the key, which fell to the edge of the wooden step.

He glanced upwards quickly—had she heard it—of course not—and then stooped and picked up the key, gleaming dully in the dim light.

The voice from the room was no longer heard, but his head seemed more than ever full of voices, a monstrous medley that pounded at his temples…it's you who are the rat…for god's sake, Mil…timid, vengeless, actionless….

# XIII

You're no good. You're no good anymore for anything. That's what you told yourself the afternoon you left the office and went to Eighty-fifth Street, the day she moved here. You're in for it now, you thought, you've let this thing ride you into a hole there's no getting out of.

She was there, moving chairs around and arranging rugs, with a silent concentration that made you laugh in spite of yourself. She changed them back and forth with an intense seriousness that was new to you, while you sat on the divan against the wall, smoking cigarettes and pretending to join in her earnestness. Later you understood that with her when a thing was once placed it was there to stay. Like the red rug she put just inside the entrance; it was so thick that every time the door opened it turned up the corner or got stuck, but when one day in exasperation you kicked it into the middle of the room you found it back in its old place the next evening, and you had to change it to the bedroom yourself.

When she agreed, on your return from the Pennsylvania trip, to leave Twenty-second Street and take a place with you as Mr. and Mrs. Lewis, she wanted it to be a furnished flat. It would cost too much, she said, to buy furniture, and would be too much bother. You were thinking to yourself that you weren't really doing it for her at all, that never in your life had you had a place that was really yours, with your own things, never once had you sat in a chair that belonged to you. In any event, no matter what happened, it would be nice to have the rooms and furniture. You were pleasantly thrilled, that first time you came up

these stairs and opened the door with your key. In a plain clean
gingham dress Millicent looked quite domestic, normal, just a
woman like any other woman, rather homely to be sure. Those
were your rugs she was dragging around, those new fat clean
cushions were yours, there was the upholstered leather chair
you had brought especially for yourself.

You went through the little center passage, with the bathroom on the left, to the rear room. The beds had already been
put up, one against either wall. You probably wouldn't be able
to sleep here very often, but there was your own bed, with its
thick new mattress and bulging pillow of down. Millicent
hadn't understood why you insisted on two beds; she said she
always slept so well that you could toss around all night as far as
she was concerned. You went over and felt of the blankets and
comforter. Then you went to the hall and got the bag you had
brought, filled with additional purchases, and unpacked it,
putting each article away in a considered spot—toothbrush,
hairbrush, scissors, slippers, comb, a carton of cigarettes, ben-
zine for your cigarette lighter.

"You got too many towels," said Millicent from the door.

Under her silent indifference she was interested in all the
pretty new things, more than she had been in her clothes. She
helped you make up a list of items that had been overlooked:
ashtrays, waste baskets, clothes hangers. She arranged the shades
on the wall lights, carefully placed the two bronze vases on the
table in front, and finally squatted on the floor and began putting
away the books in the shelves in the corner. You knelt to help
her. They were books she had brought from downtown, popular
novels and detective stories.

"It's going to be nice here," she said.

You nodded. "Aren't you glad we went ahead and bought our
own furniture?"

"Yes, it wasn't as much trouble as I thought it would be. It must have cost a lot of money."

That was in September—a year ago September. It seems like a hundred. And yet in a way not a single thing has happened since then. It was already all over. What have you learned that you didn't already know? Pathetically you knelt there and handed her the books, one by one, with your guts full of hate, knowing that whenever she wanted to she could do you in again, make you against your will lean back and close your eyes and feel that terrible tight strangling come in your throat....

It isn't in her at all—but it must be, or you're crazy. Mrs. Jordan apparently thinks she's just a stupid little woman without enough respect for herself to keep her clothes clean, judging from what she said to Grace one day. Grace likes her, likes to be with her or she wouldn't come around here so often. There's nothing queer in it, Grace is all right, just an ordinary good-looking girl like any of the girls you see anywhere.

"You're too darned lazy to live," she said to Millicent one evening, "but I love you just the same."

It sounded grotesque to hear that word love used to her. Even as a joke, and probably Grace meant it. I love you. For that matter who is there you could say it to? Imagine Erma, your dear wife! I love you. My god! Of course that was one woman to another woman. Try it on a man. Dick or Larry or Schwartz or Victor—Victor would be perfect. I love you, you damn lousy pig....

Jane talked as if she knew something, last summer when you came back from Maine, and again the other day. That telephone number...Millicent acted queer too, about the same time. So for that matter did all of them. They might as well mind their own business—what do they think you are, an imbecile that has to have his shirt buttoned for him? Jane does, you might as well admit it, she thinks just that. She thinks you ought to find an interest in life! She's dumb and futile as the rest— wanted you to go with her and her menagerie down to Nassau and lie around in a bathing suit and build forts in the sand. Thanks, you should have said, I've got an interest in life, I've got a pretty mistress in a pretty little flat, with a bowl of flowers on a stand and William the Conqueror on a table....

That was funny, the only really funny thing that Millicent ever did. You thought you were being ironic when you brought the thing here, and she went you one better. It was only a few days after you moved in that she said there ought to be more vases and things. In fact you hadn't bought any bric-a-brac at all except the two bronze bowls. The next afternoon you went to a department store and got some candlesticks, and some more vases, and two or three little bronze figures. She tried them here and there and finally got them arranged to her satisfaction, while you sat with an unread evening paper on your lap, grinning inwardly at what Erma would have thought of this display of art objects.

"It's very nice," said Millicent finally, standing in front of you and looking around to view the effect, "but there ought to be something big for the table. A big statue or something. I saw one over on Broadway yesterday of some girls, with some bunches of grapes, that was only seven dollars."

"Ha, a statue!" you exclaimed.

"Yes, for the table."

"I know the very thing. Beautiful white marble, and just the right size. I'll get it tomorrow."

The next day you went to Park Avenue, wrapped a piece of paper around the head, and carried it to a taxi. You were afraid you might have to get someone to help you, but were able to manage it all right when you once got it on your shoulder. Half an hour later, panting after the two flights of stairs, you let it down in the middle of the table, removed the paper and invited Millicent to admire.

"It's very modern, a fine piece of work," you said. "Its name is William the Conqueror."

She stood and looked at it solemnly, and then went up to it and rubbed her hand over the roughness of the column and the white smoothness of the cheek, and brow. You felt the hand as intensely as if it had been on your own skin, and with an effort you controlled an impulse to pull it violently away—to seize her wrist in both hands and twist it till it snapped.

"It looks like you." She chuckled. "I think it looks exactly like you." She turned and looked at you appraisingly. "If you were really like that," she said, "you wouldn't be afraid of me."

Startled and astonished, you exclaimed, "Good lord, I'm not afraid of you!"

"Oh yes you are. You think I'm wicked. All men do, just because I'm not ashamed of anything. That's why they don't mind if I'm not pretty."

"Who told you that? Somebody told you that."

She dismissed the question with a shake of her head, and put her hand again on the marble, caressingly. "It's very nice the way it comes out of that rock," she said.

She had taken all the flavor out of your irony, and you wished you had left it at home in its corner.

The next evening you came in and up the stairs, and let yourself into the front room, and at the first glance around you sat down on the nearest chair, with your hat and coat still on, stared incredulously, and roared with laughter. How you laughed! Millicent sat in the blue chair, reading, and on the table beside her stood William the Conqueror with a string of little yellow chrysanthemums around his neck!

"No, it's too damn good!" you choked. "My god it isn't possible! Erma darling come and look at it!"

Millicent, unmoved and unsmiling, merely said:

"I don't think it's so funny. I think they look nice there."

You spluttered into another roar. Then suddenly you became calm. "Look here," you said, "just as a matter of curiosity, exactly why did you do that?"

She had closed the book in her lap and sat quietly regarding you with her unwavering gaze.

"I don't know what you mean. I just did it."

"You did it to make fun of me, didn't you? I ask in the interest of science. Don't mind my feelings."

"Why should I make fun of you? I don't think you're funny."

"Come, you're not so stupid," you insisted, "what were you thinking when you hung that thing there?"

A chuckle came from her throat. "I was thinking that if I hadn't spent a dollar for those flowers, I'd have twenty dollars left out of the money you gave me this week."

You looked at her suspiciously and helplessly; the laughter was gone. But you felt no resentment, it was too vastly comic, even considered as a mere coincidence: and you doubted, and still doubt, if that was the truth of it. Who could be more unlike than the brilliant cynical articulate Erma and this little dumb drab insect? Yet observe the parallel! What hidden centuries of preparation led up to that identical gesture? A part of you, the part that was still able feebly to pretend that it was looking across the footlights, would have liked to tell Erma about it, would have enjoyed her exclamation of delight at this perfect confirmation of her malice.

The temptation arrived, for it was only a few days later that she returned from the mountains, in an unusually good humor and loaded with scandal. That first dinner in the apartment

with her, alone together in the luxurious and spacious surroundings—your first dinner away from Millicent in two
months—gave you an immense feeling of relief and gratitude,
an assurance of solidity and security which you felt you owed to
her. You felt that for all her egotism and her silky brutality she
was the best friend you had, and that she was strong and confident and wise; you wanted to tell her about Millicent, you
wanted to say to her:

"I'm tied somehow, I don't know how, to an ugly and ignorant little bitch whom I despise. She is dull, unhealthy, perverted, false (that would be good, Erma would smile at that),
but the intimate touch of her hands has stayed with me twenty
years in my dreams and now I'm a hopeless slave to it. For god's
sake tell me what to do."

Erma would have said, put a pillow on her face and sit on it
while you count ten thousand. At that she might have pulled
you out of it, just for the fun of showing what she could do.
What could she have done? What could anybody do except
choke her, or smother her, or shoot her? You've tried hard
enough. What could anybody do?

Erma couldn't understand why you hadn't gone to the Adirondacks, why you'd gone off alone somewhere in Pennsylvania
and hadn't even taken one of the cars. She said you looked
yellow, bad around the eyes, worse than she'd ever seen you.
What was the matter? You grinned it off and declared it to be a
combination of hard work and longing for her; and after dinner
went to your room and examined yourself carefully in the mirror.
You found yourself evading the reflection of your own eyes and
forced your gaze into them. What was back of those brown and
white balls, you demanded. What uneasy secret things were
happening back there? What rust or decay was eating into that
intricate mechanism and turning its order into chaos? Great

god, what was happening to you? Steadily you gazed, and your eyes looking back at you seemed suddenly friendly and unafraid —but there was something back of them, something that made you almost visibly shudder.—Erma was right, you looked yellow; you were in fact a fairly attractive man, but you wouldn't be very long if this kept up.

Now that Erma was returning, as you had explained to Millicent, the daily arrangement of your movements presented a little difficulty. You had always kept yourself pretty well at Erma's disposal, when she was in town, for bridge, dinners, theatre, opera, concerts, dances. Of course there had been frequent and extended periods when you were, so to speak, on vacation, but their nature made it impractical for you to expect the convenience of a notice in advance. You had a telephone installed at Eighty-fifth Street and told Millicent that whenever possible you would let her know during the afternoon whether you would be able to come for dinner— not that it mattered particularly, since you always went to a restaurant.

You had never before realized, finding time heavy on your hands, how well-filled it actually was. As the autumn weeks rolled by and the first snow came, you thought sometimes that it was coming out all right after all, that being with her continuously for two months had tied you up in a knot which was now being unraveled by the resumption of a normal routine; but then you would find yourself thinking of her, specifically, when dancing with someone at a party, or in the middle of a play, or at Jane's house with the children playing and shouting around you. You couldn't get her away from your mind. It was all in you; she didn't bother you, not her. You would telephone her from the booth in the cigar store on Broadway, not wanting to call from home or the office:

"I'm sorry, Mil, I can't make it today or tomorrow, or Thursday either. I'm pretty sure I can Friday."

"All right," her voice would come.

"Won't you miss me?" You would despise yourself for each word as you uttered it.

"Of course I will, but Grace will go to some shows with me. You might send up some more books."

Before returning to the office you would go across the street to Donaldson's and order a dozen novels sent, any novels. Once, when they put in *Lord Jim* she even read that, though you wouldn't believe it until she proved it by answering questions.

You went through the books once, looking for something to read—when was it? That weekend she went somewhere with Grace. They left Friday afternoon. You and Erma had been asked out to Shotwell's, but you begged off so you could be here alone. It was early in December, not quite a year ago. That was fun, the only real pleasure you've ever had here. Curious how still and empty it seemed with Millicent away. Friday, Saturday, Sunday, she'll be gone three whole nights, you said to yourself; and you picked up her things that were lying about and put them out of sight in the closet; you even put her hats up on the top shelf. This is my place, you thought, this is mine, as you rearranged things in the bathroom and put a new bulb in the light in the hall and took the silk coverlet off your bed and carefully folded it.

Seated in the leather chair, under the reading lamp, with a novel in your lap, you felt away from the world, peaceful, almost happy. This place would be wonderful, you reflected, if it weren't for her. To be alone here like this, in your own place, with no one in the world knowing where you were! Why didn't you think of it before—you could have done it years ago. She'll be back Monday. What if she never comes back? It was a thrilling thought; it made you stop breathing for a moment. What if she died, got killed in an accident, for instance? God that would be wonderful—absolutely dead and done for. Your name needn't appear, Grace would take care of things. Did Grace know your real name? Mil swore she didn't. You believed it on account of the way Grace acted; nothing you could put your hand on, she just acted as if she wondered who you really were. You could give her all of Millicent's things, the whole works, and give her plenty of money for the funeral expenses…get hit by a car maybe, or just simply get pneumonia or something and die….

You rubbed your hand across your forehead and reached to the table to push the lamp back a little; there was a flash of white marble in your eyes. You turned and looked at it, studied it, and spoke to it aloud:

"No such luck, eh, old man? You wouldn't wait for luck, would you? No, you're a regular hell-raiser, you wouldn't wait for anything; you wouldn't even bother to shoot her or stick a knife in her, just snap your fingers and bingo, she wouldn't exist. Do you know what you are? You're my son Paul's little joke on his father, only he doesn't know it's his father and that's a joke on him. You're a cock-walloper, you are. You look like a goddam turkey gobbler."

Later, much later, you fell asleep in your chair, trying to read.

The week preceding Christmas was filled with duties which couldn't very well be avoided. Erma had a lot of new people on the string, and it seemed to you that she was becoming increasingly insistent on your presence and assistance, though that was probably imagination. Certainly she was becoming curious about your sudden tendency to find excuses to be away; it amused her, and she didn't think it worthwhile to resent it, but she was curious.

"Just when I begin to think you are at last explored you take on a new mystery," she said. "You never objected to the Hallermans before. You always were able to tolerate bridge at least twice a week. You are developing a positive distaste for the theatre. You never before refused a weekend at Holcombe. Have you found a pretty mistress or are you learning to swim?"

"I already know how to swim," you laughed.

"By Saint Mary I'll bet it's true!" she exclaimed. "And you took her to Pennsylvania and went berry-picking with her, and by now the only question is whether it will be a boy or a girl. Bravo!"

She came over to you, smiling at you.

"Please have it a girl, and call it Erma, and I'll be godmother and give her a million dollars," she said. "Seriously, Bill, I think it might buck you up to be a father; though," she added, "I must say that the prospect doesn't seem to be helping you any—you look more done in than ever. What's the matter?"

You shrugged your shoulders. "I'm worrying for fear it will be twins."

"Then you aren't going to tell me?"

"There's nothing to tell."

"All right. But you aren't very amusing lately, you know. It rather frightens me for my old age. I had pictured us sitting on our piazza in the sunshine of the Midi, side by side, being wittily reminiscent."

You went off to the subway, bound for the office; but on arriving downtown you went first to the cigar store and telephoned Millicent. She answered in a sleepy voice; you had got her out of bed, as usual when you phoned in the morning.

"I'm sorry," you said, "but I can't make it today or tomorrow. And Wednesday there's an all-night party at home, and Christmas Day we're going out to Dick's place on Long Island."

"All right," came her drowsy voice.

"I'm sorry about Christmas—I don't know what you'll do, all alone—"

"Oh it will be all right. Perhaps Grace and I will do something."

At the office, where there was never much of anything for you to do anyway, you sat at your desk and looked out of the window at the grey sky. Was Erma going to get difficult? Not in any conventional sense, of course, but she had never yet had a strong curiosity about anything without satisfying it. That would be all, but it was too much. You couldn't bear the thought of her seeing Millicent, as she would somehow manage to do if her curiosity got strong enough; it was intolerable that she should see her, perhaps even talk to her. What might not Erma guess? Things that you yourself did not know, dim and inadmissible things which, if they existed at all, might as well remain sealed, since it would do no good to uncover them. You must be more careful, you must dissimulate more cleverly; or perhaps you could invent some tale that would satisfy her and leave her to poke her nose in some other hole where it didn't belong....

Christmas morning, not having got to bed till after five, you turned out sleepily at eleven in response to the summons you had told Allen to give you, and hurriedly bathed and dressed and had orange juice and coffee. You were not expected at Dick's until three and could drive it easily in two hours. Leaving a message for Erma that you would be back in time to leave at one o'clock, you left the house and took a taxi to Eighty-fifth Street. You hadn't seen Millicent for three days. You might be an ass, you reflected, but this was Christmas Day and she was all alone and it wouldn't hurt you any to take the trouble to drop in for a minute and give her a little present and say Merry Christmas. "Whatever else she may be," you said to yourself aloud, "she's probably human." The present was in a large package beside you on the seat; you had been glad to get it out of the house, for Erma had unfortunately seen you bring it home the preceding afternoon; you had evaded her curiosity, which would have been considerably increased had she known that it contained a woman's fur coat.

You had seen them so rarely in the daytime that the street and house seemed unfamiliar. Asking the taxi-driver to wait, for you expected to stay only a few minutes, and taking the bulky package under your arm, you ran up the stoop and up the two flights of stairs and let yourself in. The room was empty; you glanced around, called, "Hello, Merry Christmas!" and, leaving the package on a chair, started for the passage leading to the rear room. You heard nothing, but all at once there she was, in her nightgown and bare feet, confronting you at the entrance to the passage.

"Merry Christmas," she said, smiling. It was the smile that betrayed her; you had never seen her try so hard to smile; it made you alert and woke you up. You continued straight ahead, as if to go with her or past her to the bedroom.

"Don't go in there," she said calmly, putting out her hand.

You stopped and looked at her.

"Grace is still in bed," she said.

You grasped her by the arm and brushed past her, took two steps down the passage. From there you could see that there certainly was someone in your bed, against the right wall, hidden under the covers; you could see nothing but the long irregular hump. But a shifting of your glance showed you, on the floor at the bed's foot, a pair of shoes that were assuredly not Grace's; and, thrown across the chair by the dressing-table, a shirt and a pair of trousers. You took another step forward, then wheeled sharply and returned to the front room and sat

down on the edge of a chair, feeling as if you were going to
vomit, as if all your insides wanted to leave you; you swallowed,
hard, several times. You were aware that she was standing in
front of you, towards the passage; you didn't look at her.

"If you had telephoned—" she began in a slow and quiet
voice.

"Shut up!" you said. You were feeling nothing whatever about
her; your sick rage was for your place, your bed. The temple,
not the priestess, was violated. Ha, the priestess!

You stood up and looked around the room; it nauseated you
and you felt weak on your legs. The package on the chair caught
your eye and you nodded toward it.

"That's a fur coat," you said, "you're welcome to it. You're
welcome to everything. I hope I see hell before I see this place
again."

You looked straight at her; her slate-colored unblinking eyes
returned your gaze calmly.

"You should have telephoned," she said. "I never promised
you anything. You know very well—"

You had crossed and opened the door, and without replying
you went out and closed it behind you; and down the stairs.
These stairs. The taxi was at the curb. You glanced at your
watch and saw that it was only a little after twelve. "Go around
the park," you said, and got in.

In the front of your mind was a memory apparently irrele-
vant: the picture of yourself, the night Lucy went away, sitting
on the culvert in the rain, sobbing, the tears streaming down
your face. Why should you think of that? Because you wanted
to cry now? Not likely. You were much more apt to laugh; and
tried it, but managed only a croak. Why should you think of that
night? For one thing it was an insult to the memory of Lucy—it
would be an insult to any woman.

There he was, no matter who, on your mattress, under your blankets, his head on your pillow. His shoes on your rug, the rug you had carefully selected because you liked to have something soft and thick to step out of bed onto. You felt hot within, ready to burst, with helpless rage; no one had a right to do such a thing, it was inhuman. "The bastard, the bastard," you said aloud.

In the midst of your anger you felt a swift sudden sense of relief: you were free of her! With a flash of joy you became aware that your anger was against him, against the grossness and impudence of his intrusion; there was no anger for her. As the significance of that struck you the turmoil died away and your whole body became perfectly still, there in the jolting taxicab, still within and without, it seemed almost that your heart stopped beating; and gingerly and with care, so as not to disturb that peace, you began to inspect it. Could it possibly be true? Why was your rage not directed against her? You deliberately created pictures in your mind of those two—but at that you trembled, that was dangerous; after all it was there that you pictured them. Certainly you would never go back there, you would never see that place again. Nor her. Nor her. What amazed you was that you weren't merely saying it to yourself, you meant it and believed it, for the first awareness of it came up out of your heart. You felt a great freedom and cleanliness within you—you wanted to laugh aloud—the idiotic spell was broken!

You had some clothes and things there. Well, she could send them to you or sell them or give them to him, any him. Of course that wasn't the first time your new thick mattress had entertained a guest; you had been an ass not to know it. Mr. Gowan and Mr. Peft and the lord knows how many others. You had in fact known it, in a way. No, not that; not that they had been there in your house. Other places—hotel rooms, perhaps. You realized with amazement that all the time, from the very first, there had been in the bottom of your mind a certain conviction that she was continuing her relations with other men, and that you had felt neither jealousy nor resentment—had, in point of fact, simply not bothered about it. What kind of a fish were you, anyway? It had become second nature, perhaps, after ten years of Erma. The best possible training for a complacent husband. Oh blah. You'd never cared for Erma, what did it matter to you? Nor for Millicent either. Lord what a gorgeous name for her—Millicent! You'd never thought of it before. Millicent, Lady Pembroke or something, by Sir Joshua Reynolds.

You got back to Park Avenue before one, and drank a cup of coffee with Erma before starting for Long Island.

That was a merry Christmas Day. First a little taxicab ride to give Millicent her fur coat. Then in the car all the way out to Dick's, Erma gave you the devil because you'd been discourteous to that fat German when he came in the library the evening before. How could you know who he was? She didn't care anyway; she was having one of her bad days and took it out on you, as usual.

After you got there it was all right. No one was missing but Larry and Rose. Even Margaret came, with her great scientist —not a bad guy at all. At the table you sat between Jane and Mary Alaire Carew Bellowes Carr, with Jane on your right; and when she thanked you for the things you'd sent the children and patted your hand and smiled at you, you thought, good old Jane, and your throat was so full you couldn't speak. But you wanted to; you wanted to tell her of the blessed relief that had come to you; you would have liked to say to her:

"I'm happy, and clean, and free!" And then that she might not think it too important, you would grin and repeat the old Christmas morning jest of long years ago:

"Give me a cookie!"

# N

*In his overcoat pocket the fingers of his right hand, closed tight around the butt of the revolver, released their hold and tried to straighten themselves out, stretching within the confines of the pocket, then clutched the butt again, tight, tighter. Again the fingers opened, and they felt moist and sticky; he took his hand out and rubbed the palm up and down on his overcoat, several times, then brought it close to his eyes and looked at it; it seemed very white, and the fingers very short, in the dim light. He thrust it back in his pocket, and it stayed there beside the revolver, touching it, without taking hold of it.*

*You're afraid, that's what's the matter, he told himself, timid vengeless hell, you're just plain scared....*

# XIV

And not only because you're standing here on the stairs with a gun in your pocket, either. You're always afraid when it comes to doing something. You're even afraid of words if they're the kind that make things happen. Bloodless rhetoric. Bunk. "I hope I see hell before I see this place again." Surely you didn't think it up all alone? "You tell your boyfriend to get dressed, and you get dressed, and both of you be out of here in five minutes, and stay out." That sounds just like you; probably you said it and she didn't hear you.

That was good wine Dick had; better than the stuff Erma gets. Mary got drunk and silly, and when Dick told her she looked like a Salvation Army exhibit, it made her so mad she got sober again. Probably that Christmas Day was the first time they'd spoken for a month. You got a little bit lit yourself, just enough to dance well. You were really damn near pickled; when Margaret was teaching you a new step she'd picked up in Harlem, you slipped and would have fallen flat if the table hadn't been there. Jane said:

"What's the matter, Bill, I never saw you so gay; have you suddenly got a crush on the winter solstice?"

"No, this is my rebirthday," you laughed, and kissed her. Then you felt you had to kiss the others too, and Mary the little bitch took it standing up. Dick noticed her and gave her a laugh and she was so mad she could have killed him.

Margaret and her genius came back to town with you. He's all right, only it's hard to understand what he says on account of his accent. Late at night, long after midnight, you dropped them at Eleventh Street. On the way uptown Erma said:

"It must have been triplets."

"What?"

"I say, such exuberance couldn't be for anything less than triplets. How did the sexes come out?"

"All modern conveniences. One and a half of each." She laughed, but she was piqued and got nasty again. Good heavens, couldn't she see that it was nothing to make conversation about? She's never been stupid except about this—it's her confounded curiosity. She'd cut you open to get it out if she thought it would be legible.

You slept that night, what there was left of it, like a top. The next day at the office there was no word from her; you thought there might not ever be any; you hoped not. You were worried about your clothes and things; you didn't want her to have any excuse. Seriously now, after twenty-four hours and a night's sleep, it appeared definitely done, and you considered calmly the small practical problems that remained; particularly you were uneasy of the suspense in the mere negative role of silence; she should be told, yes, it's done for good. You didn't want to write her—on the typewriter, unsigned? No, she'd answer it. The obvious way was the telephone. It could be done in three curt final sentences. You went out and down the elevator, and across the street to the booth in the cigar store. But you didn't call the number; you couldn't. At the thought of hearing her voice in the receiver you felt weak; there was a revulsion in your stomach. Simply you didn't want ever to hear that voice again, and you wouldn't; you returned to the office and walked back and forth from the desk to the door, and stood by the window looking down at the pygmies in the chasm below, and evolved a plan.

A little after five you left the office and took a taxi straight to Eighty-fifth Street; held up more than you expected by the traffic, you didn't get there till a quarter to six and were afraid you might arrive too late to see her go out, but to your relief there was a light in the front windows. You had the taxi stop almost directly across the street, and sat there in its corner, in the dark. Only a few minutes had passed when the light in the windows was extinguished, and a few moments later the street door opened and she came out and down the stoop, alone, and started west toward Broadway. She looked droopy, you thought, untidy; it irritated you to see how she walked in little jerks. Oh well, you wouldn't have to look at it any more. As soon as she was out of sight you rapidly crossed the street and ran up the stoop and the stairs and let yourself in. You called out, "Hello, anybody here?" and went to the bedroom. The beds were neatly made; you approached yours and pulled the blankets and coverlet back and saw that the sheets and pillowslip were clean and fresh; and from under the pillow peeped the edge of your folded pajamas.

"The hell you say!" you remarked aloud.

To save time, so as to get in and out as quickly as possible, you had written the note at the office on the typewriter: *I'm taking everything I want. The enclosed five hundred is my going away present. I don't want to hear from you. Goodbye.* You glanced in the envelope to make sure the bills were there, then slipped it under her pillow. On the floor you spread the newspaper you had brought along, and hurriedly made a bundle of the few articles you decided to take: silk dressing-gown, slippers, comb and brush, some shirts and neckties, a little bronze vase that you liked. Then you went to the front room and looked around, and returned to the bedroom, grinning, took the envelope from under the pillow and added a postscript to the note: *You can have William the Conqueror. Let him sleep in the guest bed when there's room.* You put on your hat and coat and gathered the bundle under your arm. From the open door you looked back, thinking, this is the last time—oh hell; and a minute later you were down the stairs and in the cab on your way to Park Avenue.

"That's that," you said aloud, and repeated it, "That's that."

It annoyed you to find that you were tense and trembling. You wished the cab would go faster. When you got home you took the bundle to your room and dumped it in a closet, and mixed and drank three cocktails while you were dressing for dinner.

The first phone call was the next afternoon.

"Mrs. Lewis on the telephone."

"Mrs.— Tell her I'm not in. Gone for the day."

"Yes, sir."

Mrs. Lewis! Why the devil couldn't she say Mrs. Green? That was her name. So she was going to try it, was she?

The following morning she phoned twice; and when a third call came shortly after lunch you decided it wouldn't do; you took the call.

"Well."

"Oh—is it you, Will?"

"Yes. What do you want?"

"I don't think it's very nice of you—"

"What do you want?"

"Why I just want to know if you're coming tonight—"

"Forget it. And cut out the telephoning."

"But I have to telephone if you—"

You took the receiver from your ear and with her voice still faintly buzzing in it slowly hung it on the hook. After a minute or two you removed it again and spoke to Mrs. Carroll:

"Please tell the operators that if that Mrs. Lewis calls me again I'm not in. Or a Mrs. Green—Green. At any time. And don't bother to send me a slip on it."

Surely that was final enough, you thought. That was the way to do it. Erma would say, you should fold your arms and look masterful. All right, that wouldn't hurt either. You didn't give a damn about the gestures, the point was that for once in your life you were going to sit tight; if you'd kept that up much longer you'd have ended in a madhouse.

You half expected a letter from her, but three or four days passed without a sign. Not a sign, nothing. You were restless and uneasy and assured yourself that it was on account of the uncertainty as to what she might do. There were a dozen ways she could make a nuisance of herself, and she'd try all of them if she thought it worthwhile. She might begin telephoning Park Avenue, she might even go there, and what if Erma happened to see her and get started on her? What a morsel for her! Each evening when you went home you half expected Erma to greet you with that terrible little smile:

"The mother of the triplets was here today."

But there was no sign. Irritated to find your uneasiness and restlessness increasing, you got into a state of nerves that became almost unbearable. You jumped when the phone rang; you could scarcely dictate a letter without flying out at Miss Malloy, unreasonably—then you would apologize and dismiss her, turn the letters over to Lawson and sit there at your desk looking out of the window.

One afternoon just after you had returned from lunch you stood at your window looking down into Broadway three hundred feet below, and found yourself thinking, "If I opened this window and let myself drop over the sill, I'd hit the pavement in two or three seconds. Maybe only one second. I'd never know what hit me. If I fell on anyone on the sidewalk, it would kill them too. Not long ago a man jumped out of a twelfth story window on Thirty-ninth Street and went right through the top of a sedan."

You turned away abruptly and summoned Miss Malloy to tell her you were leaving for the day. Obviously you had better talk to someone and get hold of yourself. Taking the subway to Eighth Street and Broadway, you walked across to Jane's house. She wasn't there, but the maid said she was expected back at four o'clock, so you decided to wait, and found a book and an easy chair. Ray, your little godson, who has always been your favorite, came in, and you amused yourself asking him questions about school; then you went back to your book and he started the radio. Less than a minute of it exasperated you so that you shouted at him, "Turn that damn thing off!" With a look of surprise he did so, and turned away without a word; you resumed your reading. A little later the radio again suddenly smote your ear; glancing up, you saw Ray with his hand on the dial, looking at you with friendly roguishness. You sprang over to him, shouting, "I told you to turn it off, didn't I?" and slapped him in the face, so violently that he nearly fell. Then you stepped back aghast, and stood trembling; he looked up at you, too amazed to be hurt, as amazed as if you had suddenly turned into a gorilla before his eyes. You wheeled about and went to the hall for your coat and hat and left the house, and strolled off up Fifth Avenue.

"He'll tell Jane all about it," you thought. "What in the name of heaven is the matter with me?"

At Thirty-sixth Street you stopped at a toy store and bought a fencing outfit (you had heard him tell Jane he wanted one), and sent it to him with a note: *When you're in practice you can challenge me to a duel if you want to. Apologies and love.*

You were almost home when suddenly you stopped, hailed a taxi and gave the driver the Eighty-fifth Street address. You would satisfy yourself on one point at least. It took only a few minutes, across the park and a block downtown; as the cab slowed down and came to a halt you pressed your face against the glass and looked up. Ah, there was a light in the front room! She hadn't gone, then—no, damn her, she was still there, sitting in your chairs and sleeping in your bed. As usual, she had neglected to lower the shades; you could see a movement; that must be her arm, taking something from the mantel. She hadn't left, she was going to hang on, but apparently she had taken you at your word and decided to leave you alone. Good! Good enough, she had more sense than you'd given her credit for, the slut! You gave the driver the Park Avenue address and asked him to hurry, for you had just remembered that it was New Year's Eve and you and Erma were supposed to dine with the Shotwells at their place the other side of Dobbs Ferry; there was to be a big party afterwards, a *réveillon à la campagne*, as Flo called it on the invitations; she would; and you and Erma were to stay over the holiday.

Everybody got soused; Erma came to bed with you that night; and how you wanted to sleep! That's one time she knows enough to keep that smile off her face—well, after all, when you're hungry—being cynical is all right after you've had a good meal....

The day after New Year's you didn't get back to town in time to go to the office. The day after that, about the middle of the afternoon, the phone rang and you heard:

"Mrs. Lewis is calling."

You were momentarily confused and replied, "I thought I told you if she phoned I wasn't in."

"No, not on the telephone, Mr. Sidney; she's here, in the reception room."

"Oh. Well. Tell her I'm out, gone for the day."

So. She was there in the reception room just a few feet away...sitting there...in a minute she'd be gone....

You forced your attention back to Lawson and the two accountants who were there to discuss the handling of income tax refunds on the reserve account. You listened to Lawson, trying to take it in, well aware of his opinion of your competence at this sort of thing. What the deuce, you thought, it's a purely technical question, why do they bother me about it. One of the accountants, Perry, the little dark man with the big ears, kept kicking his foot against your desk as he crossed and uncrossed his legs, and it infuriated you.

The phone rang again; this time it was Miss Malloy, speaking from her little room back of yours.

"That woman, Mrs. Lewis, told Miss Dietrich in the reception room that she saw you come up in the elevator and knows you're here and that she's going to wait till you see her."

"Yes. Thank you. All right."

"—and if we made it a flat three point eight on the entire plant it would bring the net down to—" Lawson went on, reading from a paper one of the accountants handed him. You would have to take a position on this, one way or the other, at the Board meeting the following day; you closed your eyes and frowned; why did he have to talk so fast nobody could keep up with him?

It dragged along for another hour. When at length they had gathered up their papers and departed you pressed the buzzer, and Miss Malloy came in at once.

"I have to ask a favor of you," you said. "Will you please go to the reception room and tell Mrs. Lewis I will not see her, now or any other time, and escort her to the elevator."

"If she won't go?"

"She will. Don't make a scene. Just tell her that."

"Yes, sir."

Matter of fact and businesslike, with no sign of a knowing look in her intelligent brown eyes, she went. Good girl.

Almost immediately the door opened again and she re-appeared. She's already gone, flashed into your mind.

"She is talking to Mr. Carr," Miss Malloy said, "so I thought I'd better wait."

"What! To Mr. Carr!"

"Yes sir. They are sitting on one of the settees, talking."

"The dirty little bitch!—I beg your pardon."

"Yes, sir," Miss Malloy smiled.

You walked to the window, and to your desk and sat down, and then got up and went to the window again. Finally you turned to her:

"Please tell Miss Dietrich to send Mrs. Lewis in here as soon as she gets through with Mr. Carr."

"Yes, sir." She went to her room.

Paltry ass, you told yourself furiously, you might have known something like this would happen. A fine mess this was going to be. What could she be telling him? You could hear in fancy her slow dry thin voice, spilling the whole thing, pretending she didn't know any better: "Mr. Sidney has been very nice to me." Dick would laugh, without malice, "Sure, he's a nice man." At that, this was better than if she'd gone to the house and seen Erma. She would do that too; she'd do anything. You could have her arrested; you could get an injunction or something; you could give her a lot of money to go to Russia or Africa or somewhere.

Many minutes had passed; were they going to talk all after-noon? On the phone you asked Miss Malloy if she had deliv-ered the message to Miss Dietrich. Yes, she had done so at once. At that moment the door opened and Millicent entered; from without the blue uniformed arm of the attendant silently closed the door behind her. She came directly across to where you sat at the table.

"You made me wait a long time," she said.

For a moment you gazed at her speechless, helpless. You had a feeling that you had never really looked at her before. She was so obviously invulnerable; not as a rock, immovable; more like some elemental and indivisible atom for which no solvent or hammer could be found. Then suddenly your temples contracted and you savagely demanded:

"What did you tell Dick?"

"I didn't tell him anything," she replied.

"You were talking to him for an hour."

"Why no, I don't think so. Only a few minutes. I was sitting there and he came through and I saw him glance at me and I stopped him and said, pardon me, aren't you the Mule? He guessed who I was right away."

So that was it, an accident. Fine piece of luck. He didn't pass through that room more than once or twice a day. Was she lying? You could find out.

"So he sat down and we talked about old times. I don't think he's changed a bit. He's very handsome."

"What did you tell him you were here for?"

She chuckled. "I told him I was having a hard time, and I happened to meet you and I thought you were going to help me out."

The phone rang; it was Lawson; they had the reports ready. Could he bring them in? You said you'd ring him back. You turned to her again and looked steadily into her unblinking eyes; all but imperceptibly their expression changed, and you lowered your gaze.

"Look here, Mil," you said, "I haven't got much time. I'm busy. You have got to stay away from here. You have got to let me alone. It's all over. I'm done. If you need some money, anything within reason, you can have it."

"I don't want any money."

"Then for god's sake what do you want?"

"Well of course I've got to have a little money. I've got to have something to live on." She paused. "We ought to have a long talk about it."

"What about your alimony?"

"He's quit paying it."

"How much do you need?"

"We ought to have a talk," she repeated. "Can you come uptown tonight?"

"No. Not tonight or any other night."

She raised her shoulders and dropped them; deep in her eyes you saw a momentary flash like a point in white fire behind a curtain of mud-colored smoke.

"You'd better come," she said quietly. "You might as well come—you know you're going to come." She added in a tone of deadly finality that overwhelmed you. "What's the use of fighting about it?"

The phone rang again; Mr. Upwater of the National City was waiting to see you.

What had she really told Dick? you asked yourself. If you did go up there—well, there was no way out of it. If you didn't go what would she do? There must be some way of handling her. You couldn't think, with her sitting there looking at you.... That damned phone....

"I'll be up after dinner," you said. "Around nine."

After you had opened the door for her, just before she went out, she looked around and said:

"I think your office is very nice."

You sat down at your desk to think, to try to straighten it out in your mind and decide honestly what was happening and what you meant to do. Then Miss Dietrich phoned to remind you of Upwater, and you told her to send him in. You wanted to go down the hall to Dick's room on some pretext or other, to see what he would say; but by the time you were through, with Upwater and one or two other people, and Lawson with the reports, Dick had left. Remembering that there was to be a crowd for dinner, and hating the thought of that atmosphere of jocularity and inanity, you phoned Erma you couldn't be there and found a mildly malicious pleasure in contemplating her indignant efforts to fill your chair on two hours' notice. Let her get a surprise once in a while; it would do her good. But apparently you didn't care to eat alone either; you phoned Jane, but they were dining out; finally you dragged Schwartz off to the club.

You had said you would be there around nine; it was a quarter to when you dismissed the taxi and started up the stoop. There was no plan in your head; you were floundering in a jelly of indecision. In the taxi you kept saying to yourself, this will be final, but you might as well have been repeating the alphabet or the multiplication table, it would have meant just as much. However, you repeated it going up the stairs, this will be final.

In the blue chair, under the reading-lamp, in her lap a little pasteboard box filled with small shiny metal objects, she sat. It was your first view of the blazing purple cheap velvet negligee, with the white ostrich feathers around the neck and cuffs and down the front hems, which, flaring open, exposed the wrinkled pink stockings and the dark brown felt slippers. Accustomed as you were to her taste, it seemed that this must be a calculated grotesquerie. Was this done to impress and seduce you? Doubtless it was funny, but you didn't smile even to yourself, Significantly you did not open the door of the closet as you always had done, but instead put your hat and coat on a chair.

"Grace gave me a box of puzzles," she said, "and I can't work a single one of them. Look."

You stood in front of her, lighting a cigarette.

"I didn't come here to play with puzzles."

"They're stupid anyway." She put the lid on the box and placed it on the table. "Only it makes me mad not to know how to work them. Grace is very clever at it. Aren't you going to sit down?"

You pulled a chair up closer, at the other end of the table, and sat on it. You wished you hadn't come; wished you had done anything rather than come. Words were so useless with her; you always felt either that she didn't understand what they meant or that she already knew all you were saying, and much more. The two contradictory feelings were so blended that there was no separating them. You looked at her a moment in silence and then said quietly:

"Why don't you let me alone, Mil?"

She returned your look without replying, and you went on, "Having a man here was stupid and indecent, but it's not only that. I was ready to quit anyway. We've never really cared for each other. I suppose you've got a dozen men on the string. I'm not objecting, it's none of my business, but I'm just saying you don't need me too. We're not alike, we don't enjoy each other; there's nothing to hold us together except a practice that probably doesn't do either of us any good; it's not natural. Why don't you let me alone? If it's money why don't you be honest enough to say so, and I'll—that is, we can talk it over; I thought I was being fair enough, leaving you everything here and that five hundred dollars."

After a pause, "I don't want any money," was all she said.

"You said you did at the office, You said you had to have something to live on."

"Well, I was just trying to scare you. I don't want all this furniture and everything either. Of course I'm glad you're rich because it makes it so much nicer."

Helplessly you exclaimed again, "Then what in god's name do you want?"

She chuckled. "You're very funny, Will. I'm sorry about that man—truly it was the first time anyone was ever here and he said it was Christmas Day and he didn't want to go home and Grace was out in Jersey to her aunt's. He's no good anyway. It was Mr. Martin—don't you remember, he sells insurance, I told you about him one day."

"I don't care who he was. I'm not interested in him. I've told you that doesn't matter. Of course you're lying when you say it was the first time—but that doesn't matter either. You haven't answered my question: what do you want?"

In a new tone she said all at once, in a breath:

"I want my big brother."

Startled, you looked at her, uncomprehending; then in a sudden swift flash you remembered that she had said to you one day, long ago in your room at college, "We don't ever kiss or say we love each other, we're just like a brother and sister except when we're having fun. You're my big brother." At the time the infantile simplicity of it had annoyed you, but it had disappeared from your mind. Apparently with her it had been more than a momentary fancy....

"I wasn't lying, it was the first time," she was saying. "I made him go right away, right after you left. I told him—"

"Good god I don't care if he never went!" you cried. "Forget him!" You stopped, then meant to resume ironically, "So you're in love with me," but the words wouldn't come, they seemed too absurd and incongruous. Instead you said, "So it's me you want."

She nodded. "And it's me you want." She said it not as a challenge or a claim; she just said it, calmly, a fact.

"Like hell I do!" you shouted, and stopped short; thinking, I must keep control of myself, I'm getting childish. You wanted to laugh at her, sneer at her. You leaned forward and looked at her and said more calmly, "Listen, Mil, we may as well be frank. I can't stand you any more. You're ignorant and silly and dumb as hell. Now I'm done. I was done before I found that man here; you were driving me crazy. I was getting so that when you touched me, it made my flesh creep. I tell you I was going mad! I'm done!" You tried to keep your voice calm, but gradually it had raised until you ended with a shout, "I'm done, do you hear! I'm done!" You had sprung to your feet, and finished standing close to her, bending over her. with flushed face and clenched fists.

She gazed up at you, steadily, without saying anything, and again you shouted, shouted that you had never wanted her, you wished you had never seen her, that she was filthy, perverted, evil, that she had nearly ruined you long ago, at college, before she was old enough to have any right to know what a man was, and that she was trying to finish the job now, but she wasn't going to get away with it, you were done. You bellowed and yelled at her, pacing up and down the room, stopping in front of her chair and then going on, mopping your face with your handkerchief, stuffing it back in your pocket, pulling it out again. At last you stopped and stood in the middle of the room staring at her, hating her, trembling, silent.

She returned your gaze, but still she did not speak.

"You see, Mil," you said in a shaken voice, "you see…you see…."

Her voice was quite steady, with all its usual thin dullness:

"You've said some awful things."

"Well…I've felt some awful things."

"It's not me that's awful."

"Oh yes it is. You're damn right it is. It's both of us."

She shook her head. "You're just afraid. I don't mind what you say. I know you can't ever really leave me, I know how you act, I know what you think." The deep veiled flash came and went in her eyes. "I know how you feel when we're having fun too, but you like it, and anyway," she chuckled, "you're my big brother."

You were speechless with revulsion and disgust, and tired out. You wanted to yell at her again, tell her to shut up, to shut up, to let you alone. Was she right? Couldn't you ever really leave her? Had you come here tonight knowing that? There were your hat and coat on the chair. Couldn't you put them on and go out and never come back? Look at her, good god look at her!

"The hell I can't!" you said, and senselessly you began to yell at her again, pouring epithets and insults on her, completely out of your mind, impotence gone mad. You kicked the footstool to one side and bent over her, your face close to hers, you seized her chair and shook it; words were not strong enough, but you went on flinging them at her, a harmless shower of verbal confetti dipped in dung. Amazing that you didn't touch her, strike her, strangle her, as she sat there silent and imperturbable, breathing evenly, not shrinking from your threatening hands, unmoved by the cyclone of abuse and hatred. You spluttered, raving, your face almost touching hers, and all at once you saw two glistening drops of your saliva appear on her cheek, beside her mouth, but she did not lift her hand to remove them; they remained there, shining like silver bubbles. For an instant you gazed at them, fascinated; then, dropping your handkerchief into her lap and saying "wipe off your face," you stepped back and stood there looking at her.

"You don't need to spit on me," she said. As though suddenly hypnotized into an immobility to match her own, you stood and watched the accurate and inevitable movements of her hand as she picked up the handkerchief, damp with your perspiration, and rubbed it back and forth across her cheek; always the same, the same as when she is eating the candy you bring her or unbuttoning your clothes....

# O

Only two or three steps from the top, he could see, ill-defined in
the dim light, the features of his own hall; the door at the front
at the further end, closer, the door to the bedroom, and at the
back the open entrance, without a door, to the kitchenette. It
was really a public hall, but since it was the top floor no one else
ever used it.

There was a soft yellow glow through the shade which covered the small, single electric light in the middle of the wall.
Standing quietly, he could hear from the kitchenette the recur-
rent faint plop of a single drop of water from the leaky faucet
into the sink, a full two seconds' interval between; and from the
kitchenette also, through the window at its further end, came
the yowl of a wandering cat in the court below.

Plop…Plop….

## XV

"I know I'm not pretty," she said, after you dressed and were sitting beside her on her bed. "I know you think all those things about me."

"Don't talk about it." You took a last puff on your cigarette, got up and crossed to the ashtray on the dressing-table, and came back and crawled in behind her and lay down. You had phoned Erma you wouldn't be home. Maybe you would never go home; you were too weary to think any more of what you would or would not do.

"These pajamas are the heaviest ones you've got," said Millicent. She twisted herself around on the bed and put her hand inside your sleeve, up beyond the elbow, and patted your arm with her fingers. Then she removed it and began stroking your neck, and your chest; and then you felt its familiar warm clinging steady movement on your leg.

"What do you think I am?" you protested feebly.

"It doesn't matter, just for fun, that was an hour ago," she said.

You lay back on the pillow and closed your eyes. No matter. If there was anything left of you she was welcome to it. In the other room, an hour before, when you were still trembling with the remnants of your futile and abortive rebellion, the first touch of her hand had sent fire through you, an intense instantaneous blaze of sensation which caused you to shudder so violently that you convulsively seized her wrist and for a moment held it still. Now it seemed soothing and restful, faintly alive but not disturbing. Nevertheless, after a minute or two you stirred a little, and the hand clingingly followed your movement; you opened your eyes and saw that she was watching your face, her lips pressed together, her eyelids drooping, her head bent a little towards you; and as you sighed and closed your eyes again you heard her chuckle.

Later, alone between the sheets and under the blankets, the room dark and icy cold, you lay on your back with your eyes open, telling yourself that this was the bed in which that man was lying, that morning, only a little more than a week ago. You had no very strong feeling about it, but it was impossible to lie there and not think about it. So you could do this, here you were, without batting an eye. What, you wondered grimly, what for instance if the sheets and pillowslip had not been changed? You squirmed; but you thought, yes, doubtless, it seems that anything is possible. You were aware that among your family and friends and acquaintances you were thought to be rather a fastidious person—in Jane's verbally emancipated circle, ridiculously so. Fastidious and somewhat immaculate. This would amuse them. All of this. In a flash your thoughts were on Millicent, and you felt your brain go tight: was this a final surrender, were you—you fought it off—enough, enough! You forced your mind back to the Christmas guest as a comparatively painless subject....

In the morning, when you had dressed and were ready to leave she was still sound asleep.

You were not long in suspense about Dick, for the afternoon of that same day he went to your office with you after the Board meeting, and after you had finished discussing the reports, he suddenly said:

"By the way, what about our old college friend? Did you see her yesterday? She said you'd kept her waiting over an hour."

"Yes, she said she'd seen you," you replied readily, prepared.

"Did she tell you that cock and bull story about her husband?"

"Why...yes...she's been married."

"Married hell! I'll bet she's been the daughter of a dozen regiments. Did you fall for it?"

"Sure." You managed a grin. "I'd fall for anything."

"Funny." He turned back from the door. "I'd better be careful though, you smashed me once for insulting her innocence. Remember? Battling Bill." He laughed; and for reply you joined in. He went on:

"And I said—what did I say?"

"You said she had a nasty line."

"By god you remember it! I've often wondered—she looks to me as if she still has it. Funny woman—homely as hell and yet, she has a look in her eyes that makes you curious. You'd better look out, Bill. What does she want?"

"Money, of course."

"Sure, but how much? You'd better be careful how you give it to her. Do you want me in on it?"

No, you said, it wouldn't be necessary, it was only a matter of a thousand or so to help her out of her present difficulties. Why the devil was he asking so many questions? It was none of his business. Still it was only natural; as a matter of fact, though it had never occurred to you before, if it hadn't been for Millicent you wouldn't be here now, you would never have heard of the Carr Corporation, you would never have met Erma. Yes, your wealth and position in life, your success, your happy possession of a rich and beautiful wife, were all owing to your zeal in defending Millicent's pure childhood. A pleasantly fertile thought....For Dick too the episode had had its emphasis—though not in the same degree as for you—naturally, he would be interested in this reappearance of that little bitch—that's what he called her —after many years.

You could read Dick like an open book; it appeared certain that he suspected nothing beyond a compassionate gesture to a woman in trouble, for old time's sake.

A year ago, almost; yes, actually nearly twelve months of hours and minutes since that night, each day confronted with the next, an ordeal not to be tolerated. "It wasn't very nice of me to have Mr. Martin here," she said that night, "I won't do that anymore." So utterly weary that the force of gravity itself seemed overpowering and irritating, you were relaxed, a dead weight, in the leather chair. You weren't sufficiently interested to bother to reply. All the same, after that you slept here very seldom; sometimes you would go home as late as two or three in the morning. Unconsciously, so that at first you weren't even aware of it, your attitude toward the place was changed; it was no longer your place, the things were no longer your intimate and friendly possessions, they belonged to you no more. Whereas formerly you had shrunk only from her, only in her had felt an alienness and a threat, henceforth all was foreign, each thing here was an enemy. You never brought back the little bronze vase; it is still at home on top of the bookshelves in your dressing-room.

Preoccupation with her, or rather with yourself with her on you, more and more continuously filled your mind. At the theatre in the middle of a scene, at a bridge-table at home, at your desk at the office, you would find your thoughts on her in spite of your efforts to drag them away. Resenting her, hating her, jibing at her, more rarely trying honestly to understand her; numberless thousands of times picturing her dead, with an inexhaustible inventiveness of detail. She would disappear; in the paper you would see an account of a woman found drowned (in the Hudson? yes, that would be most likely), you would go to the morgue and there she would lie under a sheet, her face

swollen; or the phone would ring and it would be the police to say
that a woman had been killed by an automobile on Amsterdam
Avenue, in her purse had been found a card bearing your name
and address, and would you kindly come and identify her; or
merely some evening you would find her sick in bed and, on
calling a doctor, would be told that it was her heart, she had only
a few hours to live. She would breathe her last under your eyes.
These pictures would float endlessly in your head until by rep-
etition they became meaningless, and you would invent others;
death itself would grow stale, and you would imagine her gone,
for any one of a hundred reasons, to far-off and inaccessible
places—after all, you wanted her dead only to you; but these
dispositions had a lack of finality that was never satisfying.
Always she could come back.

Most frequently of all you would fancy yourself in love; this
would happen oftenest at home in bed, during the hours before
you went to sleep, especially on those nights when you had not
gone to see her. This was in all ways the most thrilling and satisfying; for one thing, you had never been in love, as you understood it. Nearest with Lucy; and now sometimes you used her;
her husband long dead, there would be a meeting, casual and
unforeseen, and one look into each other's eyes would be enough
—a complete mutual abandonment and fusion, no one else
would exist. Tears would spring to her eyes, and you would be
unable to speak, nor would it be necessary....Mostly though,
Lucy would not come to life and your lover was ideally created;
sometimes a beautiful and worldly duchess, met at the Salle
Pleyel in Paris or at a little inn in the Pyrenees; at others an
innocent and laughing virgin, a radiant girl who would over-
whelm and blind you, and who would finally gravely sigh and
confess that, despite your age, you were for her love's youth, forever. Duchess or virgin, she was always fair-haired, grey-eyed,

with clear blooming skin, as lovely as love itself; and the end was always the same. Thinking it more manly to tell her than to write, you would go to Eighty-fifth street to see Millicent, and as she sat motionless in her chair with the comprehension of an unimagined doom distending her eyes and distorting her features, you kindly but inexorably bade her farewell. Sometimes you reproached her and sometimes not; sometimes you left a large sum of money for her and sometimes you didn't; but the essentials were the same.

Gradually these fantasies came to occupy the greater part of your life. The one about Jane rarely varied. She and Victor were in a railroad accident, and though he was instantly killed, she escaped with injuries which left her a cripple for life—not exactly crippled, but her beauty completely destroyed—the physical details were blurred. You left Erma and made a home for Jane and the children and, entirely indifferent to Millicent, spent the rest of your life in that brotherly devotion. This touching drama was often rudely interrupted by your sense of humor—really it was a little too obvious—you had always resented Jane's overthrow of your generous plans for her and the girls, and this was a little too pat, usually you were smiling at yourself before you reached the finale. Nevertheless you returned to it....

Day after day at the office, leaving the routine, which was about all that was left of your duties, more and more to Lawson, you would sit at your desk or stand at the window with your mind wearily trying to drug itself with these stale and infantile stories. Sometimes at the end of the day, sometimes earlier, occasionally even before lunch, finding it no longer bearable, you would take your hat and go home, or perhaps to Jane's house or to the club. You tried taking long walks, but that was worse than the office; you were more alone, and you

dreaded to be alone. Almost equally you dreaded being with
people; everybody irritated you with their demands on your
interest in things which appeared to you utterly inconsequential. Especially Jane; never had she appeared so idiotically
active. First of all, of course, came her children, but she had a
dozen enthusiasms at once and she was always crowding them
on you. When you went to her house in the afternoon she was
always out, or there was a crowd coming to tea, or one of the
children had something wrong with him, or there was something you must do. Adler was to talk at the New School for
Social Research, didn't you want to go? Or what did you think
of the proposal for the registration of aliens, would you write
letters to senators and congressmen about it? One day when it
was too much for you and you protested irritably, not the first
time, she came over to your chair and put her hand on your
shoulder and said:

"Will, dear, what's the matter?"

"What do you mean what's the matter? Nothing so far as I'm
concerned," you declared.

"Yes there is," she insisted quietly. "You're unhappy about
something. I suppose, if it were anything that is any of my business you'd have told me about it; but whatever it is, if it's
making you unhappy it is my business. We used to tell each
other everything. Is it Erma?"

"Good lord no!" You added hastily, "It's nothing. I'm all right."

After a pause, "You won't tell me," she said, and stayed there
patting your shoulder. You made no reply, there was no impulse
to reply. As for telling her, you would rather have told Dick, or
Schwartz, or even Erma. Not likely!

Erma was too preoccupied with herself to take much notice
of you. Her difficult period. It still is; how long does it last for
heaven's sake? She's difficult all right; you've been a well-matched

pair this last year. Moved to arithmetic by the approach of this physiological phenomenon, you reflected incredulously that she was forty-three, two years older than yourself. She didn't look more than thirty. Her skin was still as fresh and healthy-looking as an apple, and the lord knows her tongue hadn't stiffened up any. When she suddenly decided to go to Florida, around the last of January, it was at first a great relief, but soon you were considering that the important thing was to get rid of time somehow, even disagreeably, and wishing her back again.

You moved to the club, and still you seldom slept at Eighty-fifth Street. Some weeks you would go there only once; others you were there every evening. You never went without phoning her in advance, and you never phoned her without a feeling of unreality, a feeling that you were doing something too implausible to be believed in. Put to the torture, you could not have answered the question, why do you do this? Seated at the desk, your hand would reach for the telephone (for you had discontinued the trips to the cigar store booth); you would draw it back and demand, why? Sometimes, you would dispose of the question out of hand with a grim and determined reaction: all right, I won't; and you wouldn't; but that merely postponed it for twenty-four hours. Oftener, you would sit and argue it. What need could she satisfy that could not be better satisfied elsewhere? How could there be any actual bond between you; and if there were none, except in your imagination, could you not control that and defeat it? Homely, vulgar, half-witted, illiterate—how could you see all that so well and still be blind to it?

Sometimes you would say, these things happen, they are fate. Many people are held together by bonds so profoundly concealed that to reason they seem idiotic, and yet so strong that no force can loosen them. Very well, if this had happened to you it was not your fault; why not accept it and have done with it? For ten years you had been complaining that life was stale, nothing interested you; you were interested enough now, weren't you? What were you ashamed of? She was homely, vulgar, half-witted, illiterate....Bah, words. She was false and treacherous. Maybe not, if you accepted her—who wouldn't be, the way you were acting? She was evil—what do you mean, evil? No, damn it, don't squirm out of it, don't evade it, don't jump away from it like a scared imbecile—what do you mean, evil? Perverted...O classic blah! Ha, Erma too then? And Mrs. Davis, especially Mrs. Davis. And everybody alive, judging from what you hear. Dick, about the only time you heard him talk of it, made no bones about it. And what that orchestra conductor said when he was on trial during the war—of course that's different, he was a European.—So you're trying to get away from it again—no you don't—oh no, you don't—what do you mean, evil? You don't mean perverted, that's silly. What do you mean?

Well. Evil is not seen, it is felt. It is not defined, it is conveyed. Deliver us from evil. It depends of course on what is evil to you. She is obscene. You always take a bath....

Grant the evil. That's why. She is evil, and you get a kick out of it. No. You get revulsion, disgust, hatred. Bitter and burning hatred. But you have harbored her for twenty years. She turned into a ghost and then she came back again. Did you hate the ghost? You hated yourself. There's no answer to that; you're crazy. Go on and telephone, you might as well. Tell her you hate yourself more than usual tonight, so you're coming up and take her to a show....

Sometimes you would go directly from the office and take her to dinner, but more often you would dine first at the club. But for her insatiable fondness for the theatre, there would have been nothing to do except sit and read, until spring came and you could drive into the country, for there wasn't a subject under the sun she would talk about. You've tried her a thousand times; she simply wouldn't talk. Did she ever, alone with Grace, for instance? Not when you were along, for occasionally, finding Grace there, you would invite her to accompany you to dinner, and Millicent wouldn't say twenty words during the entire meal. Once or twice, when Grace returned with you after dinner and you went to the leather chair with a book, you could hear them in the bedroom by the hour—Grace's low-pitched, pleasant but endless chatter about nothing, and only at long intervals Millicent's thin grave tone: "That must have been very nice."

She always seemed to be afraid of words; she wouldn't even answer questions if she could help it. Like the day you asked her about Dick. That was in late spring, around the middle of May. Erma had returned from Florida and was talking of going to Scotland for the summer, and wanted you to go along. You and she had dined with Fulton and his fourth wife, on his roof, and, allured by the mild May air, she had suggested a walk and had sent Dorst on to pick you up at Fifty-ninth Street. As you were crossing the avenue at Fifty-seventh you got caught in the center and stood there at the edge of the solid slow-moving traffic, glancing carelessly at the cars as they crept past; and suddenly your careless glance became a stare as you saw Dick and Millicent side by side in a taxicab not ten feet away. They were looking the other way and obviously had not seen you, nor had Erma seen them.

"How far are we?" said Erma. "I'm getting tired. Damn physiology anyway. Come along to Scotland and we'll ride around on ponies—we're too old to walk."

You were conscious of no particular emotion, except curiosity. It was not conceivable that Dick—and yet he had married Mary

Alaire Carew Bellowes. He had done other things too; he was weird, and catholic, when it came to women. This was rich—oh this was juicy! The homely little slut!

The next day was Saturday and Dick didn't come in. In the evening you went to Eighty-fifth Street early, before dinner, and after you had glanced through the evening paper you found an opportunity to say casually, with your eye on her face:

"Have you seen Dick since that day at the office?"

She displayed not the slightest change of expression.

"Dick? You mean Mr. Carr?"

"No, I mean Moby Dick. I mean Dick Whittington, thrice Lord Mayor of London."

She looked at you calmly without replying.

"Yes, I mean Dick Carr. Have you seen him?"

"Why yes, we saw him that evening at the theatre, don't you remember?"

"No. It wasn't me. You were probably with Mr. Peft or Mr. Rockefeller or Mr. Barrymore."

She chuckled. "I remember now, it was Grace. She thought he was very good-looking."

"Well, have you seen him since?—Oh what's the use. I just wondered how you would handle it. I saw you and Dick in a taxicab on Fifth Avenue last evening."

She picked up a book from the table, made as if to sit down with it, and then put it back again, and remained standing. The movement was unhurried and methodical, but for her it was a frenzy of agitation.

"I suppose you were on your way here?" you sneered, trying not to.

She was standing still as a statue, the way she so often does, her arms hanging at her sides, her head languidly erect, motionless as a grey dark cloud on a windless day.

"I'm sorry you saw us," she said. "I didn't want you to know until it was all done."

"Really!" You put the paper down and stared at her. "Really!"

"I think he is going to give me a lot of money," she went on. "I've only seen him twice, and we don't do anything you wouldn't like. Even if I would he wouldn't want to. He said he wouldn't. He used to give me money a long time ago—when I knew you. He's just sorry for me, and he's so rich...."

"I thought you didn't care for money."

"I didn't say that. I said I didn't want money from you. I'd take all I could get from him. I think he's going to give me one hundred thousand dollars. He says I could live on the interest."

"Where were you going last night?"

"We ate dinner at a restaurant downtown to talk it over, and he was bringing me home. He didn't come upstairs though."

"What restaurant?"

"Why, I didn't notice. He took me."

"Where did you meet him?"

"At the corner of Broadway and Fulton Street."

She turned and sat down; she was through. You looked at her, and you let the next question die in your throat; when her lips got that twisted look and her eyes turned away from you like that, with a jerk, you might as well question a tree-stump. There was a rush of blood to your head, but you fought it back. You got to your feet, shoved your hands into your pockets, and walked to the window and back again.

"I don't believe a goddam word of it," you said.

She didn't reply; she was reading; but after a long pause, seeing that you weren't going to speak again, she said, "It's all true. I wouldn't lie to you about Mr. Carr."

Always before that, in your occasional conversations about him, she had called him Dick.

Of course, you got nothing more out of her. Late that night

walking home, as you often did, you considered at your leisure the amazing fact that while you might not have been greatly affected by an admission from her that Dick was sharing her favors with you, you were furiously humiliated by the idea of his making a princely gift that would mean financial independence for her. Bah, you thought, no danger, remember her alimony tale. Anyway Dick, though generous, wasn't a jackass. Then the alternative…well, what of it, Dick or Mr. Gowan, Dick or Mr. Martin…what's the difference….But underneath was a deep and intense resentment.

She didn't mention it again. Now and then you would say, "When you get the hundred thousand let me know, we'll have a spree," but she would either not reply or would say, "I haven't got it yet," as if you were talking of the laundry. Once or twice you came near asking Dick about it, point-blank, but the words wouldn't come out. If it were true, he would certainly say so—and what then? Or if it proved to be merely one of her little inventions, it would be embarrassing and would open up difficulties. But you wanted miserably to know.…

Did you know that Dick had been here, in the apartment? No you don't know it even now for a certainty, though for a while you thought you did, that evening you found the inscription on the statue. That was June, late in June, just before Erma sailed for Scotland. You had been here before dinner, and for an hour or two afterward, before you noticed it; you saw it when you went over to take a book from the table. There it was, printed in big black sprawling letters on the rough unpolished marble of the column: BATTLING BILL. You must have betrayed your surprise by an exclamation or something, for when you turned to Millicent, she had already looked up from her book and her eyes were on you. You were furious, instantly suspicious, but you tried to control your voice.

"Who did that?" you demanded, pointing at it.

"I did, this morning, I just happened to think of it," she replied.

"That's a lie. I want to know who did it."

With no resentment in her voice, but speaking a little more slowly than usual, and a little louder, "There's no sense in your telling me I lie everything I say," she said, and resumed her book.

You approached her chair. "All right, then you did it. Why?"

She looked up, but did not answer. You stood staring at her, then went and looked again at the inscription, printed unevenly on the rough marble; then, with a shrug of your shoulders, went to the bathroom and came back with a towel. As you bent over, rubbing the letters off one by one with your back to her, Millicent's voice came, unruffled and calm:

"One of the girls downstairs that's studying art gave me the crayon. She said it was art crayon. I guess that's what made me think of it, I wanted to use it on something."

Still you thought it must have been Dick; she didn't have wit enough. Was it Dick, had he been here? Probably; but just as probably not. There's no telling—hell, there's no telling anything. You hadn't been here the evening before, he might have done it then. Or she might have been telling the truth....

With that trivial episode something seemed to break. You knew you must do something. Finally and inescapably you must do something. There was nothing to do, you told yourself in bitter despair, nothing you could do. Very well, you must do something anyhow. Anything, no matter what, but something definite, the time was past for arguing about it. Night after night you could not sleep, sometimes you didn't even go to bed. The fantasies had deserted you, and your mind was left naked and raw. One night, long after midnight, you walked from Eighty-fifth Street clear to the Battery and stood there, on the edge of the pier, wondering if you would really drown if you jumped in....A man and woman walked past, and a policeman came up and began talking to you....

Go to Scotland with Erma? Good god no. She went, more hostile and resentful than you had ever seen her, still in the midst of her difficulty, with a maid and a nurse and a dozen trunks. Why not, then, swallow the thing whole and go off somewhere with Millicent for good? That appeared to you the most definite and conclusive; it's the sensible thing to do, you said. But you couldn't even propose it to her; the prospect overwhelmed you with its surrender and degradation. Then go to Paul, in Rome; he was your son, tell him so; what was a son for? Bury yourself in his life—sure. It didn't take long to dispose of that. It's strange how clear-headed you were about it—a wonder you didn't take a ship and chase that phantom and try desperately to clutch it.

All right, but you must do something....

You were afraid to tell Millicent you were going to leave her and never see her again, afraid of the unconcerned disbelief you knew you would see in her face. You told her merely that you were going away alone and didn't know when you would be back, but she must have remarked that your manner of saying it was odd. When you told Dick, briefly, that you needed a change and were leaving for an indefinite period he didn't seem surprised, but was considerably concerned; and you didn't even write to Jane, who was at the seashore with the children. Even if you had wanted to you couldn't have replied definitely to Dick's anxious questions, for beyond the first step you had no plans. One evening around the middle of July you went to the Pennsylvania Station and got a westbound train.

The activity of the preparations had buoyed you up, the packing, the arrangements at the office, the formidable wad of

travelers' checks from the bank, this had an air of decision and
purpose; but that night in the Pullman compartment you sat in
misery and desolation, locked in your little box as the solid-
vestibuled extra-fare tram hurled itself through the night like a
screaming idiot. You were running away, a beaten coward, but
that didn't trouble you. Where were you going and what were
you going to do? The project you had formed with a thrill of
hope now appeared puerile and ridiculous, an aimless and
empty gesture of forlorn desperation; nevertheless you would
go through with it. Tomorrow morning....You invited fantasies,
but they wouldn't come; or forced to appear, there was no
blood in them, merely puppets on strings; and with a fierce
masochism your mind would dart away from them to plunge
itself into the gloom of reality. You were going—from nothing
into nothing. You were running away—from nothing; for though
unformulated and unadmitted you felt profoundly the conviction that what you were struggling blindly to escape from would
never be left behind—it was there with you, tenaciously and
eternally; it was buried in your heart, in your flesh and bones;
no matter what agonies it might bring, no matter what sacrifices you might offer or what frenzied retreats you might make,
it was literally inescapable. There was no imaginable way out.

But out of what? Good god *what* was it? You suddenly beat
your fists against your knees, frantic, and shouted against the
roar of the train:

"But it's terrible, it's terrible! I'd do anything, by god I'd do
anything!" And then sat there looking at the black window,
ashamed and afraid, wondering in sober earnest if you were
going mad.

## P

*The cat yowled again, and again, in the silence that followed, he heard the plop of the water dropping into the sink, as he stood in the middle of the hall under the dim wall light. Through force of habit rather than necessity (for he could really identify it by touch just as well) he stood close under the light and looked at the key in his hand to make sure that it was the one with the two large teeth at the end; the other was for the street door downstairs. He looked up quickly as a sound came from the front room, the muffled sound of a chair being dragged across a rug; and he thought, she's pulling it closer to the table, to read; that's good, she'll be sitting down.*

*That's good, he thought, what do you mean that's good, what's the difference, go on in....*

# XVI

Go on in. Yes, she'll be sitting down, and you'll take off your coat and hat, and she'll say, "You're late, did you remember to bring some candy?" and you won't answer, you'll stand and look at her and presently say, "Mil, this time I'm going to get the truth out of you," and you'll keep it up for an hour or two and then put on your coat and hat and go home. Or maybe you won't even go home....

In a vague sort of way that's where you thought you were going when you got on that train. You didn't think the word, home, but the idea was something like that, you were trying to find a root somewhere, and blindly you went back to that. At first there seemed to be something in it. After a sleepless night you got off the train a little before noon, on a blazing hot July day, and took a taxi to the hotel. In spite of the vast changes since your boyhood days it all looked familiar and friendly, for only two years had passed since you had been there, at the time of your mother's funeral. No one at the hotel remembered you, but after lunch, walking to Cooper Street, you were recognized by one of your own schoolmates with whom you had renewed acquaintance on your previous visit, and you met old Doctor Culp, grey-haired and bent over a cane, who insisted on stopping for a chat...memories of your father....

There was the house, decrepit and apparently not painted for years, but essentially the same. The bay window where you had sat winter afternoons working at algebra, the porch pillars where the hammock had been attached, the spot under the maple tree where Jane had put the little table on summer afternoons, serving weak tea to her girl friends, oblivious to the derision of the boys of the neighborhood, the window where you had stood and looked out the day your father died....

The real estate agent informed you that the old Sidney house, as he called it—after twenty years!—was now owned by Mr. Masenstod of the First National Bank and was being rented by the month, not on lease, to a man who ran a butcher shop and had eight children. It could be bought cheap. The following day you closed the deal and paid cash, a New York draft for sixty-two hundred dollars. But the butcher had paid his rent till the end of July and insisted on being permitted to stay a month beyond that. Your plans must wait. You went however to a contractor and made arrangements for a complete renovation, repairs, painting, new furnace, plastering—the work to begin promptly on the first of September. By that time you began to meet with questions: were you going to live there? You replied evasively. There was an article in the paper, now a daily, about the extensive improvements Mr. William B. Sidney, the prominent New York capitalist, was planning for the old family residence on Cooper Street, which he had recently purchased. Nothing left to do, you wandered about day after day, with half the town obviously wondering what the devil you were there for; you took walks into the country and went on a fishing trip to Lake Harmon....

Around the middle of August you took a train to Dayton, and hired a car with a chauffeur and directed him west, on the Millvale road. It was graded and paved, a wide thoroughfare; gone the pleasant country road over which you had bumped with Lucy, in her roadster. On this smooth, efficient surface the miles sped by so quickly that you reached the farm long before you were ready to expect it; you rushed past; at your shout the driver stopped, turned around, and returned to come to a halt directly in front of the house. The place was changed hardly at all, except for new stables in the rear; the house was still a dazzling white among the evergreens and all the other buildings yellow. Just the same: the orchard at the back, and the tennis court. You would have liked to get out and walk up through the meadows, over the wooded hill, and down the bank of the stream to the pool, where you had sat with Lucy on that summer afternoon; you shrugged the impulse away. As you sat there, a figure on horseback appeared around the corner of one of the stables and came trotting down the driveway. It was Lucy's father, older, smaller it seemed, but as erect as ever. At any moment you expected to see his wife follow him, but she did not appear. When he came through the gate and went off down the road alone, you said to yourself, she is dead. Nothing less would have kept those two apart, even for a short morning gallop.

You nodded to the driver, "Back to Dayton," and leaned out of the car and looked until the legend in enormous red letters on the side of the big yellow barn, *Millvale Stock Farm*, faded from view. Undecided, all ends loose, you sat in your hotel room that night and tried vainly to read. You thought of Idaho, but you didn't want to see Larry; you didn't want to see anybody. Yet you must see someone, and you must move. You shuddered as you thought of the evening you had spent with your Aunt Cora a week previously, sitting on the narrow side porch, her rocker creaking back and forth as she talked interminably in her penetrating rasping treble of your mother's last hours, and the impending kitchen manufacture of tomato ketchup. No, it would be pointless to go back there; not now; not for another month at least. Where was someone to talk to? Where was someone to whom there was anything to be said?

In the morning you took a train up to Cleveland; and, arriving in the middle of the afternoon, went with your bags to the Hotel Ohio, and registered. It was hot and sultry, with no saving breeze from the lake, and you wandered around the

streets for a while and finally brought up in front of the entrance
of the Jayhawker Club—but you did not go in. You stood there
a moment, then with a drop of the shoulders turned and went
off. Before long you were back at the hotel, where you spent
ten minutes with the porter going over railroad schedules, and
then went up to your room and packed the bags which you had
unpacked only three hours before. Sitting there on the edge of
the bed, you got the contractor on long distance, and were
informed that everything was in readiness to begin operations
promptly on the first, the minute the butcher and his brood
departed. An hour later you were on an eastbound train.

You had to get off at Albany at five in the morning, and wait
till eight for a train to Boston, where again you changed, this
time headed north. For lack of a connection you spent the
night in a hotel in Portland, and early morning found you on a
rattling local with its nose pointed toward the Maine woods.
Descending at the Pineville station around noon, and following
the directions you had written down at the office two months
before, you hired a Ford at the little roadside garage and were
jolted twelve miles over a narrow dirt road, into the heart of the
forest. At length the Ford came to a stop at the roadside in
front of a small cottage set in the middle of a clearing; at one
end was a pile of sawed wood considerably larger than the cottage itself; and from behind the woodpile a man appeared and
leisurely approached. Yes, he said, this was Steve Wilson's, and
he was Steve; and yes, the trail to Bucket Lake went off to the
right down the road a piece, just beyond the edge of the
clearing. You couldn't miss it; about three miles in was an old
wood road off to the left; for Bucket Lake you kept to the right.
Certainly, you could leave your bags with him, but he couldn't
very well take them in tomorrow, the next day he might manage
it. You extracted a toothbrush and a comb and turned the bags
over to him, paid the driver of the Ford, walked down the road

a few hundred feet to where the entrance to a trail was marked by a felled tree, and plunged into the woods.

The trail was plain the first mile or two, but then there began to be spots where you were a little doubtful; at one place, where it suddenly emerged into a large clearing which apparently was a swamp except in late summer, you searched for nearly an hour before you could be sure you had picked it up again. It was hot even in the shade of the woods, and the sweat ran down your face and the middle of your back as you strode along with your coat and vest over your arm, incongruous and uncomfortable in your business suit and polished calfskin shoes. You had passed the wood road far behind; the trail seemed endless. Seven miles it was supposed to be and you began to be a little uneasy; you glanced at your watch; had you by any chance gone wrong somewhere? You went ahead, faster; and in another few minutes there was a break in the tree-wall, an unwonted light, and all at once you found yourself at the edge of a carpet of grass which sloped gently downward only a few yards to the shore of a lake—a miniature circular lake not more than three hundred yards in diameter, with the green forest hugging its shore on every side. Not far away, on your right, was a little cabin, and you started for it almost running and shouting, "Hello there! Schwartz! Hello!"

He was lying on the grass in the shade at the edge of the woods, back of the cabin, reading a book. At your shout he jumped up, and came toward you with a grin of surprised pleasure.

"Bill! My god you look funny!" And as he violently pumped your hand, "So you really came!"

During those three weeks, there were a dozen times when it was on the point of your tongue to tell him the whole story; that was what you had thought you were going there for. You had a feeling that it would be an immeasurable relief to tell it, to say it in words aloud, all the details and incidents, and then say, "There, what do you think of that? How's that for nonsense?" Maybe that's why you never breathed it, because that was the only tag you could conceive for it; if it seemed inexplicable and preposterous to you, what would it have sounded like in the telling, what could he have said except that you were obviously crazy? Maybe you expected something else from him; there's a light in him somewhere that he never shows to anybody; you just know it's there. He has a secret of some kind, always has had; every summer he goes off for two months to that little cabin, absolutely alone—you're the only person that's ever been invited to visit him.

As you swam and fished, explored the woods, read his books, and lay of an evening talking, on the grass with the stars overhead and the breeze whispering in the forest at your elbows, you had a feeling that you had in sober fact been possessed of an evil spirit and were finding the spell that would exorcise it. Tired out after the day's exertions, for Schwartz was extremely active and you had a hard time keeping up with him, you would sit on the gunwale of the boat at the water's edge, smoking, with dusk falling around you, and after a silence he would perhaps say:

"No, I don't think that matters, but of course no one can prove it. It's merely that I can't conceive of an organism having any spring of action outside of itself. A stimulus, of course, but that's different. If you touch me with a hot iron I jump away, but the iron is merely incidental; the spring of my action is from within, the desire to keep from getting burnt. All moral and ethical dicta are nothing but incidental hot irons—and the Christs and Mahomets and Kants and Calvins and Anthony Comstocks— essentially they're all the same—they're the neurotic blacksmiths that stick them in the fire and work the bellows and then pull them out and thrust them at us. Ha! At least some of us know why we jump—but all we do is hide behind a tree and make faces at them...."

That was his favorite theme. You sat and smoked and idly listened, wondering, at peace almost. Hot irons...words...Blah!

His time up, on Labor Day Schwartz had to go. You accompanied him over the trail to Wilson's. Pleased and amused that you had decided to stay, he arranged that Steve should keep you supplied with provisions, and also that he should prepare the cabin and boat for the winter at such time as you should decide to leave. The Ford came for him around noon, and after waving goodbye and watching them bump away down the road out of sight, you started back along the trail alone.

You stood it for two weeks. After the very first day and night you grew frightened—if not frightened, uncomfortable and apprehensive. Everything that had seemed so friendly and peaceful when he was there, the woods, the placid little lake, the wide enveloping silence broken only now and then by a bird's song or the rustling unseen movement of a squirrel or muskrat—all became by insensible degrees hostile and threatening. You didn't want to go out with the boat, the water seemed bottomless, forbidding and terrifying; and as for the woods, one day when you started for the top of the ridge to the east, where you and Schwartz had often gone, you turned before you were halfway there, stood a moment, breathlessly, in the midst of the forest, and then precipitately retraced your steps, almost running by the time you saw the clearing and the lake through the thinning trees. It was worst at night; you would stir out of a dream, and then, fully awake, lie in the darkness and gaze at the faint square of the window, listening to the silence....

Just at the thickening of dusk one evening you sat at the water's edge and found yourself wondering what would happen if you rowed out to the middle of the lake and jumped in. Naturally, if you didn't swim you would drown; but could you keep yourself from swimming? The boat would be there within a few feet of you. Could you resist the impulse to cling to it? Even if you managed to capsize the boat and sank, the shore would be at the most only two hundred yards away, and you could swim a mile or more. Could you keep your arms and legs still and let yourself go under? What if you put rocks in your pockets or tied some in a sack around your neck? That would be horrible, you couldn't do that. The second time you came up, perhaps the third, you would be able to open your eyes and see the cabin and the woods and the sky....You reached down and dabbled your hand in the water, shivering, then got to your feet and went into the cabin and fixed your bed, putting on an extra blanket, for the nights had become quite cold.

The following morning, immediately after breakfast, you took the trail to Wilson's. He couldn't go in for your luggage that day, and in order to summon the Ford he had to ride six miles to the nearest telephone. You were forced to stay at his cottage until the next day, when, around noon, the Ford came and took you to Pineville. Steve had arisen at dawn to go in for your bags. At Portland you just made the connection to Boston, arriving there late at night. You spent the night at a hotel, intending to go across to Albany the next day and from there on to Ohio; but when morning came, you decided it would be just as well to go to New York and catch a fast train west from there.

As the Merchants' Limited sped dizzily along the shore of the sound, you reflected that it was past the middle of September, and the work on the house was probably completed—he had said it would take only two weeks. But the reflection was forced, there was no life in it; you were in fact already aware, though you hadn't admitted it, that you were not going back to that husk. As usual, you weren't going to do anything. Were you then going to stay in New York? No. That is—no. Jane and the

children would of course be back from the seashore; school had
begun two weeks ago—no, not their school, it didn't start till
early October. Erma was probably still in Europe, you had
heard nothing for more than a month. Dick—oh what did it
matter?

At Grand Central, you got your bags to a taxicab and gave
the driver the Eighty-fifth Street address. The traffic barely
crawled, seeming scarcely to move at all, and you grew more
and more impatient—and you realized that a tension which
had long been progressing within you was tightening, tightening to the bursting point. You forced yourself under control—would she be there? Would she be alone? You should
have telephoned her from Boston. But at Boston you were supposed to be on the way to Ohio....Why didn't the damn fool go
around that limousine that thought it owned the avenue?

She was there. Alone. The taxi-driver refused to help you,
presumably on account of the observations you had made
regarding his driving, and you puffed up the stairs with the two
heavy bags—it was unseasonably hot—and your hand trembled
as you put the key in the door. She was sitting with both windows wide open and nothing on but the purple negligee, sewing
on buttons and drinking lemonade.

"Hello," she said, "you should have sent me a telegram, I
might not have been here."

After you had put the bags in the bedroom, and sat down
and mopped off your face, she brought you a glass of lemonade
and said you'd better get into a tub of cold water. She also said
that she hadn't been away at all, and it had been very quiet;
Grace had gone to Atlantic City, but was now back; and there
was a new musical comedy that was very nice, she had seen it
three times. You sat and listened to her and looked at her,
thinking surely it was impossible that such a creature existed....

After you got out of the bath she joined you in the bedroom....
Later you went to dinner.

That was two months ago, two months to a day. By the following morning nothing seemed to have changed; instead of
ten weeks you might have been gone overnight. The first day or
two there was a little freshness, perhaps, in the streets and the
people in the office, even in this place and her, but it soon disappeared. Schwartz at his desk—well, there was nothing new
or exciting in that. Nothing new anywhere. Until the middle of
October you stayed at the club, but spent nearly every night
here; then Erma came back and the same old round started all
over again. Dinner parties, bridge, Board meetings, Lawson
running in and out with that knowing sly glint in his eyes—perhaps he isn't at all aware of it....

Yet there was a change. You couldn't have put it into words,
not indeed feeling it, except as a vague sense of a concluded
fate. Hope was gone, and with it irony. "Here I come with my
radiant princess," you used to say to yourself as you opened the
door and stood aside for Millicent to enter the little restaurant
on Broadway where you usually take her. That was gone   a
grim but spontaneous spark of humor replaced by something
perhaps less grim but infinitely more profound. The jest was
too stale. Once you had tried to persuade yourself into a deri-
sive acceptance of the caprice of fate; now the acceptance
forced itself dully upon you, but the saving derision was gone.
Only four nights ago, in that same restaurant, you sat and
watched her methodically breaking her bread into little pieces
and dropping them into her soup, and when she said, "I think
bread is very nice in soup," there was no smile in you, no twinge,
no reaction at all; that oft-repeated statement, like all else,
seemed to have lost even the significance of banality.

Another winter; in a month it will be Christmas again. You'd better get her another fur coat and bring it Christmas morning. You will at that. If you're here. Erma says you look like hell and that you've got a disposition like the camel she rode that time at Ghardaia. She says you ought to go abroad for a year. Why not? Dick has mentioned it too, three or four times, though he seems to be embarrassed about it; that's the first time you've ever seen him act like that. Is he trying to get you out of the way? What for? For Lawson? For himself? Not likely; that's not like him. You should ask him about it, straight, and then you'd know; you should have asked him this morning when he came in your office and didn't seem to know what he'd come for. He said something about Jane's good judgment, but that doesn't prove anything.

Even if they don't know, even if she was telling you the truth last night, what business is it of theirs? Jane, with her superior air of seeing things which you can't be expected to see! Oh she knows what's good for you! Sure, she knows everything, just as she did thirty years ago—more than that—when you'd run up from the lot, trying not to cry, and she'd have that look on her face—oh it was kind enough. How kind she was, how kind and understanding, while your mother would stand there with that silly meaningless smile....

If not Dick, why couldn't you ask Jane? Does it matter so much? But you must know if they know. You're not going on like this, like a helpless imbecile, with them discussing you behind your back, trying to decide what they'd better do about you....

Exactly what did she say? Did she say she had seen Jane? Yes. Night before last—seems a year ago. You came up after dinner, rather early, and she wasn't back yet. You remembered you hadn't told Schwartz about that car, and you got the telephone book out of the closet to look up his number, and as you sat, waiting for him to answer, with the phone book lying upside down on the table, in front of you, you noted indifferently the chaos of numbers scribbled in pencil all over the cover; it was a habit of Millicent's that had at one time amused you; and suddenly you saw among that chaos a number that riveted your attention: Chelsea 4343. You hung up the receiver and grabbed up the book and looked at it closely; of course you hadn't put that number there; but it was quite plain, unmistakable, Chelsea 4343.

It was half an hour before you heard her key in the door. You waited till she had got her hat and coat put away, and then you held the book in front of her, pointing to the scribbled number, and said:

"Did you put that there?"

She looked at it without replying. "Look here," you said, "if ever you told the truth you'd better tell it now. Did you write that number there?"

She nodded. "Yes, I remember now, I wrote it one day—"

"What for?"

"Why, sometimes I look a number up and then forget it so I write it down—"

"Whose number is it?"

She didn't glance at it again; she looked steadily at you, and finally shook her head, "I don't remember."

During the half-hour you had waited for her to come you had sworn that you would beat the truth out of her, choke it out of her; now you were determined and perfectly calm; you were not even angry; you just wanted the truth.

"You might as well sit down, we're going to have this out," you said, and took a chair in front of hers, close to her. "You'd better be careful what you tell me, because this is something I can check up on. I want to know when you telephoned my sister Jane, and what for."

"I really had forgotten it was your sister's number," she said. "All right. Go on."

It took an hour to get it out of her, and before she was through she had told it a dozen different ways. Was Erma in it? Sometimes she was and sometimes she wasn't; anyway she hadn't seen her. At first she said she'd seen Jane twice and then she said only once. It was mostly Dick. As long ago as last spring, Dick had sent for her and offered her fifty thousand dollars if she would let you alone, go away somewhere, and not let you know where she was. When she wouldn't take it he had doubled his offer. This fall, just recently, he had been after her again; this time when she refused the money he threatened her. Then Jane came, and begged her. "She begged me all afternoon," she said. She took a day to think about it, and she put that number there only a week ago, when she phoned Jane that she had decided not to go.

At first you believed it. After you had got all you could out of her and tried to piece it together and decide how much of it was true and how much she had invented, you put on your hat and coat and started for Tenth Street. She didn't ask where you were going or whether you'd be back; she just sat there, solemn, quietly watching you. Probably two minutes after you left she was reading a book. You never got to Jane's house; you walked past it, but you didn't go in. You couldn't decide what to say. What if it were all a lie? No, there was too much detail in it; in spite of the way she had contradicted herself, she couldn't have made it all up, there was an essential verity in it. When you finally turned definitely away from Jane's house and took a taxi to Park Avenue, you were telling yourself that you would ask Dick about it in the morning, that would be better; and then, by god, you'd let them all know that you didn't want them poking their noses into your affairs.

And then, yesterday, like a lousy coward you didn't go to the
office at all. You packed trunks! And you found the revolver
and sat on the edge of the bed for an hour, holding it in your
hand and looking at it, as if that was going to put muscles in
your guts. In the afternoon you went to Jane's house; she was
out and wouldn't be back till after dinner. That didn't matter.
Don't kid yourself.

Last night Millicent was surprised to see you. Of course, you
hadn't telephoned, but she was surprised more than that; you
could tell by the way she looked at you, though she didn't say
anything. You told her you hadn't asked Jane and Dick about it,
but you were going to, and if you found she'd been lying you'd
make her pay for it. She said you wouldn't ask them. She said it
as if it didn't make any difference one way or the other, "You
won't ask them about it." You replied quietly that she was
wrong this time, you certainly would, you most certainly would;
and then all of a sudden there was that tiny flash deep in her
eyes, and she said, with no change at all in her voice:

"Anyway, I made it all up."

Good god, what does it matter what she said? You ought to
know by this time. What she says! You knew it too, really you
didn't give a damn, but you jumped on her, you began it all over
again, tearing yourself to pieces….She declared calmly that
Dick had never mentioned you, she hadn't seen him for months.
She had never seen Jane, nor telephoned her; she had put that
number there one day, during the summer, when she wanted to
write you about something and couldn't get your address from
the office, because they didn't have it, and she thought of
phoning to Jane for it, and after looking up the number had
remembered that Jane was at the seashore. Dick had never
offered her money to leave you, but she still thought she might
get some from him, just because he felt sorry for her….

And at the end, after all that, after you'd made a whining fool of yourself, she actually thought she could touch you. By god, she did. Her eyes looked like that, not really starting to close, just ready to, tightened up a little. A thousand times you've seen them like that. Then they do begin to close, and her lips get straight and thin and very quiet, and her eyes get narrower and tighter....It was vivid and terrible, in your dream that last night in Schwartz's cabin....

There goes her chair again, pulling it across the rug. Now would have been the time, now that you know she's sitting down. Go across to the windows and pull down the shades. You pitiful paltry coward. Last night it sounded like she was telling the truth. If she wasn't, if Dick and Jane—begging her—no matter. What do they matter? If they came up the stairs right now and all three of you went in together—ha, that would be the way to do it. Erma too, the whole damn outfit. You could sit in a corner and listen to them, and by heaven they could keep it up all night and all day tomorrow, and forever, and they wouldn't get anywhere. Begging her. No matter what they got her to do; they could send her to the top of the world or the middle of the jungle and you'd find her. And that's what she knows. That's why; that's what she knows. So swallow it, swallow it at last, and open the door and go in and tell her so. She'll respect you for it. That's why she despises you, she sees you wriggling and squirming, that's why she said Jane begged her....

She'll respect you! Jesus! The bitch, the filthy bitch!

Oh cut it out. Cut it out! Steady....

Steady....

# Q

*He turned the key in the lock and opened the door; and, entering,
quietly closed the door behind him. Millicent, with a magazine
in her hand and a box of candy in her lap, was in the blue chair,
close to the table, under the reading-lamp. That's funny, he
thought, the blinds are already down, she must be getting
modest.*

*"You're late," said she from her chair. "You didn't telephone,
so I nearly went to a show. Take off your hat and stay a while."*

*Then, as his left hand went into his trousers pocket and out
again, returning the key, and as his other hand suddenly left his
overcoat pocket and hung at his side, she said in the same even
tone:*

*"What have you got there?"*

*His right hand lifted, and a tremor ran through him from
head to foot as he realized that the revolver was in it. He was
watching her face; he had not said a word; but now he spoke:*

*"What does it look like, huh? What does it look like, Mil?"*

*At the same moment he was saying to himself, be careful, you
damn fool, why did you take it out, you don't know what you're
doing, what's the matter with you? And also, he was going
towards her. He stood in front of her chair, almost touching her.*

*"Are you trying to scare me?" she said, her eyes level and
unwavering, fixed on his. She sat motionless.*

*He said, "You don't think I'll shoot, do you?"*

*"Yes, I think you might. I think you might shoot." Without
letting her eyes leave his face, she moved her hand to indicate
the marble head, glistening white, on the table beside her, and*

added slowly, "Why don't you shoot Battling Bill? You hate him so."

He moved his eyes to look at it, and then, without replying, but with senseless vast relief surging through him, he deliberately pointed the revolver at the thing and pulled the trigger. There was a deafening report; the statue faintly tilted and came to rest again with its nose splintered off; the revolver fell from his hand and clattered to the floor. Like a flash Millicent stooped and then was erect on her feet beside him, the revolver in her hand. She looked at him and chuckled; and hearing her chuckle and seeing the gun in her hand he suddenly smashed his fist hard into her face; she staggered against the chair with a little cry, and he hit her again, and she fell to the floor; and then, with a swift and terrible precision, he reached over and seized the heavy statue as if it had been made of cork and, lifting it high above him, hurled it upon her head as she lay there at his feet. There was a cracking sound like the breaking of a brittle board; and the statue, spattered with blood, rolled gently onto the rug and came to rest there with its broken nose pointing toward the ceiling.

Christ no, he thought, Christ no....

He stooped and picked up the revolver from the floor and stood there an instant with it in his hand, then suddenly darted for the door; and as he opened it, he heard Mrs. Jordan's clumsy steps starting rapidly up the stairs, and her voice: "Mr. Lewis, was that you? What is it?" He stepped back and stood there two paces from the open door, the revolver still in his hand, unable to speak or move; he caught a glimpse of Mrs. Jordan's face in the dim stairway, heard her scream, and heard her clattering downstairs again and yelling, "Police! Help, police!"

He slowly lifted his hand and looked at the revolver—inquiringly, as if it could tell him something he wanted to know; then *with a violent convulsive shudder he relaxed his fingers and it fell. He rushed to the hall, to the head of the stairs, but hearing voices below returned to the room; and, not looking at what lay beside the statue on the floor, went to the window and raised it and leaned out. He heard shouts and, in the dim light from the street lamps, saw forms of people moving swiftly. He closed the window and deliberately and precisely pulled down the shade; then he turned and walked rapidly to the little table in the corner where the telephone stood, and lifted the instrument and took off the receiver and put it to his ear.*

*The sound of voices, and of heavy and hurried footsteps on the stairs, came through the open door as he said into the mouthpiece:*

*"Chelsea four three four three."*